CW00971342

Books by
MARGERY SHARP

NOVELS
Rhododendron Pie
Fanfare for Tin Trumpets
Four Gardens
The Flowering Thorn
Three Companion Pieces
The Nutmeg Tree
The Stone of Chastity
Cluny Brown
Britannia Mews
The Foolish Gentlewoman
Lise Lillywhite
The Gipsy in the Parlour
Something Light
The Eye of Love
Martha in Paris
Martha, Eric and George
The Sun in Scorpio
In Pious Memory
Rosa
The Innocents
The Faithful Servants
Summer Visits

SHORT STORIES
The Lost Chapel Picnic

FANTASIES
The Rescuers
Miss Bianca
The Turret
Miss Bianca in the Salt Mines
Miss Bianca in the Orient
Miss Bianca and the Bridesmaid
Miss Bianca in the Antarctic
The Magical Cockatoo
Bernard the Brave

SUMMER VISITS

MARGERY SHARP

SUMMER VISITS

LITTLE, BROWN AND COMPANY • BOSTON • TORONTO

COPYRIGHT © 1977 BY MARGERY SHARP

ALL RIGHTS RESERVED. NO PART OF THIS BOOK MAY BE REPRODUCED
IN ANY FORM OR BY ANY ELECTRONIC OR MECHANICAL MEANS IN-
CLUDING INFORMATION STORAGE AND RETRIEVAL SYSTEMS WITHOUT
PERMISSION IN WRITING FROM THE PUBLISHER, EXCEPT BY A REVIEWER
WHO MAY QUOTE BRIEF PASSAGES IN A REVIEW.

LIBRARY OF CONGRESS CATALOG CARD NO. 77-15364

FIRST AMERICAN EDITION

T 02/78

PRINTED IN THE UNITED STATES OF AMERICA

To
Geoffrey Castle

Chapter One

THE BIG HOUSE in East Anglia, half-rectory half-manor, had been in the hands of the Tabors for some two hundred years before old John Henry Braithwaite bought it from the last of the line in the 1850s; it was he who made the place absurd by attempting to add the more striking features of a mediaeval castle—crenellating the roof, digging a moat, and throwing three ground floor rooms into one to make a great hall complete with minstrels' gallery. He also, more in the spirit of his own age, had a lodge built to imitate a bee-hive, and another to resemble a Swiss chalet. Then he changed the name to Cotton Hall, for he'd made his money in Lancashire and wasn't going to turn his back on his origins.

It may be said at once that the moat was a failure, it not having been properly revetted. Whatever water seeped in seeped out again, leaving a ribbon of chickweed round two sides of the house, so John Henry had it filled in again and was glad of the occupation.

Cotton Hall in his time never had a mistress. His wife, whom he'd married when she was a lass with a shawl over her head, after bearing him four children died a few months after his apotheosis into East Anglia. Perhaps it was just as well: she'd done her gallant best to keep pace with him as he rose in the world, but Cotton Hall could have proved too much for her. John Henry brought with him only his two daughters, Charlotte and Flora; his two sons, Harry and George, were already out and prospering in a world wider than Lancashire, for the old man had made gentlemen of them both—sent them to a famous Grammar School, thence to the University, then, both inclining to the Law, into chambers in London. However Charlotte, for

7

the two years before she married, made him an excellent housekeeper.

Flora when she took over proved less competent. Plain (she resembled her father) and aware of it, painfully shy and inclined to read poetry, she found the mistress-ship of Cotton Hall nothing but a burden; and however inadequate as a housekeeper would have been still less adequate as its hostess, but fortunately there was no entertaining to be done. Indeed it sometimes seemed as though John Henry had settled in Suffolk simply to disoblige his neighbours. He didn't shoot and didn't preserve; naturally no local squires or their wives called; the great hall with its minstrels' gallery began to feel like a room in an empty house. Much cared John Henry; his only aristocratic trait was *le plaisir de déplaire*; and as for shy plain Flora, she was only thankful that the only guests she was called upon to receive were her own kith and kin on their annual summer visits from London. Even these always rather agitated her; and a certain August Sunday in 1860, when she'd reached the age of twenty-nine, found her even more agitated than usual.

In the little fifteenth-century church above the salt-marshes a marble tablet on the wall commemorated the Rev. Nigel Tabor's lifetime of service to the parish. (How thankful he'd been to leave it and retire to the academic groves of Cambridge!—where his laying down of six dozen of port for his old college earned him universal approval.) Other memorials to the Tabors included a Crusader's brass in the aisle, and an elaborate Elizabethan family group in the chancel. But *sic transit gloria mundi*, and it was now the Braithwaite clan who filled the front pew.

John Henry naturally occupied the corner seat next to the aisle. Then came his daughters-in-law Clara and Adelaide, then Charlotte (now Mrs Stacey), all wearing such voluminous crinolines their husbands had to sit in the pew behind alongside Flo. Their numerous progeny sat further back still, to make it easier for their nurses and nursery-maids to take them out before the sermon.

'I choose my text,' opened the Vicar—no Tabor, but a young man recently down from Oriel—'from the Epistle of St John. *"If we say we have no sin, we deceive ourselves."*'

John Henry took out his watch and laid it rather con-

8

spicuously on his knee to see that the regulation half-hour wasn't over-run. Clara and Adelaide and Charlotte, comfortably aware that *they* had no sin, adjusted their shawls and dropped into a semi-doze, as did their husbands behind them. Only Flora, who besides having so much on her mind was in love with the young man from Oriel, remained fully awake.

The London party had arrived the previous day, by special train. It was unthinkable that they should travel otherwise: John Henry had it laid on for them. He could do things in a big way when he liked. From Bayswater and Belgravia and Bloomsbury, Braithwaites and Staceys—parents and children, nurses and nursery-maids—assembled at Liverpool Street Station and there found their special train punctually awaiting them. For such a numerous party two coaches had to be provided, one so superior that its lavatory had swans painted on the china basin just above the water-line, and this was always appropriated by the Harry Braithwaites, Harry being old John Henry's elder son. But his own elder son Alan, and his daughter Sybil, were generous enough to let their cousins from the next coach come in to look and even pull the plug.

'For though we may believe ourselves to be without sin,' enjoined the young man from Oriel, 'if we look searchingly into our hearts, what do we find there? No such sin as would bring us before a court of magistrates, perhaps; we don't steal, or poach, or—heaven forbid!—commit murder. But there are other crimes almost as bad. Have we ever been un-neighbourly, for instance—for aren't we bidden to love a neighbour as oneself?— or refused a helping hand in time of need?'

'I'm sure *we* didn't!' murmured Adelaide to Charlotte.

For their journey down had been for once marked by an unusual incident. All were aboard, the special train was about to draw out, when suddenly, past the deferential station-master, the deferential porters, shouldered a scarecrow-looking young man with a portfolio under one arm.

'Is that the train for Suffolk?' he demanded.

'Aye; but 'tis a special,' said the station-master repressively.

'Let me get on! I'll pay my fare!' cried the young man.

All on board looked shocked. No one ever paid a *fare*, on the special train ... Even the station-master was shocked.

'I'll travel in the guard's van!' cried the young man.

9

'Out of the question,' said the station-master—not even adding 'sir' and preparing to blow his whistle.

'My wife's in childbirth!' cried the young man.

Through the breasts of the females of the party ran a perceptible shudder. Of course Clara and Adelaide and Charlotte knew all about childbirth—hadn't Clara been two days in labour before the delivery of a daughter?—but to hear a man pronounce the word, and in so public a place as Liverpool Street Station, offended every feminine instinct. Still their breasts (or how should they have shuddered?) were not of stone.

'As he seems in such distress,' murmured Charlotte Stacey, 'why not let him—you agree, Clara, you agree, Adelaide?— come with us?'

So for once the train steamed out with a supercargo on board. He didn't create any further scandal; stayed in the guard's van all the way, and in the bustle of the Cotton Hall party's arrival at Ufford station, disappeared.

'My dear people, I beseech you,' finished the young man from Oriel, 'search your hearts!'

It wasn't a bad sermon, also it ended well within the half-hour. John Henry put his sovereign in the plate, and the rest their half-sovereigns, willingly enough. But of them all it was only Flora who had truly listened, and who in the last moments on her knees truly prayed.

'O Lord,' prayed Flora, 'if it be Thy will let them all not irritate father too much, and let them not squabble too much, and please, O Lord—if it be Thy will—let them not find out ...'

What Flora apprehended the rest of the family's finding out was that old John Henry had recently taken a mistress.

Her name was Hilda, and she was the daughter of one of the gardeners—old Ham, who occupied the lodge that resembled a Swiss chalet: in person a purely East Anglian type, with blue eyes, light hair, and a blooming complexion that bloomed additionally under a fine down of fair hairs like the fluff on a peach, but already, at nineteen, beginning to put on fat. She had originally entered Cotton Hall by way of the laundry, then been promoted first to house- then to parlour-maid; when not only her neat-handedness at table but also the swing of her rump as she carried out dishes attracted John Henry's eye. (Even at seventy there was still a goatish gleam in it.) The first time he followed Hilda up to her attic bedchamber Flora had sighed, but thought little of it, for she had become hardened to closing her ears to her father's nocturnal prowlings; and when it became a regular thing, night after night, was hardly surprised that he tired of climbing so many stairs and decreed Hilda should shift to the first floor bedroom once Charlotte's.

'I hope you don't mind, Miss Flo?' asked Hilda with some delicacy. 'I know it was your own sister's room, but all those stairs are just too much for an old un ...'

Flora found she didn't mind. Nor did she mind when Hilda gradually took over the mistress-ship of Cotton Hall as well. Hilda was far more competent than herself in dealing with the big, ill-trained staff, and with the tradespeople and odd job men—got the chimneys swept, for instance, for half the price Flora had been used to pay. But all this had come about within the last eight or nine months, and with summer visitors imminent there obviously had to be some re-adjustment.

'Miss Charlotte's room for her and Mr Stacey,' said Hilda. 'I'd better shift back upstairs.'

'Thank you, Hilda,' said Flora.

'And I'd better not wait at table,' continued Hilda. 'If I caught your Da's eye I mightn't be able to keep a straight face. I'll teach Bessie Cable.'

'Thank you, Hilda,' repeated Flora.

The two women became in a sense accomplices, and Flora showed her appreciation of the other's tact by the gift of a silver teapot; and Bessie Cable served at Sunday dinner handily enough.

'So here you all are again,' said John Henry, surveying his clan across the laden table. (Roast beef, naturally, roast potatoes and brussels sprouts, to be followed by apple tart and cheese, then for the men nuts and port.) 'I don't know what you'll find to do with yourselves.'

If they hadn't come he would have been deeply offended. He'd laid on a special train to ensure their punctuality in coming. Now that they were arrived, he appeared to regard them with at the best tolerance, as though suffering an imposition. It was entirely in his Northern-bred character, the ethos of which equated softness with weakness, not to show pleasure or affection. In his cotton-mill he'd been known as a hard master, and was proud of it. So were his hands, however hardly he bore on them, proud of it.

'I'm sure, Papa, we always have a very enjoyable time here,' said Charlotte. 'Don't we, Clara, don't we, Adelaide?'

'Very enjoyable indeed,' said Clara.

'Perfectly lovely!' said Adelaide.

John Henry regarded them cynically. They didn't, as both he and they knew. During that obligatory month in East Anglia, with no calls to be paid to or received from county neighbours, they were bored to death. The men of the party usually found some business to call them back to London, at least during the week; Charlotte and Clara and Adelaide, lacking this recourse, brought down quantities of needlework—Clara a patchwork quilt, Charlotte a *gros point* cushion cover, Addie a reticule she was netting with beads; and if each took back a completed quilt, cover or purse, that was the best they could expect.

Their expectations from John Henry were as precise as the pattern of a bedspread or cushion-cover. Several years before all had been summoned to a solicitor's office in Ipswich to hear his Will read out. Harry, as eldest son, got Cotton Hall; what else the old man left in the way of assets—and it was believed he'd invested in railway stock—to be divided equally between his second son George and his daughters; and all agreed it was a very fair Will indeed. Nonetheless his grip on his family tightened; for if there was no question of getting into his good graces, by that annual visit, how graceless it would have seemed not to pay it!

'We quite love coming here, Papa,' lied Charlotte, meeting her sisters-in-law's eyes across the dinner table. 'I'm sure the children love coming here above all things!'

Which at least was true. As soon as they were all together at Cotton Hall the children took up the wonderful game where they'd left off last year and re-formed themselves into The Tribe.

Alan, son of Harry and Adelaide, at nine the eldest (and most imaginative), was its head: the Grand Panjandrum Mato-Topa. He had no consort, but his sister Sybil was his Handmaid, and Alice, eldest daughter of George and Clara, Wet-Nurse—an appellation so surrounded by mystery, to children whose mothers still promoted the myth of the gooseberry-bush, it made her some kind of Soothsayer. Timothy Stacey was the Scapegoat—a rôle less onerous to a seven-year-old than might be imagined, for the children thought it meant a goat that had escaped, so that he was licenced in any sort of tomfoolery, like a court jester. The rest of John Henry's grandchildren were too young to take part, and lived so to speak in purdah in the ample quarters of Cotton Hall, impinging on the attention only of their mothers. The nursery party formed a sub-culture of its own, enlivened, so far as the nursemaids were concerned, by a running feud with cook and the indoor staff.

The Tribe's headquarters, its Holy of Holies, was the bee-hive-shaped lodge. No one else ever went there; but as an additional precaution all magic-making paraphernalia—an Old Moore's Almanac, a rabbit's skull, a pack of cards and a Guy Fawkes mask—was hidden in an old croquet box. Only the Grand Panjandrum Mato-Topa was allowed to open it, when after assuming the mask he invoked the spirit of Hiawatha and repeated the Lord's Prayer backwards.

The Tribe lived surrounded by mysterious taboos. There was a different one for each day. Sometimes, for example, every sentence uttered had to begin with a designated letter, such as M: so that to the suggestion, 'Shall we play croquet?' the answer couldn't be Yes or No—Y and N, for obvious reasons, were never chosen—but 'Marvellous', or 'Mouldy', or 'Must we?' This particular taboo applied even to questions put by adults. Once when the letter for the day was P, and Hilda asked what they'd like for supper—

'Prunes,' replied Alice.

'Potatoes,' suggested Sybil.

'Prawns!' added Timothy the Scapegoat, remembering his duty to amuse.

'I have never heard such nonsense!' cried Hilda. 'Prunes and potatoes and prawns! You shall just have boiled eggs!'

'Parboiled,' capped Alan; and why the children went into such fits of laughter Hilda couldn't imagine.

On other days, known as Days of Doom, sacrifices were demanded: a favourite doll or picture-book to be cast on old Ham's perpetually smouldering bonfire in order to preserve the Tribe's safety, during which ceremony all were required to repeat the Ten Commandments. The Tribe's religious beliefs were as much of a mish-mash as the architecture of Cotton Hall.

But the really secret days were the Days of Mato-Topa's Rest.

In these only Alan and Sybil took part. Two or three times a week, in the afternoon, the bee-hive lodge was declared tabu to the others, and only Sybil, at a secret sign from her brother, followed him there to lie at his side on a heap of old potato sacks. First, however, Alan took off his shoes and stockings, while Sybil knelt before him and rubbed his feet. This ceremony usually lasted some ten minutes, or even longer: Sybil loved to feel his narrow insteps warming between her hands, then the small bosses of his ankle bones as she rubbed even higher. Then world-wearily Mato-Topa stretched out on the sacks and summoned her beside him. 'Now the songs of our far country!' ordered Mato-Topa; and Sybil would hum over and over *The Last Rose of Summer*, which plaintive melody certainly suggested yearnings for some far country, until, just before he fell, or feigned to fall, asleep, Alan drew her beside him to lie cheek pressed to cheek, while outside the quiet garden, the quiet and warmth of a summer afternoon, enclosed them as if in a womb. Then—the roles of Sleeping Beauty and the Prince reversed—Sybil waked him with a kiss and they both, still a little *distrait*, went back to the house for tea.

It was the peculiar fact that only at Cotton Hall, in the ambiance of the Tribe, did Alan and Sybil play out such fantasies. At home in Bayswater they were as normal a brother and sister as any others.

Chapter Two

THE RITUAL SUMMER VISIT settled into its usual dull routine. As has been said, during the week the menfolk of the party escaped back to London, on the plea of business—and business indeed they had: Harry, the barrister, having inherited both his father's drive and his hard-headedness, was now quite a leading light in the bleak world of heirs versus mortgagees, with an occasional foray into the Divorce Courts; George, the less ambitious, had become a solicitor, so was often able to lend his brother a helping hand.

The husband of Charlotte, Arthur Stacey, was the rising architect who'd transformed Cotton Hall. It was a stroke of luck for her—how else could she have found a match, handsome girl though she was, marooned in the East Anglian wastes?—that he was a bachelor; for though rising he couldn't afford to marry, as he frankly explained. 'If you need a bit of backing,' said John Henry, with equal plainness, 'I'm ready to back you—that is, as a son-in-law ...'

In the event the marriage turned out a very happy one, and Charlotte, unlike many Victorian wives, could speak quite freely to her husband.

'Why we come here,' she once complained unfilially, after John Henry had been more disagreeable than usual, 'to endure bad temper as well as boredom!'

'In case your respected papa takes it in mind to make another Will,' said Arthur Stacey.

'What, after we all went to Ipswich to hear his—what do you call it?—testamentary intentions read out to us?' protested Charlotte.

'I don't believe he'd ever leave the house away from me,' said Harry.

The husbands and wives—it was a Sunday—were playing a desultory game of croquet after church before lunch. Only the croquet lawn was in fairly good shape, the garden being otherwise rather neglected; John Henry employed two gardeners, but Hilda hadn't yet got round to taking the outdoor staff in hand, and in any case one was her own father—old Ham, who cared for nothing but his perpetually smouldering bonfire.

'Nor do I anticipate being cut off with a shilling,' said George.

'Of course not!' cried Clara. 'It would be quite abominable!'

'But if he inclines to be charitable in his old age,' meditated Arthur Stacey, 'he might well like to have a Life Boat named after him ...'

'And we could all go to the launching!' cried Addie. 'Charlotte and Clara and Flo and I, all in our best bonnets!'

What a frivolous woman she was! How on earth had Harry come to marry her?

In fact it was her very frivolity that had attracted him. While making his way in London as a young barrister he was now and then invited out to dinner as a sufficiently personable (and promising) spare man; at one of which entertainments, as the least important male present, he had been allotted his hostess's equally unimportant orphan niece. (Her only expectations from an uncle in India who after surviving two barren wives had just married a third.) To begin with Harry didn't find much to say to her, but Addie knew her business.

'Are you shy? So am I,' she confessed. 'How nice to find a *man* who's shy too! What shall we talk about? For we must talk about something, or Aunt will scold me! Do you hunt?'

'No,' said Harry.

'Nor do I,' regretted Addie, 'though I've always longed to. There's absolutely nothing so becoming as a riding-habit. Are you fond of music?'

'I'm afraid not,' said Harry.

'Then we must just eat our dinners,' decided Adelaide, 'and listen while our betters speak!'

So she sat prudently eating her dinner—yet still with a spark of gaiety and frivolity in her eye; and it was she the High Court Judge, the guest of honour, sat down beside in the drawing-room when the men joined the ladies for coffee.

'You must have been uncommonly bored,' said Harry, when he had a chance to speak to her again.

'Not a bit!' declared Adelaide. 'Though perhaps because it was I who did all the talking!'

'What about?' asked Harry, with genuine curiosity.

'Crinolines,' said Adelaide promptly. 'I told him that except in a box one simply can't go to the opera any more, the seats are too narrow. And I asked him if he remembered the time when ladies wore damped muslin draperies—*à la Grecque*—to show off their ... best points; and he said—the old pet!—indeed he did, and however many got consumption, to the masculine eye it was well worth it!'

'You were flirting with him,' accused Harry—struck by a suspicion that she'd been flirting with himself too.

'Well, of course!' said Adelaide.

Any young woman who could flirt with a High Court Judge naturally attracted Harry's serious interest.

'I wonder if you'd let me take you to the Royal Academy?' he suggested.

'I'd be delighted—if Aunt can find time to chaperone us!' said Adelaide.

Though flirtatious, she was evidently no flibbertigibbet—no modern girl who used slang and aped her brothers' ways—and this also attracted Harry. He began to pay serious court to her, and in due course won her hand.

Again, it was a happy union. With the Staceys, particularly after the children came, they lived in as much intimacy as the distance between Bloomsbury and Belgravia allowed.

Only poor George, marrying Clara, made a bad bargain. He married chiefly because his brother had. There was always a certain sibling rivalry, and without a wife of his own he felt even more inferior. So he married the daughter of his senior partner, who turned out to be demanding, fretful and a *malade imaginaire*. Though Adelaide and Charlotte were always on excellent terms, they tended to cold shoulder Clara except at Cotton Hall, where intimacy was inevitable. The attitude of all three married women towards Flora—poor Flo, the daughter at home—was a mixture of pity and slight contempt.

'Does she even run the house?' wondered Clara, as she and her sisters-in-law (Flora not being present) sat over their needlework and netting in the great hall. (John Henry liked to see it in use, even though the presence of a few women couldn't much animate it. 'We must look like figures in Madame Tussaud's!' once exclaimed Adelaide.)

'*I'*d say the house is run by Hilda,' she observed now—for discreet as Hilda meant to be, her empire over servants and tradespeople alike couldn't have failed to be noticed.

'She is the daughter of one of Papa's gardeners, and came to us first as a laundry-maid,' said Charlotte—as it were implying that so old a family retainer might quite properly be expected to run the house. 'One is only glad Flo has such a good servant to relieve her of domestic cares.'

'I only wish I had someone to relieve me of *my* domestic cares!' said Clara self-pityingly.

'But then you never had a laundry-maid, dear,' said Charlotte. 'What about a little croquet?'

They put aside their work and went out into the garden. It was always a needle game when the men weren't there, and neither Addie nor Charlotte nor Clara ever refrained from swinging the flounce of her crinoline to conceal a bad lie. But even the pleasure of croqueting Charlotte couldn't make Clara hold her tongue for long.

'I suppose she isn't *more* than just a servant, to Papa?'

'Certainly not,' said Charlotte, with more conviction than she felt. 'I wonder who that young man could have been who got on the train with us?'

'I wonder too,' said the easily diverted Adelaide, 'because for all his dreadful clothes he looked to me like a gentleman ...'

'If Papa is in any danger of becoming *entangled*,' persisted Clara, 'shouldn't one of our husbands speak to him?'

'Certainly not,' repeated Charlotte. 'I agree with you, Addie: he did look like a gentleman. We must ask Flora if any young couple have come into the neighbourhood, the wife expecting a baby.'

'Flo won't know,' laughed Adelaide. 'Flo never knows anything of anything—except where to meet Mr Price!'

It was another thing her sisters-in-law couldn't have failed to notice: that Flora's morning walk, which she always took between ten and eleven whether there were guests at Cotton Hall or not, regularly coincided with the young man from Oriel's round as he went his pastoral way visiting the sick or distributing the Parish Magazine. 'Good morning, Miss Braithwaite,' said Mr Price. 'Good morning, Mr Price,' replied Flora. *'Bid me to live and I will live/Thy Protestant to be,'* she might have added, *'Or bid me love and I will give/A loving heart to thee,'* but convention forbade.

'A very fine morning,' said Mr Price, if it wasn't actually pelting with rain.

'For the time of year,' agreed Flora; and that was all her hungry heart had to live on till next Sunday.

For Mr Price knew better than to come calling at Cotton Hall. He'd tried once—trotting in as ingenuous as a spaniel pup—and received, John Henry was happy to recall, a right flea in his ear. 'I come to church on Sunday,' had pronounced John Henry, 'to set an example to the lower orders. To me it's naught but mumbo-jumbo and I want no more of it on weekdays. You get my sovereign in the bag like clockwork: let that be enough.'

Naturally Mr Price never called again, and Flora as naturally never attempted to take part in any parish activities, dearly as she'd have liked, for instance, to teach in Sunday School, where Mr Price always looked in if only for a few minutes. John Henry indeed admitted the utility of Sunday Schools, as a means of getting children out from under their parents' feet, but otherwise lumped them with the rest of good works as mumbo-jumbo. 'Pay a man a decent wage,' said John Henry (which he'd never done in his life), 'and that's all the good work needed ...' So however loving her hungry heart, Flora had a hard row to hoe ...

Nevertheless her prayer in church that Sunday was answered. None of her kin actually *found out*. Adelaide and Clara guessed at, Charlotte strongly suspected, a more than servant-and-master relationship between old John Henry and Hilda, but none actually *found out*. Charlotte indeed was far from anxious to probe into her father's domestic arrangements; Adelaide had her reticule on her mind; and though Clara occasionally tried to revert to the subject, Charlotte regularly snubbed her—and had moreover always a red herring to hand.

'One can't help wondering who he was,' said Charlotte, 'that young man on the train with us?'

They even enquired of Flora, but as Adelaide had foretold, fruitlessly. They wondered, they speculated, but never encountered him again—how should they, he berthed in quarters

19

so alien to Cotton Hall as the Fisherman's Arms down on the rim of the salt marshes?

But Flora, all unawares, had encountered him only a week after his arrival.

Chapter Three

FOR ONCE—it was an overcast day in any case—her morning walk had ended in frustration, no Mr Price to be met. Flora couldn't imagine him neglecting his duty in the way of pastoral visits or magazine distribution; when she remembered it was Saturday she guessed him shut up in his study preparing his Sunday sermon. So she walked on further than usual, out of the village and down to the rim of the salt marshes, and there just above the tide mark observed a young man seated before an easel. To her he didn't look like a gentleman at all, he looked like an artist; she made no mental connection with the subject of her sister's and sisters-in-law's curiosity. But as everyone does, encountering an artist, she approached and looked over his shoulder.

The young man's name was Alexander, and as suited his age (about twenty-four), he was a bachelor: the wife in childbirth had been a brilliant improvisation to get him onto the train as the first stage towards the Fisherman's Arms, a small, rather disreputable inn situated some two miles from Cotton Hall on the salt marsh's edge, there to foregather with a couple of fellow painters, do some sketching *en plein air*, drink too much of the excellent local ale and abuse the Royal Academy. But when he reached his destination, first by way of a carrier's cart (all the Cotton Hall party were met at the station by flies), then on foot, disappointment awaited him.

'No one else here?' he asked the landlady.

'None o' your lot,' accused the landlady.

She was a Mrs Strowger, and had led a hard life: husband and son both lost at sea, an only grandson gone for a soldier, and of her widowed daughter-in-law the less said the better. In its prosperous days the inn had been frequented by smugglers, but the excisemen caught up with them, and now a few fishing-gentlemen helped pay the rent, but not in August. In August she'd come to rely on painting-gentlemen—and where were they now?

Alexander could only shrug. To swear to meet every year, as to swear eternal friendship, is not uncommon amongst artists; but didn't even the Pre-Raphaelite Brotherhood disintegrate? Days passed, and neither of Alexander's cronies turned up. (In fact both had accepted their fate and become drawing-masters.) But since he'd got there, he settled down before the wide prospect of marsh and estuary without any distraction until Flora impinged upon his eye.

'Magnificent, isn't it?' said he to Flora looking over his shoulder.

Whether he referred to the prospect or his paint-bedaubed canvas, Flora wasn't sure; and since both struck her as equally drab, she merely remarked that perhaps soon the sun would come out.

'Pray heaven it doesn't!' said the young man. 'I suppose you're a Constable admirer?' he added. 'Of leaping horses and Willy Lott's Mill and so on?'

'Constable, as everyone knows, is our greatest painter,' said Flora repressively.

'What about Turner?' countered the young man. 'D'you know what *you*'re like?' he added, suddenly regarding her with interested bright brown eyes. 'A Holbein!'

It was true, though no one had ever remarked on it before. With her father's high narrow forehead under a receding hair line, narrow cheeks and prim mouth, Flora indeed resembled a Holbein portrait of a gentlewoman—his masculine portraits were more realistic—only no one had ever noticed it before.

'I could paint *you*,' said the young man, 'and perhaps get into the Royal Academy after all!'

For despite his contempt for that institution he knew what a portrait on its walls—the portrait of the year?—could do for him. It could put him in the money. Moreover Flora's Holbeinesque appearance had genuinely struck him.

'I'm sure I hope you will,' said Flora politely. 'Good day.'

'No, stop a moment!' cried the young man. 'Who are you, where do you live?'

'At Cotton Hall,' said Flora.

Evidently the address meant something to him; he grinned wryly.

'Then I suppose it's no use asking you to sit for me?'

'Certainly not,' said Flora. 'Now I must go home to see to lunch.'

Actually it was Hilda who saw to lunch, as she saw to everything. (As she was always to see to everything.)

'Stop just a moment!' begged the young man, abandoning his canvas and reaching for a sketching-block. 'At least let me get your eyebrows down!'

'Good day to you,' said Flora.

As has been said, she made no connection with the person who had so aroused her sister's and sisters-in-law's curiosity; and made no mention of the encounter.

Meanwhile Alexander tried to draw her from memory, made a botch of it and cursed his luck, and lingered on at the Fisherman's Arms chiefly because he could run up a bill there, without hope of Flora's return.

But of course Flora returned. No one had ever taken any interest in her eyebrows before. She returned once even while there were still guests at Cotton Hall; almost absently, dreamily extended her morning walk to the edge of the salt marsh and again glanced over a shoulder at an easel.

Ever an opportunist, Alexander again reached for his sketch book and without a word, as though not to waste a precious moment, began to draw.

In silent concentration the stick of sanguine chalk moved rapidly over the paper; and equally mute Flora stood watching its swift fluent motion: the common silence produced a peculiar effect of intimacy. She stayed only five minutes, or perhaps ten, before making to turn away again; when still without speaking, as though not to break a spell, Alexander turned the book towards her and let her see.

'Do I really look like that?' marvelled Flora.

'Only more beautiful,' said Alexander. 'You'll come back?'

'Perhaps,' said Flora, feeling for the first time in her life a sensation of power over a male.

*　　*　　*

23

A fortnight later the summer visitors thankfully departed. Charlotte took home a completed cushion-cover, Clara several square feet of patchwork, but Adelaide only three inches of beaded reticule. The complicated artifact was altogether too much for her, and as soon as she got home she guiltily hid it in the bottom of her rosewood work-box. Now and again she took it out and looked at it, but always put it back; and in time the needles rusted among the tangled beads.

Flora was now at more liberty; her daily walk now took her regularly beyond the village, down to the rim of the salt marsh; she fancied the extra exercise must be beneficial, for she felt in unusually good spirits. Of course she still timed herself to encounter Mr Price, and still exchanged a few words with him, but they were no longer so precious as they used to be; fatuously, but nonetheless very agreeably, Flora pretended to herself that she had now two strings to her bow ...

Of her two admirers (so Flora taught herself to think of them—and Alexander certainly admired her), the latter was indeed the more reliable. He was always waiting for her—once, in drizzling rain, under an umbrella. So was Flora under an umbrella; and it was on this occasion that he persuaded her into the derelict shed behind the inn, where smugglers had once stabled their horses, to give him a proper sitting. He kept his paints and canvases there, an abandoned truss of hay afforded a model's throne—all was ready to hand!—and with genuine excitement he settled down to work. 'Mayn't I look again?' asked Flora, as after twenty minutes or so she rose to go. 'Not yet; I'm only blocking in,' said Alexander. 'Not till I've shown you as beautiful as you really are!'

It became an accepted thing (so does flattery disarm even the most prudent female breast) that their subsequent meetings took place not on the rim of the salt marshes smelling of sea-lavender but in the shed smelling of musty hay. However to Flora either scent was equally heady ...

For of course besides painting her Alexander made love to her. He was a natural lover, a woman was necessary to him, but though his amorousness was easily aroused none of the lumpish local young women aroused it. Flora was to his painterly eye beautiful, and her primness enticed; but he had no idea to start with of taking her maidenhead. He began with but kissing her hand, and immediately apologized. 'Forgive me, I've picked up

24

foreign manners!' he explained. 'I've lived too long in Paris!'

Flora opened wide, beglamoured eyes. To her, it was like hearing he'd lived in the moon ...

The first time he kissed her throat she shuddered—but it was a pleasurable shudder. When he kissed her on the mouth she closed her eyes and sighed—but as it were unawarely, as though it were happening in a dream. She became used to the dream-like caresses that terminated each sitting; and when the inevitable happened, and she lost her virginity on a truss of straw, that was dreamlike too. She didn't even know what had happened; was aware only of a piercing pain, then of a piercing pleasure, while Alexander, after an equally piercing pleasure felt no remorse, because so often, after a first time, nothing happened. He was still careful, and took credit to himself for it, not to invade her womb again.

It would have considerably startled him to know how Flora's thoughts were engaged on a fully conscious level. She never asked herself whether he was in love with her, she simply assumed it, as she assumed also that he would love her for ever, as she would love him for ever; and when two people loved each other for ever, they got married. Even doubly seduced—seduced first into the rôle of artist's model—Flora remained conventional to the bone; and confidently looked forward, as soon as Alexander was celebrated and successful enough (thanks to her portrait?), to ask her father for her hand, to a white wedding with perhaps Sybil and Alice as bridesmaids.

Meanwhile the portrait had exceeded Alexander's expectations. Flora with her Holbeinesque eyebrows inspired him indeed; he was painting brilliantly, far beyond his usual capacity, and when he looked at the finished canvas saw the picture of the year at next summer's Royal Academy indeed. Then the thought occurred to him, why wait? Like all artists who have produced (they believe) a masterpiece, he was eager to put it on display. The Salon d'Automne this year, the Royal Academy next, thought Alexander vaingloriously; and as soon as the paint was dry packed his traps and flitted.

He didn't tell his landlady he was leaving. He owed her too much. He meant to shoot the moon while she snored.

He didn't tell Flora either. He felt it would be kinder not to. He simply left a note for her with Mrs Strowger.

'Won't you be seeing her yourself?' asked she, pausing in surprise on her way up to bed.

'Tomorrow I'm going to have a long day painting on the estuary,' said Alexander. 'It's to tell her not to wait for me, and in the morning I might forget.'

It was a very pretty note he left for Flora.

'*My very dear Miss Flora*', it ran,

'*How can I ever thank you? Now alas urgent business calls me to Paris, and when we shall meet again who knows? Je te baise les mains*'—he thought Flora probably had enough French for so much—'*and shall ever remember you in the scent of sea-lavender.*

Your always devoted admirer,
Alexander.'

It was a very pretty note indeed. It could hardly, in the circumstances (that he intended going off for good), have been more prettily phrased. But even before she opened it the following morning, as though the envelope were transparent, Flora paled; and when she read its contents paled still further; and Mrs Strowger jumped to the right conclusion.

'So he's gone off!' cried she indignantly. 'I wondered, when I saw no breakfast things about! He's gone. off!'

'On urgent business,' said Flora, recovering herself.

'Owing me thirty-five shillings!' cried Mrs Strowger.

Flora took out her purse.

'It must have been an oversight, in his hurry. Of course you must let me pay, and when I see him again we'll settle accounts.'

But already she suspected she wouldn't see him again—ever. For all its prettiness there was a note of finality in the message—as Alexander had intended there should be.

And what was thirty-five shillings to pay, thought Flora coldly, for two months' happiness? She was only glad she had enough money in her purse to spare her the necessity of any further visit to the Fisherman's Arms.

Then her heart broke; and the images of Sybil and Alice dressed as bridesmaids mopped and mowed beside her deridingly all the way back to Cotton Hall.

'A fine day, Miss Braithwaite,' said Mr Price.

'I would call it rather overcast,' said Flora.

It was a curious sensation, having one's heart broken; of coldness and emptiness; like a lunar landscape. Immediately, it was numbing, which Flora was glad of; she wished to feel as little as possible. The letter and envelope were still in her hand; she didn't passionately crumple them, or tear them in shreds. She could wait until she got home, to put a match to them, or toss them onto Ham's bonfire ...

In the event however she did neither. To remind her (Flora told herself) never to be such a fool again she locked Alexander's farewell letter in a secret drawer of her writing-desk.

Alexander gone, summer visitors gone, life at Cotton Hall settled into its usual torpid round. Autumn, the shooting season that invigorated the whole countryside, might as well have been winter; as his neighbouring squires polished and oiled their guns John Henry had nailed up on the boundary of his own demesne the notice USE OF FIRE ARMS STRICTLY PROHIBITED. Hilda injected a little excitement by proposing to keep goats—so wonderful a nanny's milk was, she'd heard tell, for making cheese; if John Henry allowed the whim, it was with some idea that they might stray into his neighbours' properties and there wreak goatish havoc. But the Billy and Nanny acquired by Hilda nibbled peaceably in their own paddock, and Hilda produced a few small malodorous cheeses, and that was the only result.

Winter came down like a wolf. The wind over the marshes blew so icy cold, Mrs Strowger shut up shop in the way of bedrooms to let altogether. Icicles hung by the wall, Dick the shepherd blew his nail, greasy Joan (if she were lucky and not forced to ask for poor relief) keeled her pot. Spring, with its promise of new birth, seemed aeons away ...

Only Hilda, who still kept an eye on the laundry, noticed something.

'How long have you been missing your periods, Miss Flo?' asked Hilda.

Chapter Four

'HOW LONG HAVE you been missing your periods, Miss Flo?' asked Hilda.

'Oh, just a month or so,' replied Flora.

'More like three or four,' said Hilda.

'But I'm perfectly well,' Flora assured her.

'Never a bit of sickness in the mornings?'

'Just now and then,' admitted Flora.

'You needn't mind telling *me*,' said Hilda.

'Tell you what?' asked Flora.

'Why, that you're going to have a baby!' said Hilda.

In her innocence and ignorance Flora had never suspected it; and now could only hide her face in her hands.

'You poor innocent!' said Hilda compassionately. 'Who's the father? Not—what a joke *that*'d be!—Mr Price?'

'Of course not!' cried Flora.

'Well, someone's got at you,' said Hilda, 'so I suppose it was that painting chap?'

How simple of Flora not to have realized that her visits to the stable-studio, in so small a community, would be common knowledge! She dumbly nodded.

'He didn't ... force you?' asked Hilda interestedly.

'No,' said Flora. 'He was always so gentle, I suppose that's why I scarcely realized what was happening ...'

'I only wish your Da had some of his gentleness,' said John Henry's mistress. 'I might be a prize heifer and he an old bull. Do we let *him* know?'

'Never!' cried Flora. 'He'd turn me out of doors!'

'I dare say he would at that,' agreed Hilda. 'He's a very hard man. I could send you to Granny Cable, but I don't recommend

28

it; two of the last poor young things that went to her died in dreadful agonies. I'll try with a knitting-needle myself if you like?'

But Flora only shuddered.

'Then if you mean to bear the child,' said Hilda practically, 'you ought to have a husband to give it a name. I suppose the painter-chap isn't wedded already?'

'I don't know,' said Flora. 'But it doesn't matter. He's gone. He's gone back to France ...'

Hilda sighed. Was ever such helplessness as poor Miss Flo's? Then her eye brightened.

'What if we make out it's mine? So fat as I am,' chuckled Hilda, 'Granny Cable's asked me time after time if I'm not expecting! And it's quite a wonder I *haven't* been caught; only your Da's not the man he once was. I dare say he'll be pleased as a dog with two tails!'

So once again the two women became accomplices.

The crinoline, as the Empress Eugenie amongst others recognized, is a wonderful camouflage. Its swelling outline seemed designed to conceal approaching maternity; John Henry noticed no change in his daughter's figure save that her bosom improved, and complimented her on plumping out a bit.

By Hilda's reckoning Flora was almost four months gone already, so that the birth would take place long before the summer visitors arrived again, and that was one mercy. Another was that Flora's pregnancy ran its course with complete ease. Indeed, as soon as her morning sickness stopped, she enjoyed rather better health than usual—partly, perhaps, because in the interests of concealment she took just as long walks as she'd always done, also on Hilda's recommendation, in the interests of the unborn child, now took a glass of port with her father after dinner. 'Th'art getting quite companionable!' said John Henry.

The months passed, Flora's condition still unsuspected. Hilda watched over her like a mother. 'You're carrying it low,' said Hilda. 'That means a boy ...'

But as the birth-date began to be reckoned in weeks, she thought it prudent to give John Henry a bit of warning.

'What would you say if I were to have a little one?' she asked.

For a moment he stared.

'What, of mine?'

'Whose else?' said Hilda. 'Th'art a proper patriarch!'

For once his hard features softened.

'I'd see right done by it ...'

'Then keep out of my bed for a bit,' said Hilda. 'Better still, to put temptation out of thy way, I'll shift in with Miss Flo.'

'Does *she* know?' asked John Henry, surprised.

'She does; and's been right nice about it,' said Hilda. 'You've never given Miss Flo her due. There's a second bed in her chamber already, and that's where I'll shift to.'

'Just as you say,' agreed John Henry, 'if she's willing. Shall you want a doctor,' he asked, with rare consideration, 'or a midwife woman?'

'If my mam could do without either,' said Hilda, 'so can I.' (For the matter of that, so had John Henry's wife, four times over, done without either.) 'Just leave all to me and Miss Flo ...'

'I'm still surprised at her,' ruminated John Henry.

'You've never given her her due,' repeated Hilda.

Another piece of luck: the birth took place at night, about midnight. Behind a bolted door Hilda had all prepared: a pot of boiling water simmered on the hob, towels and napkins wreathed the fireguard, as Flora began her short labour. It lasted only three hours, and she scarcely cried out at all; when she did, Hilda stuffed one of the napkins into her mouth, then pulled it away to give air for the final effort. 'Push!' adjured Hilda. 'Push with all thy might!' Flora did so; and out from her womb emerged a Christian soul in the likeness of a small crumpled red wriggler.

'Th'art a right Hero!' said Hilda, snipping the umbilical cord with a pair of scissors steeped in boiling water. (She knew better than to use scissors not so steeped; hadn't one of her sisters-in-law died, so the doctor said when they called him in, of a dirty knife?) 'Now lay quiet and leave all to me!' Then she gave the child a good slap on the buttocks to start it breathing on its own account, swaddled it in a warm towel and gave all her attention to Flora; and only when the latter was comfortable in a clean nightgown, sponged the babe clean too and laid it in Flora's arms.

How often has it been told that, however undesired, as soon as a babe is laid in its mother's arms, maternal instinct springs up to greet it with delight! No such instinct sprang up in the breast of Flora: she regarded the infant with faint but definite distaste. Nor did her milk flow with any abundance, and Hilda swiftly substituted for the nipple a rag dipped in sugar-water. 'If th'art not to nurse it, tha'll have to bind thy breasts up,' warned Hilda, 'but they say goat's milk does even better ...'

Then suddenly the infant wailed, and as suddenly (he must have been listening at the door), John Henry knocked.

'Is it come?' he demanded.

'Aye,' panted Hilda—in the panting tones of one who has just given birth—'but we want none of you yet awhile!'

'Just tell me lad or lass?'

'Lass,' said Hilda—her prognostication had been wrong after all. 'Now begone till tomorrow morning!'

And in the morning she presented to him the little atomy cradled against her own breast, while Flora, in the neighbouring bed, still slept.

'Don't wake her,' warned Hilda. 'She's tired out after helping me through the night ... but if you want to look at your daughter, here she is!'

John Henry looked, but without enthusiasm.

'I'll see right done by her,' said he. 'Anything you fancy, in the ways of oysters or port wine, you've but to ask for ...'

But it was apparent that he was disappointed. He'd hoped for a lad. For two or three days more Flora and Hilda remained so to speak in purdah; then Flora was on her feet again—hadn't Queen Charlotte opened Parliament within but hours of giving birth to the Prince Regent?—and it was Hilda, bowing to convention, who lay in bed a week on a diet of oysters and port wine. Flora bound up her breasts as Hilda advised, and if a little milk—not that there was much—seeped through her bodice, the customary shawl, as useful as the crinoline, concealed any damp patches.

'Don't you mean to nurse it yourself?' asked John Henry of Hilda.

'The gentry don't,' replied Hilda resourcefully. ''Tis said to be bad for the figure ...'

At which John Henry chuckled but was content. The child wasn't a lad, it was a lass.

However deprived of a mother's milk, the infant, on a diet of goat's milk and sugar-water, throve sufficiently to be christened at the end of the first month.

It was a rather meagre ceremony; Hilda carried the babe into church one morning with but Flora to stand godmother, and Mr Price performed the ritual with unusual dispatch. But the father's name was given correctly: John Henry Braithwaite; though himself not present he had no wish to deny paternity, which Mr Price found both praiseworthy and slightly scandalous. Also it was he who ordained the infant's name: Margaret.

'Call her Margaret after my Granny,' said he. 'She's got her Granny's brown eyes.'

If there was any reason why John Henry had flighted into East Anglia, it was so sentimental he usually preferred to forget it; but East Anglia was where his mother had originated, and in the lean days of his urchin-hood she'd always found him a ha'penny to buy sweets.

Chapter Five

'NOW THAT'S OUT OF THE WAY,' pronounced John Henry to Hilda and Flora, 'I've something to say that's best said before the pair of you. Hilda here has borne me a child, which though only a lass I'll do right by. She shan't be portionless.'

'Didn't I always say you were good at heart!' cried Hilda— not altogether tactfully, nor indeed truthfully; but John Henry brushed the interruption aside.

'And I mean to do right by Hilda too,' continued he. 'I'm going to wed her.'

The faces of the two women reflected one to the other a look first of incredulity, then of complicated dismay. For a moment neither could utter a word, whilst John Henry, perceiving only the first emotion, watched complacently. Then Flora found an argument.

'But Papa, even if you and Hilda do get married, it won't ... legitimise ... little Margaret.'

'As well I know,' said John Henry. 'It's something to be put up with. But mayn't Hilda bear me other children, and let's hope a son?—and *he*'ll be legitimate. How shall you like to be mistress of Cotton Hall?' he asked Hilda.

'I'd be despised,' said Hilda stoutly. 'Whatever would everyone think—Mrs Stacey and the rest? That I'd caught—' she was about to say 'a silly old man', but prudently changed it to 'a man old enough to be my father'—and even so had had to check herself again, she'd been about to say 'grandfather'—'and done Miss Flo out of her rights.'

'I don't think you'll find Flora forbidding the banns,' said John Henry. 'You might tell Mr Price to see about 'em,' he added to his daughter, 'and we'll be wedded the day after they're through. At my age, I've no time to lose.'

33

It wasn't impossible that he also remembered the impending visit of the Harry Braithwaites and Georges and Staceys, and preferred to present them with a *fait accompli*.

'I never meant it, truly I didn't, Miss Flo!' wailed Hilda, almost in tears.

'I'm sure you didn't,' said Flora. 'We must think ...'

'As for bearing him other children, didn't I tell you I was never caught in all those months and months? Whether 'twas him or me who knows, but never once did *I* miss a period! I used to be quite surprised!'

'Then he'll be disappointed,' said Flora grimly.

'And take it out o' *me*!' wailed Hilda. 'What a dog's life I shall lead! I suppose we couldn't tell him even now, Miss Flo, little Margaret's really yours?'

'No, we couldn't,' said Flora.

And Hilda too knew in her heart they couldn't—not after the comedy they'd played in complicity, not after John Henry had crept to the birth-chamber door to ask lad or lass ... However awkward the present situation, it was too complex to be so easily resolved.

The banns were called, the wedding ceremony took place— again without show. Flora, so recently a godmother, could hardly be expected to act as bridesmaid, but she was there, and to give the bride away old Ham the gardener, Hilda's father. It was a trifle awkward that when he signed the register he could do so only with a cross, but Mr Price kindly inked in his name above it, and the however disparate pair were legally wedded.

This was towards the middle of July. They were barely under the rope, as John Henry put it, before the Harry Braithwaites and Staceys and Georges arrived for their summer visit.

'You tell 'em, Flo,' said John Henry.

Flora sensibly did so as soon as they entered the house just before dinner—in the hall, even before they'd got their wraps off. The first greetings over, the children dispatched upstairs—

'We have a new step-mother,' she told them. 'Papa— Adelaide, what a pretty bonnet!—married Hilda last month.'

Their surprise was naturally great, and their immediate anger no less, but Flora was prepared for both.

'Why didn't you stop it?' demanded Harry, only half out of his travelling coat. 'Why didn't you send for us, to stop it?'

'Because you couldn't have stopped it any more than I could,' said Flora. 'You surely know Papa better than that?'

'I always knew that woman meant to get her claws into him!' cried Clara.

'No,' said Flora. 'You mustn't blame Hilda. It was entirely Papa's own doing.'

'One would think you were on her side!'

'There's no question of "sides",' interposed Charlotte practically. 'I think Flo is being very sensible. Of course we couldn't have stopped Papa, and if the thing is done we must make the best of it—and certainly without any sort of friction.'

'You'll also see a baby girl about the place,' continued Flora—determined to clear everything up at once.

'Oho!' said Arthur Stacey.

'Papa's and Hilda's?' enquired Harry resignedly. 'I suppose it was only to be expected.'

'His marrying the mother won't legitimise the child,' said George.

'But perhaps he anticipates more progeny?' suggested Arthur Stacey.

'At his age? I think it's quite disgusting as it is!' cried Clara.

'Be quiet, Clara!' ordered Charlotte. 'Be quiet, Clara!' ordered all the rest—even her husband.

'But what on earth are we to call her?' asked Addie. 'Step-mamma-in-law?'

'Just go on calling her Hilda,' said Flora. 'Now come up to your rooms and take your things off.'

The whole important conversation, as has been said, took place in the hall, and Flora was wise to get it over so soon.

'Only as there *was* a wedding,' said Adelaide, 'it's a pity we weren't at it. I've a much prettier bonnet than this, Flo, that I didn't bring in case it was too smart; but I could have worn it at a wedding!'

Hilda took the foot of the dinner table with some dignity. ('Must I?' she'd appealed to Flora. 'Won't you or Mrs Stacey?' 'We must begin as we mean to go on,' said Flora. 'You'll have Harry on your right and Mr Stacey on your left, and whatever they say you've only got to agree with.')

35

But first Harry had a few words to pronounce, it having been agreed upstairs that he should act as spokesman for all, and take the bull by the horns at once.

'Flora has told us,' said he. 'And may I only say, speaking for all of us, we wish you many years of happiness.'

'Hear, hear,' said Arthur Stacey.

'Very nicely put,' grinned John Henry. 'Hilda, my girl, say something pretty back.'

It was something Hilda and Flora, in their own colloquy upstairs, hadn't thought for; but Hilda rose to the occasion off her own bat.

'If I'm able to make your father happy that's all I ask,' said she. 'I know my good fortune and only hope to be worthy of it. The fish was got specially from Yarmouth and though not Dover sole is the next best, which I hope you will find acceptable.'

Fresh plaice is always acceptable. So was the saddle of lamb acceptable, and the apple tart smothered in cream, and more than acceptable the claret; and if conversation didn't exactly flow there were never more than a few pauses in it, as Hilda agreed with everything Harry or Mr Stacey said, and Charlotte told her father about her husband's new building plans, and Addie, urged on by Flora, chattered about the latest London fashions. Only George and Clara scarcely uttered, and then but to regret, with their usual lack of tact, that the saddle of lamb was slightly overdone.

All however were glad to separate as soon as coffee had been served in the drawing-room. 'After such a day's travelling,' suggested Flora—they'd actually been in the train only two-and-a-half hours—'I'm sure you'll all want to get to your beds!'

'I didn't say a word wrong, did I?' asked Hilda, slipping into Flora's bedroom before seeking the connubial couch she now openly shared with John Henry.

'You were perfect,' assured Flora.

'I still think we'll have to set 'em otherwise,' reflected Hilda. 'That Mrs Clara didn't at all like not having a man on her t'other side, *I* could see. I suppose we couldn't have Mr Price in? After all, he married us ... and wouldn't *you* like Mr Price asked in, Miss Flo?'

36

She made the proposal not only from a budding sense of hostess-duty, but from good-heartedness. Though Miss Flo might have slipped with the painting-chap, Hilda suspected the Vicar her real love.

But Flora said no. In the bleak climate in which she now dwelt, that shallow-rooted bloom of foolish sentiment had withered so completely, whether Mr Price were there or not was indifferent to her. But since his presence would undoubtedly annoy her father, she said no.

'Then I'm afraid it's you who'll have to shift,' said Hilda, beginning to unhook her stays. '*You* wouldn't mind sitting by Addie?'

Flora was both touched and amused to see Hilda wrestling with the problem of a family dinner table. She herself was well content to sit next to Addie, whose irrepressible frivolity afforded the only spark of gaiety to enliven the long, over-plentiful meals. Addie blithely told John Henry all about her bonnets—particularly about the new one with humming-birds on it which she hadn't brought because she thought it would be too smart, but which she'd have been so pleased to wear at his wedding!—and just as a High Court Judge had done, John Henry smiled on her benevolently.

Charlotte was his elder daughter, and he'd done right by her and never regretted it, her husband being in a fair way of making his own fortune. John Henry always appreciated a man who could get on, and Arthur Stacey was getting on indeed—as one of the architects to the City of London, no less, when after the Crimean War money flowed easily again. Not only rows of houses were built to his plans, but squares and crescents; he adumbrated, so to speak, West Kensington. John Henry came to have as great a respect for his son-in-law Arthur Stacey as he had for his elder son (he never thought much of George), while Adelaide often actually made him laugh, as when she asked him what was she to do, if the humming-birds were to lay eggs and have chicks on her bonnet?—for they shared the same simple sense of humour.

'By the way,' Adelaide asked Charlotte, 'have you noticed the change in Flora?'

'Now that you mention it, I have,' said Charlotte. 'She seems so much more ... in charge. Which on the face of it seems

37

absurd, now that Hilda's legitimately mistress of the house. But I must say I was struck by the way she handled the situation the moment we came in.'

'She handled even Harry!' giggled Adelaide.

'I suppose that now what she must have always feared—Papa's marrying Hilda—has actually come about, she feels less need to tread carefully,' said Charlotte. 'I'm very glad. When one thinks what poor Flo must have gone through when that little bastard was born—!'

That Charlotte could employ the word 'bastard', even to a sister-in-law, was a measure of her own release from inhibitions.

Neither of them could guess that Flora's heart had been broken. A broken heart, if it does not altogether destroy, can liberate. She was developing an altogether new personality: no longer shy and self-effacing, but rather tough and abrasive.

Hilda meanwhile kept little Margaret discreetly out of sight in a cradle in the kitchen by day, which by night was deposited alongside Cook's bed in the attics. Cook quite doted on little Meg (as she came to be called), and a kitchen-maid was seconded from the pantry to take on the offices of nurse—warming goat's milk and sugar-water, then beating up an egg with honey, then introducing infant lips to porridge and a smitchet of bacon fat. Actually none of the party from London ever set eyes on her, and all in all the visit passed off pretty well, except for one ill-considered Day of Doom.

Once again the Tribe assembled in its Holy of Holies the bee-hive lodge, once again Alan and Sybil resumed their secret communion, once again the Grand Panjandrum Mato-Topa ordained the initial letter for each day or proclaimed a Day of Doom; only on this occasion he rather over-reached himself by demanding as sacrifice Alice's new china doll with the wax head.

'But Aunt Addie gave it me for Christmas!' protested Alice. 'It came from Paris!'

'Am I or am I not the Grand Panjandrum Mato-Topa?' demanded Alan coldly, 'and isn't my word law?' (So it was, in the peculiar society the children had organized themselves into.) 'Do my bidding or be expelled from the Tribe!' threatened Mato-Topa, in the icy tones that were later to subdue many a rival expert at the Treasury. (After Winchester and Oxford he was to go into the Civil Service.) Easily enough was subdued Alice, and though with bitter tears onto the bonfire went her precious doll; where its waxen head so fired the embers, the whole smouldering heap flamed into such a blaze that a garden hose had to be employed to put it out. The attention of adults was attracted—of Charlotte and Clara and Addie playing croquet—as old Ham wrathfully raked apart the cinders, and since china isn't consumed like wax, the limbs and torso of the sacrifice were all too observable and identifiable.

'Good heavens!' cried Clara. 'Why, it looks like part of the doll Aunt Addie brought you from Paris! Alice, how could you be so careless?'

'I wasn't,' wept Alice. 'I *loved* my doll!'

'Then how on earth did it get onto the bonfire?'

Throwing all tribal loyalty to the winds—

'Alan told me to!' wept Alice.

'Alan told you to? Alan told you to put your doll onto the bonfire? But why? And why did you obey him?' demanded Charlotte.

It was obviously impossible to explain to an adult that if she hadn't she'd have been expelled from the Tribe. Alice could only hang her head.

'To tell your cousin to do such a thing!' exclaimed Adelaide to her son. 'Alan, whatever possessed you?'

Actually Alan had been possessed by the spirit of the Grand Panjandrum Mato-Topa; but again no adult could be expected to understand.

'I just thought old Ham's bonfire needed a bit of help,' said he—as smoothly and disingenuously as he'd have defended an unpopular Treasury estimate. 'I'm very sorry if anyone's upset ...'

'And I'm very sorry too,' said Adelaide. 'I shall have to tell your father!'

Which meant that as soon as Harry Braithwaite returned to Cotton Hall—the next day; this happened on a Friday, so that the sword of Damocles hung but a mercifully short time—Alan was soundly thrashed. He bore the punishment stoically, as befitted a Grand Panjandrum: not a whimper passed his lips. But Alice was expelled from the Tribe for having told, and none of her cousins, except under the eye of adults, would speak to her

39

for the rest of the month, so that she in fact became the Scapegoat.

This incident apart, the visit passed off pretty well.

Chapter Six

THEIR SUMMER GUESTS DEPARTED, John Henry and Hilda and Flora enjoyed for a while a rather halcyon period. As little Meg grew and throve the old man regarded her benevolently, as earnest of further healthy progeny to come, and took pleasure in discovering a resemblance to himself. (Actually, so far as so young a child could be said to resemble anyone, Margaret resembled her mother, but since Flora herself had a look of John Henry, the error was natural enough.) He in fact took rather more notice of Margaret than either of the women did: Hilda had all the household cares on her shoulders, and Flora, as has been said, lacked all maternal instinct, and when the child in time began to prattle, and was taught to address her as Aunt Flora rather than Godmother, was perfectly content. Little Margaret wasn't neglected, but only John Henry occasionally rode her cockhorse on his foot, or chucked her under the chin and asked where she got her brown eyes ...

This happy period was however brief. As months passed, and then almost a year, and Hilda showed no signs of a fresh pregnancy, he grew impatient, and just as she'd foreseen began to lead her a dog's life indeed, snarling and snapping at her all day, or else relapsing into long periods of angry silence. He led them all a dog's life, for neither Flora nor the child escaped his ill-humour; by extension John Henry took a scunner to them as well. He took a scunner to everybody, and for once the annual summer visit of the Braithwaites and Staceys was cut short, Addie and Charlotte and Clara, in rare alliance, declaring that his bad temper had become quite intolerable.

'It's not my fault, I'm certain sure it's not!' wailed Hilda. 'I never told you, Miss Flo, but while I was in the laundry I had to go twice over to Granny Cable! The truth is, your Da's past it.

Why, I could go with any lad behind a hedge and be caught!'

For a moment the two women looked at each other; then averted their eyes, and Hilda's dropped to her wedding ring.

'We can only hope,' said Flora.

Certainly there was no lack of hedges for Hilda to stray behind, and now that John Henry, well over seventy, was more and more housebound, in the matter of her goings-out and comings-in she could do pretty well as she pleased; if she fancied a stroll in the dusk, in the dusk she strolled. But she was also the mistress of Cotton Hall, whom no local lad would dare to attempt to tumble; and Flora felt her father's honour safe.

By that Christmas he'd settled into a mood of dogged surliness. Not that he'd ever made much of Christmas: a season of unbridled jollity, any kind of Saturnalia, offended his deepest instincts. He'd never in his life given Flora a Christmas present, and now didn't give Hilda one. Christ's birth was celebrated, in that respect, only by Cook, who gave Meg a paper doll and popped a sugar-plum into her mouth.

In the village however jollity rather unusually abounded, centring on the return of Mrs Strowger's grandson as a swaggering sergeant. Though all agreed he must have been drunk when he 'listed—bugles might sound, and drums beat, East Anglians mostly stayed at home unless drunk or press-ganged—now he returned a proper hero, having charged at Balaclava. Some ten years to be sure had passed since that famous military defeat, but what was a time-lag of ten years in East Anglia? There were greeting gatherings without number at the Crown; Mr Price, in a much appreciated sermon, spoke of the soldiers of Christ embattled against Russian tyranny. Moreover Sergeant Butley looked just as a hero should: tall and swaggering, hair clipped short behind but bushy-bearded and moustachio'd up to his bright brown eyes—so bright and brown indeed, so unusual in those parts, some thought his mother (of whom it may be remembered the less said the better) must have made a slip with a gipsy. But what if she had, her son now a hero? At the Fisherman's Arms gifts of geese and hares flowed in, and the Crown rocked to its rafters with more than Christmas carols ...

Naturally Hilda and Flora on their walks abroad encountered this cynosure of all eyes; and he, hearing Flora addressed by

42

Hilda as Miss Flo, asked if she had the same name as Miss Nightingale.

'No; my name is Flora,' said she. 'But I dare say many little girls will be christened Florence in the future! Was it very terrible, in the Crimea?'

In plain soldierly language the sergeant replied in the affirmative—indeed in such very plain soldierly language, Flora immediately passed on, though Hilda loitered a little behind, possibly to hear more of Miss Nightingale.

Sergeant Butley however disrupted the village's quiet way of life for no more than a couple of weeks before he was off again leaving not a dry eye behind him—at least among the women, though several swains, let alone husbands, were glad to see him go.

The women had cause to weep. Not a handkerchief, not a button did Sergeant Butley leave behind him in the way of keepsake to any one of those he'd tumbled behind a hedge on his staggering way home from the Crown. Come one, come all was his motto; and being usually tipsy at the time served each and all as mindlessly as a bull a heifer or a billy goat a nanny, and couldn't have told a goose-girl from the mistress of Cotton Hall. All he left behind him was a Russian cartridge-pouch picked up in the Crimea, and that by accident.

Chapter Seven

THE FOLLOWING APRIL Hilda had good news at last, after missing three periods she was certain of it, and John Henry, all the more delighted for his previous disappointment, for the ensuing six months made, as Hilda said, a proper nuisance of himself. There was no need this time for secrecy, for the all-concealing crinoline or protective shawl; he watched his wife's stomach swell with fatuous pride and would have kept her on a sofa all day long but that Hilda refused to be so tied by the leg and called him a proper fusspot. She could now say pretty well anything she liked to him, and did.

But on one point John Henry was adamant: no summer visitors.

'I'll not have you bustled about in your sixth month,' said he. 'They must be put off. Flo, write and tell 'em.'

It was unheard of, that the summer visit, even though last year's had been cut short, should be put off altogether: the Harry Braithwaites and Georges and Staceys received Flora's letters with indignation—particularly as they were forced to the expense of taking seaside lodgings instead. (At a pretty little fishing village called Broadstairs.) However all the children loved the sea, and the menfolk found it much easier to go back and forth between Kent and London than from East Anglia; in fact (relieved from the tedium of Cotton Hall), found they needed to go back and forth far less. Harry Braithwaite and Arthur Stacey took up fishing, while George found a new interest in studying the marine life of rock pools.

'I'm more sorry than I can tell, Miss Flo,' apologized Hilda, 'that it's on my account you can't see all your kin here.'

'I don't mind,' said Flora—and it was true. She didn't care whether her relations came or didn't. She was on good enough

44

terms with all of them, except perhaps Clara; rather respected Charlotte, and for Addie had the slight affection one might feel for a canary.

As the birthing approached John Henry was prevented from having a famous man-midwife down from London only because there happened to be an equally famous one holidaying at Ipswich; who when summoned to pronounce on Hilda's imminent parturition rather coarsely observed that it would be as easy as shelling peas. (He had many and richer clients in town.) And in fact Hilda gave birth just as easily as Flora had done, though—as if the child in her womb was aware there was no need for discretion—at high noon; and to a lad.

'Benjamin!' pronounced John Henry. 'That's what he shall be named: Benjamin.'

There was no question, this time, of the mother's not nursing the child herself. The milk flowed rich and copious from her full breasts, and John Henry delighted to watch the infant's greedy lips nuzzling at a teat. 'He pulls like a real good'un,' said John Henry. 'Why, he gives me a taste for a drop myself!'

And he put down his grizzled head and sucked for a moment in turn. By this time he was almost as toothless as a babe himself: Hilda didn't flinch. Flora, just then happening to enter, turned away in disgust; but Alexander, as Hilda lay benevolently passive and the greybeard nuzzled, would have been reminded of a Murillo—*Charity*, or *Saint Ursula succouring the imprisoned Simeon* . . .

For a son, and legitimate, John Henry naturally made the christening an occasion of some consequence.

'Take a fly to Ipswich,' he instructed Flora, 'for I'll not have Hilda jolted about, and ten pounds in your pocket, and buy the finest christening robe to be had.' (So she did; some hundred years later it was accepted by the Victoria and Albert Museum as a particularly fine example of nineteenth-century Honiton lace.) 'And if they've a cashmere shawl,' instructed John Henry, 'you can buy Hilda that too—though I dare say there'll be a cheque needed . . .'

Then came the question of godparents. None of Hilda's connections would do—certainly not old Ham who'd signed with a cross at her wedding.

'My eldest son and Addie,' ordained John Henry, 'and

45

Charlotte and Arthur Stacey. We'll make a right Christmas party of it. You write to 'em, Flo—and tell Addie this time to bring her best bonnet!'

So Flora wrote; and the immediate result of her letters was a family council at the Harry Braithwaites.

'This is where we do or don't make a stand,' opened Harry. 'Do we go or don't we?'

'After he put us off for the summer, certainly not!' cried Clara.

'And we always have such nice Christmases at home,' said Addie, 'with all our parties and the Pantomime on Boxing Day.'

'That's not the point,' said her husband. 'It would be at the most for a week, if that, and the children can be taken to the Pantomime later. It's not Christmas we're being invited for so much as the christening, to stand godparents to our half-brother.'

'Flo said nothing of that in her letter to *us*,' observed Clara jealously.

'No doubt the old man feels four will be sufficient,' said Arthur Stacey. 'Harry and Adelaide and Charlotte and myself; but I take my brother-in-law's point.'

'So do I,' said George, 'if he means we should seem to be not only countenancing, but actually approving, what Clara and I have always considered a most unfortunate marriage. All the same ...'

'All the same, the fact remains that we now have a legitimate half-brother,' said Harry, 'and father is undoubtedly going to make a new Will. I don't believe he'd ever leave the house away from me, as eldest son; but it may make a difference to George and Charlotte—and Flo, of course.'

'What he gave Charlotte when we married was very handsome,' stated Arthur Stacey. 'I don't know how you feel about it, Charlotte—'

'Just as you do,' said Charlotte. (It was for her dowry, as she knew, that her husband had married her, but they were by now a thoroughly attached couple.) 'If Papa leaves me nothing I shan't complain; and of course he'd always make provision for Flo.'

'So only George is to be left out in the cold?' said Clara bitterly. 'George, who's never had a penny from his father!'

'He had his professional training, and an allowance till he was

46

earning enough to marry on,' said George's elder brother.

'Only just,' complained Clara. 'If it hadn't been for *my* allowance, from *my* father, I'm sure I don't know how we should have managed!'

'Be quiet, Clara,' said her husband. 'You know we should have managed perfectly well—as we do now that he's withdrawn it. Of course he's perfectly within his rights—'

'Papa couldn't *help* losing all that money!' interrupted Clara.

'In my opinion, and I've always held it, any solicitor who dabbles in the Stock Market is asking for trouble,' said Harry. 'Either he's acting on inside information given him confidentially by his clients, or he knows nothing about it.'

'What all this has to do with our going or not going to Papa's for Christmas and the christening I fail to see,' said Charlotte. 'And for heavens' sake, Clara, let George speak for himself.'

Thus tangentially adjured, George did so.

'As Harry says, I had my professional training and an allowance so long as I needed it. Obviously anything more Father leaves me would be welcome; but not if it's to be got by kowtowing to him. I'm only glad,' he added, 'that Clara and I weren't required to be godparents.'

'Oh, so am I!' now declared Clara. 'Very glad indeed!'

'Then we none of us go?' said Harry. 'I agree it would be more dignified to stay away.'

Yet in the breasts of all a doubt lingered. To stay away would undoubtedly be more dignified; but apart from Cotton Hall, apart from the claims of the little new-born half-brother, hadn't John Henry still a great deal to leave?

It was Addie who got them off the hook.

'Flo wrote he said to tell me to bring my best bonnet,' said she, 'that I didn't wear at the wedding. If he's looking *forward* to seeing my best bonnet, I'd hate to disappoint him!'

It was a flimsy enough pretext. Addie herself was surprised to find it universally adopted as a reason for sending letters not of refusal, but of acceptance.

So once again, though this time not in mid-summer but in midwinter, the family assembled in the little church overlooking the salt marshes. There was quite a large congregation as well from among the villagers, whose admiration was almost equally divided between the infant's Honiton lace christening robe,

47

Hilda's cashmere shawl and Addie's bonnet. (Not her newest bonnet: the one with the humming-birds on it. Addie's newest bonnet was a rather more restrained affair, trimmed with marabout, but she rightly imagined John Henry would prefer the humming-birds, though humming-birds were at least three years out of date.) At the ceremony she and her husband, and Charlotte and Arthur Stacey, played their parts with all due decorum, while Clara and George sat looking into their service books; and once again it was only Flora who on her knees truly prayed.

Even in the heart-broken, old habits die hard.

'O Lord, if it be Thy will, let Papa not have been cuckolded,' prayed Flora.

She had given no hint of her suspicion to Hilda. As Hilda rejoiced at the prospect of pregnancy, so had she.

'It must have been a last uprising of the old Adam in him,' said Hilda. 'They do tell such things happen, Miss Flo, just when you think a man's past it altogether!'

'So I believe,' said Flora. 'I'm very glad.'

'Not half so glad as I am,' said Hilda. 'It's going to mean an easier time all round ...'

No one could have been more thoughtful of Hilda during her pregnancy than Flora (as once Hilda had been thoughtful of her). But the confidence between the two women had subtly diminished. They were still on the best of terms, but less confidential.

'Or if I do Hilda a wrong,' prayed Flora—

(And indeed the end of December, or the beginning of January, when the infant Benjamin must have been conceived, was a cold time enough to lie with a lad behind a hedge. But perhaps not behind a hedge, but on a truss of straw in some byre warm with the breath of kine?)

'—forgive me my trespasses as I forgive them that trespass against me.'

She wasn't thinking of Alexander, to whom the formula might well have applied. It was just—a formula. Flora by this time rarely thought of Alexander at all.

For once, that Christmas, Cotton Hall was lavish with turkey and plum pudding, mince pies and pound cake, almonds and raisins, nuts and wine. There was even too much abundance;

48

under John Henry's pressings to take second portions of every dish, the elder members of the party began to feel like Strasbourg geese, and the children, at their separate table, often had to get down before a meal was properly over. But even more trying was John Henry's exuberance of parental pride.

Hilda herself would have been discreet enough, nursing the babe in strict privacy and never taking it out of its cradle for exhibition. But—

'Don't the women want to take a look at him?' suggested John Henry.

'Haven't they all seen a baby before?' said Hilda.

'Aye, but not a little uncle younger than their own youngest!' joked John Henry.

His jocularity was almost more trying than his fatuous pride, and offended particularly the eldest children.

'Don't you want to rock your uncle's cradle a bit?' he asked Alice. 'I dare say you'll be thinking of wedding before he goes to school!'

Under her mother's eye Alice gave a perfunctory shove.

'Now you'll be able to tell him you rocked him in his cradle!' joked John Henry.

In the bee-hive lodge, the Holy of Holies, the elders of the Tribe gathered to watch the Grand Panjandrum Mato-Topa assume the Guy Fawkes mask and take the rabbit's skull out of the croquet-box and cast ritual anathema on their new little uncle.

'Down on your knees,' ordered Alan, 'and hear the words of doom!'

Sybil the Handmaid, Alice the Wet-nurse, Timothy the Scapegoat all obediently knelt. It was so cold in the bee-hive lodge their knees chattered on the stone floor.

'May his shadow never grow longer than a toadstool's,' intoned Alan.

'Amen.'

'May he suffer all the ills the flesh is heir to before being cut down like grass and put into the oven.'

'Amen.'

'May he be hammered on the Stock Exchange.' (This particular curse derived from a conversation overheard between his father and Arthur Stacey with regard to George's father-in-law.

49

Alan had no clear idea what the Stock Exchange was, but imagined it a sort of anvil.)

'Amen.'

'Well, that ought to settle *him*,' said Alan. 'Now let's go and roast chestnuts.'

Chapter Eight

THE CHRISTMAS VISIT, its purpose served, was never repeated. Nor were the summer visits repeated, for before the party broke up John Henry had very plainly stated his testamentary intentions to the three husbands.

'I'll not ask you to come to Ipswich to hear my new Will read,' said he, 'because you're none of you concerned in it.'

It was an unpropitious opening. George looked hang-dog, Harry, for all his confidence in the right of primogeniture, slightly uneasy. Only Arthur Stacey was unmoved.

'What you gave Charlotte when we married was more than generous,' said he, 'and I for my part have never expected anything more.'

'Well said,' approved John Henry. 'Th'art a clever chap, that I always knew given a boost would make his own way in the world. And I don't suppose George looks for anything either, after his education and articles paid for and an allowance for how many years?'

George could only mumble, untruthfully, that no he didn't.

'Which leaves my eldest son Harry,' proceeded John Henry, 'who doubtless expects, and I don't say unreasonably, to get Cotton Hall.'

'As you say, not unreasonably,' agreed Harry, with some dignity.

'I understand you make a very good income?'

'Fairish,' admitted Harry.

'I'd say no more myself,' grinned his father. 'And George I'll warrant is making a pretty good income too?'

'Fairish,' mumbled George.

'Whereas Benny I shan't live long enough to see on his feet,' said John Henry, 'so I'm leaving him the lot. There'll be a portion put aside for Flora, and if more brothers or sisters come they shall be looked after out of his patrimony.'

There was a considerable pause. Then—

'And who are to be the Executors of such a Will?' asked Harry coldly.

The old man grinned.

'As I thought you'd have no fancy for the job yourself, the solicitors at Ipswich.'

Again there was a prolonged pause.

'You mean,' said George, almost incredulously, 'that Harry and Charlotte and I are to be cut off without a sixpence?'

With grim humour John Henry took three silver coins from his pocket and laid them on the table.

'If you want 'em, here they are ...'

Only the son-in-law, Arthur Stacey, had the matching humour to pocket the coin; the others let theirs lie. (In fact Arthur subsequently had a hole drilled and hung it on his watch-chain.)

'And of course Cotton Hall is open to you each summer as usual,' added John Henry.

'Actually we found we all rather enjoyed Broadstairs,' said Harry.

'Please yourselves,' said John Henry, 'as I please *my*self, leaving Cotton Hall to my son Benjamin ...'

Only Benjamin wasn't his son; and thus it was a twisted turn enough John Henry's newly planted roots had taken.

Then the husbands had to relay the news to their wives. Charlotte, already to some extent prepared, took it with philosophy, and Addie with good humour, but Clara fretted herself into a condition of nervous irritability that boded ill for George. However on one point all were united: Broadstairs each August it should be. Charlotte made some attempt to persuade George and Clara to continue to accept the hospitality of Cotton Hall, pointing out that it was at least free, which Clara took as an insult.

'If you think George and I can't *afford* Broadstairs,' said she angrily, 'I assure you you're quite mistaken—poor as we are, we aren't as poor as all that! Of course we shall come to Broadstairs with you!'

'*I*'m only sorry for poor Flo,' said kind Addie. 'How she's going to miss us!'

52

Actually Flora didn't miss them at all, but was rather relieved.

There now came to be a division in the family. At Cotton Hall dwelt old John Henry and Hilda and Flora and little Benjamin (little Meg in the background), unvisited from Bloomsbury and Bayswater and Belgravia: in Bayswater and Belgravia and Bloomsbury dwelt the Harry and George Braithwaites and Staceys, taking their annual summer holiday at Broadstairs. There was no open breach: occasional letters were exchanged between Flora and Charlotte, and once Addie in her good nature invited Flora to stay in London for a fortnight. But the prospect of new surroundings, new faces, filled Flora merely with distaste.

Year by year a very pleasant time was had by the party at Broadstairs. Harry Braithwaite and Arthur Stacey fished, George discovered an unidentified shrimp (that is, until it was found to have been identified already), the women sat under their parasols on the beach not now doing needlework, as at Cotton Hall, but reading novels, while the elder children bathed and the younger built sand-castles. The children, agreed their parents, were happy as sand-boys!—and so in a sense they were; but their lives had lost a certain richness.

In marine surroundings, Alan at first reorganized the Tribe to suit. He himself became Neptune, Sybil Mistress of Mermaids, Alice Keeper of Shells and Timothy (ex-Scapegoat) a sea-urchin, a role for which his short stature and snub nose well suited him; their Holy of Holies was now a disused bathing-box where sand seeped through the floor-boards. But a derelict lobster-pot couldn't replace the croquet-box altar, nor a desiccated starfish the rabbit's skull. A pack of playing-cards was easily procurable, but lacked the old magic. It wasn't the same. In particular there were no more days of Mato-Topa's Rest: Neptune, it seemed, had no need of them. Perhaps the children were growing too big for the play of the Tribe in any case. Perhaps it was even a good thing that they forgot the play of the Tribe before the boys went to boarding-school.

Between their elders Cotton Hall and its denizens were rarely mentioned. Only occasionally did Addie wonder how poor Flo was getting on, and once only did Clara, suddenly looking up

53

from her novel, make an oblique reference to Benjamin.

'Of course he mayn't live,' said she.

So accurate was family telepathy that Addie and Charlotte, a moment before immersed in *Framley Parsonage* and *Silas Marner*, instantly realized that she referred to the baby at Cotton Hall.

'Hold your tongue, Clara,' said Charlotte. 'Why shouldn't he live?'

'Papa-in-law was almost eighty when he was born,' said Clara.

'Seventy-five,' corrected Charlotte, 'and Hilda twenty-four. Hold your tongue, Clara!'

But however snubbed down, Clara with her family for a number of years more still trailed after the others to Broadstairs, until Addie, in collusion with Charlotte, decided that Sybil and Tim had weak lungs.

'Which I suppose means Bournemouth?' complained Clara. 'Of all the expensive places—!'

'Not Bournemouth, dear: Menton,' said Addie.

Thus the Harry Braithwaites and the Staceys were amongst the first English to descend on the Riviera in the summer. Monte Carlo, and Menton, and Nice, were well known as the proper resorts in winter for sufferers from weak lungs—but then in winter both families were happy at home; during the London winter, with all its fogs, Sybil's and Timothy's lung-trouble was so to speak suspended, but every August Charlotte and Addie returned to the Riviera, and in due course became quite well-known and popular figures on the Place de la Mairie. Their husbands always joined them for a fortnight (for the remaining two weeks putting up, not unenjoyably, at their Clubs), and then they made little excursions round about. Once they went as far as a little fishing-village called St Tropez, where all exclaimed at its picturesqueness—but three-quarters of a century were to pass before St Trop' came into its own ...

The George Braithwaites however stuck to Broadstairs. 'At least everyone there knows us,' said Clara with false complacency, when her husband told her that the Riviera was quite out of the question, 'and at least none of *our* children have weak lungs!'

So the George Braithwaites were shaken off at last, and George at least was content to be. The days when he could put business in Harry's way were long past, since when the effort of trying to keep up with his brother had always rather harassed than stimulated him; a smallish but solid practice was just about what he could cope with. He could have been a happy man, if he hadn't married Clara.

The difference in the lot of the two brothers could be explained only by the fact that Harry had the mark of success on him, and George hadn't. So had Arthur Stacey the mark of success on him; as architect of more and more London squares and terraces his income rivalled Harry's, and as Harry with Adelaide he dwelt with his Charlotte in perfect amity. It amused him, now and then jingling John Henry's sixpence on his watch-chain, to declare that it had brought him luck, but he had no need of any extra luck, the mark of success so strong on him already.

There was no mark of success on Alexander. His Portrait of a Lady being unfortunately refused by the Salon d'Automne, and he being as usual on his beam ends, he sold it to the madam of a brothel who fancied it would lend her establishment tone. She told her clients it represented Diane de Poitiers, mistress of Henry IV, *Le Vert Galant*, and many a respectful glass was raised to Flo's likeness hanging between *Léda et le Cygne* and *Le Petit Pantalon Rose*.

The rest of Alexander's story was sad. Paris, the mistress-city, recaptured him once for all; he couldn't tear himself away. For a while, even though his lodging was necessarily a garret and a square meal a rarity, he scraped a living painting views (latterly always the same view) of the Seine, which his acquaintances among the bouquinistes on the quais offered for sale on commission. But there were few buyers, and he took to sponging on English visitors, casting his line for them like an expert angler as they promenaded the Tuileries Gardens. 'Can I show you round a little?—I live here,' Alexander would open; and though the men sometimes tried to shake him off, their womenfolk were usually hooked—he looked so like a gentleman! Indeed looking like a gentleman became Alexander's sole asset.

But not for long. Too much Pernod, too much red wine, played their havoc, and he finally ended up under the Pont d'Alsace still proclaiming, to any other tramp who'd listen, the supremacy of Turner. Then he sank without trace.

Chapter Nine

MEANWHILE THERE HAD ensued another halcyon period at Cotton Hall. Despite Clara's forebodings, or hopes, despite even the anathema cast on him by the Tribe, little Benny grew and throve. He was a sturdy child, with Hilda's build also her lint-fair hair, but his eyes were brown. 'He's got my Grannie's eyes, like Meg!' declared John Henry. 'It's easy to see they're brother and sister!'

If the child didn't look as much like him as Meg had done at the same early age, Hilda promised that the resemblance would come soon enough; and certainly Flora hoped so. As soon as he could talk he addressed her, as did Meg, as Aunt Flora.

The position of Meg also at this time improved, she so adoring of little Benny. Alice had but given his cradle a shove; Meg hung over it with delight, crooning lullabies; then teaching Benny to play with his toes, then, scarcely more than a toddler herself, guiding his infant steps from chair to chair, and was actually the first to proclaim that he could stand alone. She called to John Henry to come and see, called to Hilda, called to Flora—beaming with innocent joy as she stood ready to catch him if he fell.

'Th'art a right good little lass!' said John Henry. 'We'll have to make thee his nursemaid!'

No one saw any absurdity in it. In the families from which John Henry and Hilda originated, children but a year or two older than the little ones looked after them as a matter of course. The important result was that Meg was taken into John Henry's favour again, and at Christmas he gave her a proper doll with a wax head—not so *chic* as the doll from Paris Alan Braithwaite had been thrashed for consigning to a bonfire, but still an object of almost awesome delight to little Meg.

56

Young Benny grew to be a boy big enough to go fishing. To go fishing was his chief joy, especially if he could stay out at sea all night with the Strowger brothers. (Only tribally related to Mrs Strowger of the Fisherman's Arms, but Hilda's cater-cousins.) It was a pleasure Hilda rarely allowed, however, John Henry being always nervous when Benny was out after dark. He so doted on Benny, even by day he could hardly bear to let him out of sight, even to go to the dame school in the village; and indeed Flora made quite as adequate an instructress as the old woman who ruled there. Flora taught Benny to read and write, and to do addition and subtraction (though not long division), and to recite poems by Ann and Jane Taylor, which last accomplishment filled John Henry with fatuous pride. But when the child was eight or nine she admitted herself at the end of her scholastic tether (also the whole project had bored her ex-tremely), and declared that some more competent tutor must be found if he wasn't to be the dunce of Ipswich Grammar-School.

'He's not going to Ipswich Grammar to be switched,' said John Henry.

Both George and Harry had been switched regularly, at their grammar-school, and their father hadn't cared a button. But Benjamin was his Benjamin.

'But he must get an education somewhere, Papa,' protested Flora, 'if he isn't to grow up a complete ignoramus!'

'As I'd have no son of mine grow up to be,' agreed Hilda—who fond as she was of Benny accepted switchings as a natural concomitant of childhood. She'd been switched herself as a child, often and often, for no more than losing a ball among old Ham's seedling lettuces ...

'A tutor, didn't you say?' chuckled John Henry. 'Then a tutor he shall have, just like a gentleman's son! We'll have in Mr Price to teach him Greek and Latin!'

So it was that at long last Mr Price became a familiar of Cotton Hall. What John Henry offered in the way of payment was a substantial increase to his stipend, and his parish duties were only as onerous as he chose to make them. Each afternoon between half-past two and half-past five he and Benjamin struggled together not only with Greek and Latin verbs, but also with the elements of history and geography, both of which subjects Flora had omitted from her curriculum. Greek and Latin in fact both rather went by the board, while Mr Price got his pupil as far as the Tudors and belts of vegetation. There was so much leeway to be made up, in young Benny's education; but he was a good-natured, willing boy, if neither particularly bright nor painstaking, and Mr Price grew genuinely attached to him, and John Henry in fact did far better for the lad than if he'd sent him to Ipswich Grammar.

Ten years earlier, how happy would Flora have been, Mr Price so accepted at Cotton Hall! Now she no longer felt even embarrassment in his company, and the fact that Mr Price was still a bachelor was a matter of complete indifference to her.

Margaret too profited by Mr Price's instructions, chiefly because she and Benny were so attached to one another, and so used to being always in each other's company. ('Mind, I'll pay no more for two than for one!' John Henry warned Mr Price.) Margaret was by far the apter pupil; she knew the names of all Henry the Eighth's wives long before Benny did, and belts of vegetation were meat and drink to her; and if in a class of two Mr Price had a favourite, it was undoubtedly Margaret with her long, serious face and intelligent eyes.

'How like your Aunt you are!' he once observed.

There was of course every reason why Meg should resemble Flora, though Flora herself often forgot it.

'Only you've brown eyes like a squirrel's,' added Mr Price.

He began to think of her as his little squirrel; and indeed as Margaret sat erect holding the history or geography book a few inches from her nose—she was rather short-sighted—there was something about her of a squirrel with a nut which Mr Price found quite charming.

Benny's scholastic progress was slow enough, but he had at last conquered Gaul with Caesar and could repeat at least the Lord's Prayer in Greek before Sergeant Butley reappeared.

The interim was some thirteen years, but he was still a fine figure of a man, still as brown moustachio'd and swaggering and bright-eyed. Some wondered why he'd returned at all, his grandmother dead and the Fisherman's Arms no longer offering him a free billet; but apparently his boyish haunts still had charms for him, and he was put up almost for free at the Crown, as an attraction, with his tales of martial deeds (and of course of the Charge of the Light Brigade), to the drinking part of the community.

Flora, who had first encountered him in the company of Hilda, this time re-encountered him alone. (She still took a regular walk each morning, though no longer as far as the rim of the salt marsh, nor in hopes of meeting Mr Price. She could meet Mr Price any afternoon she wanted to, between half-past two and half-past five, only she didn't want to. She took her walk purely from habit.) At the sight of her Sergeant Butley clicked his heels and gave a semi-military salute.

'Why, if it isn't Miss Florence!' exclaimed he. 'And looking not a day older!'

'Flora,' corrected Flo drily. 'Good day, Sergeant Butley. You know of course that your grandmother is dead?'

'Aye, I feared 'twas so,' said the Sergeant, 'but 'twas on my mind to come and make sure.'

'Now you may be,' said Flora.

'One departs, another arises,' said the Sergeant piously. 'There's now a lad, I hear, at Cotton Hall?'

'Good day to you,' said Flora, walking on.

'Sergeant Butley is back,' she told Hilda, on her return to Cotton Hall. 'I've just met him in the village.'

Did Hilda's face show a momentary look of disarray? Flora couldn't be sure.

'Bad ha'pence always turn up again,' said Hilda cheerfully. 'Did he speak to you?'

'I think he intended to be impertinent,' said Flora. 'Not that it mattered.'

'Handsome and swaggering still?'

'I see you recollect him.'

'I recollect once setting eyes on him—in your company,' said Hilda. 'You needn't fear he'll be made welcome at Cotton Hall!'

'He asked after Benny,' said Flora.

Hilda could sometimes be quick enough.

'As if a boy knowing Greek and Latin would take up with a common soldier!' she derided. 'Get your things off before lunch, Miss Flo!'

In point of fact the Sergeant never went near Cotton Hall. He stuck to the Crown. But of course Benny took up with him. So dashing a stranger in the village naturally excited first his curiosity, then his admiration; and a boy of twelve couldn't be tied by the leg. He slipped off to the Crown at every oppor-

59

tunity, to admire the Sergeant's moustachios and hear him expatiate on the glories of a military life. And the Sergeant seemed to take a liking to the lad; all his best tales (including of course that of the Charge of the Light Brigade) were repeated as often as Benny asked for them. Nor was it only the heroic past he dwelt on, but an equally heroic future: the Regiment was bound for India—there was always trouble in India!—and then what loot, what houris, might not fall to a cavalryman's sabre! Benny listened with eyes like saucers, and often had to be fetched home from the Crown at long past his bed-time.

Hilda and Flora were both uneasily aware of his infatuation. It was the last thing either had wanted to happen, but how could they stop it? The boy couldn't be tied by the leg. Thus it was a considerable relief to both that Benny chose the day of Sergeant Butley's rejoining his regiment to go off fishing, so missing the emotional scenes attendant. Once again, there was hardly a dry eye in the village (except amongst swains and husbands, Sergeant Butley, even thirteen years older, having cut his usual perfunctory swath through the village's womenfolk), but this time many a rheumy masculine eye dropped a tear as well, the day Sergeant Butley was sent off with a three-times-three from the drinking part of the community.

When Benny said he was going fishing Hilda and Flora expected him back before nightfall. But night fell without Benny reappearing.

'Off with those Strowgers no doubt!' grumbled Hilda. 'I'm going to give Jemmy Strowger a right flea in the ear. Benny'll come in soused as a herring and hungry as a hunter, and who's to sit up for him?'

'For once we'll neither of us sit up for him,' declared Flora. 'He can come in the back way and get himself bread and cheese while we go to bed.'

Both slept, but with as it were an ear a-cock, until midnight; after which both slept soundly. (One of the beneficent qualities of East Anglian air is that it almost inevitably induces sound sleep.) Thus it wasn't until the following morning that Benny was definitely missed; nor had he been missed long before one of the village urchins appeared offering a scrap of paper folded into a cocked hat.

'*Dear Mam, dear Aunt Flora,*' had scrawled Benny, '*I am gone for a drummer-boy.*'

60

Chapter Ten

FLORA, INTO WHOSE hands the missive first fell (she was always up early), saw it all. Had Benny openly attempted to leave in the dashing Sergeant's company, of course he'd have been stopped. So he'd feigned to go fishing, and instead (probably by way of carrier's cart) had made his way to join the Sergeant at Ipswich station. Flora was quite surprised at the boy's ingenuity, until she realized it wasn't Benny's ingenuity but Sergeant Butley's, that was responsible for so clever a plan.

Then she had to inform Hilda, who was still in her bedroom.

'However are we going to tell his Da?' wept Hilda. 'It'll be the death of him!'

'We mustn't tell him,' said Flora. 'At least not yet. And perhaps, if we say Benny's gone fishing, we shan't need to tell him at all. Benny must be got back.'

'How? By now he'll have 'listed,' wept Hilda, 'and all along of that wicked man! Oh that I'd never set eyes on him, that I'd died first and lay cold in my grave!'

Flora had no need to ask to whom she referred: the villain of the piece was all too obvious. And what more would Hilda have blurted out, perhaps to confirm Flora's suspicions as to Benny's parentage? But she pulled herself together, even if it was to take refuge in hysterics. Flora picked up a jug of cold water and threw its contents in her face.

'Now you're as soused as we thought Benny would be,' she said briskly. 'If he's really enlisted—'

'If who's really enlisted?' asked Margaret, just then appearing with her pinafore strings untied. 'Good gracious, Mama, Aunt Flora, whatever's the matter?'

'Your mother is having hysterics because one of her cousins

has gone for a soldier,' lied Flora resourcefully. (If John Henry were to be kept in ignorance, obviously Margaret must too.)

'How strange,' said Meg indifferently. 'Where's Benny? I can't find him.'

'Off on a fishing trip,' said Flora. 'Is breakfast laid?'

When Margaret had dutifully pattered away—

'Now listen to me and try to control yourself,' Flora adjured Hilda. 'If Benny has really enlisted, he must be bought out, but it's a matter for Harry: I'll telegraph. In the meantime tell Papa he's gone fishing—maybe for a week—and didn't say so because he knew he'd have been stopped.'

It was obviously the best, the only plan. John Henry, as Hilda told him the lie, found her tear-stained face quite natural. 'Off thy apron-strings for a week?' he grinned. 'Good luck to him! Who's he with? The Strowgers?'

'I dare say,' whimpered Hilda.

'They'll look after him all right,' said John Henry. 'Stop blubbering!'

This unexpected reaction of the old man's at least gave, so to speak, breathing-space. Flora's telegraphed message was brief but explicit—BENNY GONE FOR A DRUMMER-BOY COME AT ONCE; upon receipt of which there ensued for Harry Braithwaite the most irritating, frustrating and time-wasting episode of his whole life.

At great inconvenience he took the next morning train to East Anglia, and there (the first of his frustrations) found he might as well have stayed in London, his idea that the boy had enlisted locally, and could be swiftly and easily bought out, proving all too false a hope.

'When I said gone, I meant *gone*,' said Flora bleakly.

'What, on his own?'

'We think probably with Sergeant Butley ...'

'Sergeant Butley?'

'You won't know of him,' said Flora, 'but he charged with the Light Brigade, and then last week came back, and we're afraid Benny was ... beglamoured by him.'

'The Charge of the Light Brigade,' pointed out Harry, not unnaturally at a loss, 'took place more than twenty years ago.'

'I know,' said Flora. 'But he's traded on it ever since, and he's still so fine and swaggering one can hardly blame Benny . . . who is after all your godson.'

'If you imagine I have forgotten, you are mistaken,' said Harry bitterly. 'What's the regiment?'

'I'm not sure,' admitted Flora.

And no one in the village was sure either. Some thought it was the Dragoons, some the Lancers—or Hussars? No one in the village had questioned the Sergeant with any strictness.

'Give me the facts again,' said Harry.

'Sergeant Butley left on Tuesday,' recapitulated Flora, 'but Benny certainly wasn't *with* him, because he'd played truant to go fishing. Or so we thought, but now I think perhaps to join the Sergeant at Ipswich, and it wasn't till Wednesday morning that we got the note.'

'And now it's Thursday; by this time they may be on a troopship bound for India,' said Harry discouragingly. 'However, I'll do what I can.'

And what he could do for his godson he did. On his return to London he went straight to the War Office, which in its customary state of inefficiency would have had difficulty in tracing a mule-train, let alone a drummer-boy. That it was a mere drummer-boy Harry was forced to enquire after stuck particularly in his gullet, and after the first visit he sent his clerk to wait about in the War Office anterooms.

'A drummer-boy gone off with a Sergeant?' checked a War Office underling to Harry Braithwaite's underling. 'What Regiment?'

'That we're unfortunately not certain,' said Harry Braithwaite's clerk, 'but he charged at Balaclava.'

'If all the sergeants, let alone troopers, who charged at Balaclava were laid head to arse,' said the War Office underling, 'they'd about girdle the equator. But I'll keep the name in mind. Butley, did you say it was?'

'Not the boy's,' said Harry's clerk. 'The boy's name is Braithwaite. Though of course it's possible he may have given another.'

(This was one of several awkward points that had occurred to Harry Braithwaite.)

'You're looking for a needle in a haystack,' said the War Office underling.

So Harry Braithwaite realized, and only his extreme conscientiousness impelled him to tackle a very senior officer drinking port in his Club.

'I dare say a lad gone for a drummer-boy might be pretty difficult to trace?' he suggested.

'Not if you know the regiment,' said the senior officer loyally.

'That's rather the trouble,' said Harry. 'All we know is that they charged at Balaclava ...'

'Balaclava!' snorted the senior officer. 'Balaclava, did you say? The flower of our cavalry thrown away by that old fool Cardigan! If you're a friend of his, sir,' snarled the senior officer (who had undoubtedly been drinking port too long), 'you're no friend of mine!'

Harry was so incensed he didn't set foot in the Club again for a month.

Meanwhile he had been forced to inform the family. He didn't want to, he'd have far rather kept the whole scandalous business under his own hat, but he'd had to tell Adelaide the reason for his sudden excursion to Cotton Hall, and Addie, before he returned, told Charlotte, and Charlotte (actually with the idea of taking some of the nuisance off Harry's hands) told George, who told Clara; and once again, as on the occasion of Benny's christening, all assembled in a *conseil de famille*.

'Dear Harry,' mourned Clara, pressing his hand sympathetically, 'how very, very horrible and tiresome for you! I always knew the boy would come to no good.'

'As I remember, you always envisaged him dying young,' recalled Charlotte.

'And perhaps *better* dead,' sighed Clara, 'than making such a dreadful scandal! The only wonder is why Harry is so eager to find him ...'

Harry looked at her inimically.

'I am not "eager" to find him, except in the sense that it's my obvious duty to attempt it, and the sooner the whole confounded business is over the better I shall be pleased.'

'In a way it's rather a pity,' reflected Adelaide, 'he'd look so sweet in regimentals!'

For once her husband snapped at her.

'Whether the heir to Cotton Hall would or wouldn't look sweet in regimentals is beside the point. Try for once to show some sense!'

'Addie has a point all the same,' Arthur Stacey defended his sister-in-law. 'Why shouldn't even the heir to Cotton Hall embrace a military career, if that's the way his tastes lie?'

'By purchasing an ensignship into some good regiment, yes,' said Harry, 'though even so I'd deplore it. But an ensign in a good regiment one can always lay one's hand on; as it is I'm reduced to looking for a drummer-boy who in fact may be even now dead of diarrhoea on a troop-ship bound for India.'

The rude word diarrhoea (like the crude word childbirth) produced among the ladies such a definite shock, for a moment they were silenced. Then it was Charlotte who spoke, voicing indeed the thought in every mind.

'Harry.'

'Well?'

'Suppose he never turns up again at all? Suppose the poor boy has ... succumbed?'

There was a considerable pause while all envisaged not only the possibility, but what would be the consequences.

'Then probably my father's first Will would stand,' said Harry Braithwaite. 'That is, unless he makes another equally unjust.'

It was John Henry's second Will, leaving all to Benny, Harry meant when he called it unjust, and he had never called it so before; now the long suppressed emotions of twelve years found vent.

'Or unless he dies first?' suggested Clara. 'Indeed I'm only surprised the shock hasn't killed him already!'

'Benny's father at the moment believes the boy gone on a fishing trip,' said Harry. 'Flora and Hilda, and I agreed with them, felt the truth had better be kept from him as long as possible.'

'But when he does know?' persisted Clara. 'Good heavens, he must be over eighty! Of course the shock will kill him! Then you'd get Cotton Hall, and poor George at least a pittance—'

'Hold your tongue, Clara!' said Charlotte—and so the *conseil de famille* broke up, but not before Clara had murmured, in a sympathetic aside to Addie, that it was no wonder Arthur Stacey (equally Benny's godfather) left all the nuisance to his brother-in-law, so worried about his own Timothy as he must be.

Undoubtedly the ownership of Cotton Hall would have

meant much to Harry Braithwaite. It was greatly to his credit that he still persisted—if only through his clerk—in his attempts to fetch Benny home again. He was by far the best of the Braithwaites. George was a nonentity, Charlotte a good wife to her husband, Flora's heart had been broken. If he'd washed his hands of the whole business no one, least of all his own kith and kin, would have blamed him. Harry was a thoroughly good and conscientious man.

As for Arthur Stacey, he was indeed worried about his eldest son Timothy, for Timothy on leaving Cambridge, instead of stepping into the place kept warm for him in his father's firm, announced his intention of going on the stage.

'I hope you'll at least take a *nom de théâtre?*' had said his father, when this ambition was first mooted.

'Well, of course,' said Timothy, hoping to place a dagger in his parent's breast. ' "Stacey" isn't a particularly euphonious name ...'

Though not mortally wounded, Arthur Stacey was at least annoyed.

'It has served well enough for a not unsuccessful architect,' said he coldly. Then he met Charlotte's speaking eye, and added, though still coldly, that he was prepared to allow Timothy a hundred a year until he found his feet.

'Thank you very much, Papa,' said Timothy. (He always called his father Papa, to irritate him. Two younger brothers, both perfectly prepared, even eager, to join the family firm, addressed him as Pater.) 'And thank you too, Mamma,' added Timothy perceptively. 'I shan't ask you to come and see me till I'm playing leads ...'

So Timothy went on the stage under the name of Roger Trevannion, entering upon it, traditionally and respectably, as a spear-carrier in one of the lavish Shakespearean productions currently being mounted at the Lyceum. Timothy had no objection to carrying a spear—that is, until he graduated to Second and then First Gentleman before understudying Mercutio and Laertes; he was prepared to serve a realistically long apprenticeship to the rôles of Romeo and Hamlet. But it was not to be. His physique was against him. Short and snub-nosed, even among spear-carriers he was assigned the rôle of raw recruit, to add a touch of comedy by getting his spear between his legs; and Charlotte (who naturally stole in at a matinée) was glad his father hadn't come with her.

Actually the only understudy ever offered Timothy was Young Gobbo in The Merchant of Venice, which he mistakenly turned down. There is always room for a good Shakespearean clown. But his sights were set on higher things, and after a couple of years spear-carrying he left the Lyceum altogether to join a touring company offering him, on the strength of his tenuous connection with that illustrious establishment—'Of the Lyceum, London' against any actor's name added lustre to a provincial play-bill—juvenile leads.

'It's barnstorming in the provinces one really gets experience,' Timothy told his mother. 'I made a mistake starting in Town.'

'But where will you live, dear?' asked Charlotte.

'In theatrical lodgings,' answered Timothy. 'They're dirt cheap. I dare say I'll be able to live on my salary and save Papa a hundred a year.'

'As if your father cared about that!' exclaimed Charlotte. '*I* think you're being altogether too impetuous and impatient!'

Arthur Stacey however thoroughly approved Timothy's new decision, less from any prospect of saving money—as Charlotte had implied, a hundred a year was neither here nor there to him—as because he'd grown extremely tired of sitting up to listen for Timothy's latch-key often until well after midnight; until Timothy came in he couldn't bolt and bar the door as a householder should, and wouldn't trust Timothy to do it. He even offered to up Timothy's allowance to a hundred-and-fifty, now that Timothy wouldn't be living at home, an offer which Timothy refused.

'But you'll always be sure to let us know where you are?' begged Charlotte.

'Post cards shall flow from the length and breadth of the land!' grinned Timothy.

He no less than Arthur Stacey was glad to be quitting the parental roof where his father sat up for him every night.

Harry Braithwaite's purgatory over Benny's escapade was mercifully of short duration. Inside eight days the whole imbroglio was sorted out, not by any effort on his part but by a sudden upsurge of common sense in young Benny.

He'd indeed joined Sergeant Butley at Ipswich, confidently looking forward to being put into regimentals without delay; but at Ipswich the Sergeant met with some old acquaintances in the town, and lingered there (while Harry Braithwaite and then his clerk assailed the War Office). The joke of carrying Benny off began to lose its savour; the boy became rather a nuisance, as they halted in Ipswich, and Sergeant Butley consigned him to the temporary care of a very nice woman with several nieces.

Benny, to his credit, didn't much like any of them. The girls pulled him about and teased him, he was always being pushed out of the way whenever a soldier came in, and simple as he was it dawned on him that it might be longer than he'd thought before he and Sergeant Butley went to war together, they still having got no farther than Ipswich.

So he went home. It was as simple as that. He had enough money with him to pay a carrier's cart, and at Cotton Hall was received by Hilda with such tears and embraces as though he'd returned from the battlefield indeed instead of from an Ipswich brothel, and by John Henry with no more than an affectionate cuff.

'So you slipped your mother's apron-strings after all?' joked John Henry. 'How many fish did you get?'

Undoubtedly his escapade had sharpened the boy's wits. Catching his Aunt Flora's eye—

'Lots and lots!' declared Benny.

BENNY BACK HOME NO FURTHER ENQUIRIES NECESSARY telegraphed Flora.

Harry Braithwaite didn't often use coarse language, but he used it then.

Chapter Eleven

THUS BENNY RETURNED to the kindly tutelage of Mr Price, and for some four years more wrestled with Greek and Latin—not that he exactly wrestled; compared with a Cornish wrestling-bout, for instance, it was more like friendly horse-play. But he acquired a fairish general education; knew most of English history, especially the dates of battles, and the geography of Europe as far as Russia; he wasn't the complete ignoramus Flora had apprehended. But the day came when Mr Price honestly refused to accept his fees any longer.

'I never thought he'd make a scholar,' said John Henry philosophically, 'but for what's he to do now?'

'Go fishing,' said Mr Price.

If it wasn't a particularly brilliant prospect for the heir to Cotton Hall, it was at least better than going on the stage—for Addie, in one of her letters to Flora, had of course relayed the news, and (Timothy still at the Lyceum) with some pleasurable excitement, for Addie was always an optimist.

'At least better than consorting with rogues and vagabonds,' said John Henry, remembering this circumstance.

'At least a healthier life,' agreed Mr Price; and the next moment took his ex-patron's breath away by asking permission to make Margaret an offer.

He wasn't rebuffed. The old man had never given any thought as to what was to become of Margaret—why should he? She'd always have a home at Cotton Hall. But his first surprise over, the idea of her translated into Mrs Price at the Vicarage pleased him very much—as it pleased Hilda very much, when John Henry called her in to hear Mr Price repeat his intentions. Like her husband she was surprised, but with feminine art concealed the inappropriate emotion.

'You'll be a lucky man,' said she, 'for Meg's the best girl in the world! And as to all linen needed—for I dare say the Vicarage closet is bare as a bone—she shall bring under her arm!'

'By way of portion,' added John Henry—remembering a rash promise made on the day of Margaret's birth.

Though Mr Price was almost forty to Margaret's eighteen, they saw the marriage as in no way inappropriate. They saw it as a wonderful stroke of luck for the girl—and so in fact did Margaret. She already loved Mr Price as a tutor, and as a husband was prepared to love him more dearly still. His licensed courtship of her was little more than a formality, though very agreeable to both parties: to walk arm-in-arm—sometimes hand-in-hand—gave both a high degree of innocent pleasure, as did Mr Price's shy kisses when they parted. There was nothing in his addresses to alarm even a virgin of eighteen (indeed he was a virgin himself), and Margaret actually came to look forward to more intimate embraces; in short, came to adore Mr Price just as much as Flora had once done, before her heart was broken.

His pet name for her was Squirrel.

'I hope you don't mind, Miss Flo?' asked Hilda delicately.

'Why should I?' said Flora. For a moment she couldn't think what Hilda was talking about. 'I'm only glad Meg's not going to be left an old maid.'

'It does seem as if it was intended,' meditated Hilda obscurely. 'Will you or I see to her wedding things?'

'Oh, you,' said Flora indifferently.

It sometimes seemed she had forgotten Meg was her daughter, as Hilda occasionally forgot she wasn't really hers and John Henry's. Hilda threw herself into the marriage preparations with enthusiasm: Margaret's wedding dress was procured from Ipswich, white satin, with a bustle, and net quilling sprayed here and there with orange-blossom, in imitation of Princess Alexandra's wedding dress when she married Queen Victoria's heir apparent. Such a wedding dress would never have been seen in the village before, rejoiced Hilda, nor such a wedding breakfast as was to be spread at Cotton Hall!

But indifferent as Flora was, as though her physique had a better memory than her conscious mind, when the happy day arrived she had a headache and was unable to take part in the ceremony. Benny distinguished himself; from his end seat in the front pew he waited his opportunity, and as his kind tutor and beloved sister walked back down the aisle as man and wife, scattered in their path a pocketful of rice over the Tabor crusader's brass.

'You bad boy, why couldn't you wait till they got outside?' chided Hilda.

'I wanted to be the first,' said Benny.

It was weeks, even months, before the last grains were swept out of the Crusader's moustache; even after a year, Margaret occasionally spied a lingering particle and picked it tenderly into her palm ...

Wisely, the happy pair weren't to start on their honeymoon until next day. Margaret simply walked back with Mr Price to the Vicarage, where that night he took her virginity—after a few fumbles, for wasn't he a virgin himself?—as his lawful wedded wife. Actually that same night John Henry had another go at Hilda, but with less success. He'd grown too old for it.

The honeymoon was in fact spent in Paris on one of Messrs Cook's celebrated package tours—four days, Tuesday to Friday (so that Mr Price wouldn't have to miss Sunday duty): first-class railway carriage, first-class accommodation on the cross-channel steamer, board and lodging at a good family pension, guided tours to Notre Dame and the Chapelle Royale and a visit to the Comédie Française all thrown in for under a pound a day. Happily the Prices settled into their pension (which owing to its tie-up with Cook's had become almost an English pension; hardly a word of French was spoken except by the proprietors and staff), reverently they inspected Notre Dame, and almost as reverently attended *Athalie* at the Français; but the most delightful moments were those they spent by themselves on the quais beside the Seine, looking at the bookstalls and anglers, or in the Tuileries or Luxembourg Gardens. It was as they sat on a bench in the Tuileries, on the last day of their stay, that the shabby old man sidled up to them.

He wasn't particularly unkempt, but for some reason neither much liked the look of him; possibly because his red-rimmed brown eyes were at once so ingratiating and sly, and his teeth so yellow, and his straggling beard so stained with nicotine that it looked like a goat's. However he spoke perfect English.

'I imagine you are visitors in Paris?' said he.

71

Mr Price nodded—but repressively.

'Then perhaps I could show you some aspects of the city Mr Cook's couriers know very little of?'

'Oh, no, thank you,' said Margaret.

The man looked hurt.

'I meant, of its artistic life. I have the entrée to many studios here ...'

'I'm afraid we aren't artistic people at all,' said Mr Price.

'And so of course prefer Constable to Turner, God help you!' suddenly snarled the old man. 'The English don't deserve such a genius!'

His manner was suddenly quite wild, almost threatening. He began to gibber and gesticulate. With perfect calm—how Margaret admired him!—Mr Price rose to his feet and quelled the fellow with a fine British stare.

'*Allez-vous en!*' said he. 'Come, Margaret, for a last little stroll!'

Their last little stroll was again along the quais. There had been a run-of-the-mill tragedy there: some drunkard fallen into the river who now lay under a gendarme's cape awaiting removal to the mortuary. 'Don't look, dear,' said Mr Price. 'Now we must rejoin our homeward bound party!'

After Margaret's removal to the Vicarage she and Flora came to be on far closer terms than while both were living under the same roof. In the first place, they had now more topics of conversation: all Meg's new duties were interesting to Flora, and the young wife enjoyed detailing them to a sympathetic ear. Flora not only listened and advised but helped in the parish work (John Henry having perforce lifted his ban on such activities), and at last sometimes took a class in Sunday School. No maternal instinct sprouted belatedly in her breast, she still only rarely remembered that Meg was in fact her daughter; but watching so inexperienced a young girl so painstakingly learning her business as a parson's wife, Flora conceived a genuine liking for her, and they became if not intimates, friends.

Margaret in her early twenties grew so tall and slim, it was often remarked that she favoured her aunt more than she did Hilda. Her high narrow forehead however was John Henry's, except that there was a look of benignancy about it—derived heaven knew whence, unless from the grandmother who'd sometimes given him a penny to buy sweeties.

Chapter Twelve

MEANWHILE THE PROMISED flow of post cards from Timothy
had first dwindled and then ceased altogether. Even in the
provinces his physique was against him. The merest amateur,
with a classic profile, would have been acceptable to provincial
audiences as a juvenile lead—the noses of the heavies, or
villains, were traditionally hooked, so Timothy fell between two
stools—and it wasn't long before the manager of the touring
company recognized that he'd made an error.

'You get laughs,' he complained.

'I'm sorry if I don't give satisfaction,' said Timothy.

'I'm sorry too, but far from it,' said the manager, who was
paying Timothy two pounds a week. (Even the heavy got only
four-pounds-ten.) 'But I tell you what: with winter coming we'll
be putting on Panto, and you can have your choice of Baron
Hardup or First Broker's Man.'

Timothy, sooner than return home, opted for Baron Hardup.
Once again, he made a mistake; as First Broker's Man he might
have become applauded and beloved throughout the northern
circuit. Even as Baron Hardup, however, he couldn't help
stealing the broker's men's laughs, until one of them played on
him the oldest and dirtiest theatrical trick known, that of
pushing a pin up his stick of greasepaint and waiting until in due
course it wore through to the surface and scarified him. No
wonder the flow of postcards ceased.

There were still compensations. His landladies one and all
spoiled him. His father had waited up for him only to see the
front door locked, but now after a performance what lavish
suppers of cows' heel or tripe or pigs' trotters awaited him—and
then how slyly would a landlady's daughter slip from her room
to snuggle in his bed! It was no wonder, either, Timothy didn't
come home.

'But what on earth can have happened to him?' worried Charlotte.

'I've no idea,' said Arthur Stacey.

'But shouldn't we at least try to find out where he is?'

'I remember some scare over young Benny,' recalled Arthur Stacey, 'that put your brother to a good deal of trouble before he turned up safe and sound. It was the only time I ever heard Harry use bad language.'

'Of course I remember that too,' said Charlotte impatiently, 'but this is entirely different.'

' "Went off for a drummer-boy",' recalled Arthur Stacey. 'Of course there's a difference, my dear, between a child of twelve possibly bound for the wars and a young man of twenty-five forgetting to send a post card. He's made his bed and is evidently content to lie on it.'

'But to have a son in England and never hear from him!' protested Charlotte. 'Why, he might as well be in Australia!'

'Best place for him,' said Arthur Stacey obscurely.

But he was less lacking in paternal affection than he pretended. When a year had passed without any sign of life from Timothy he however reluctantly had recourse to a private enquiry agent.

'On the stage somewhere in the provinces,' noted the enquiry agent. 'It may take a little time, Mr Trevannion ...'

For Arthur Stacey so disliked having any contact with a private detective, he too had taken a *nom de guerre*, or *théâtre*, and as it was a son he was looking for, Trevannion was the obvious choice. But since Timothy had by this time adopted another *nom de théâtre*, the search naturally proved fruitless. Arthur Stacey paid the chap off, and attempted, not unsuccessfully (he being at this time involved in a development scheme by one of the great London boroughs), to put Timothy out of his mind. 'If he'd emigrated to Australia or New Zealand,' Arthur Stacey reasoned with himself, 'would we worry if we didn't hear from him over a twelve-month?' The answer in fact would probably have been yes: certainly on the part of Charlotte. Amongst other disagreeables, she was always having to tell lies to her sisters-in-law.

Addie turning out her rosewood work-box before she gave it to a charity bazaar found therein the rusted needles and tangled

beads of a half-finished reticule; and the next time she visited
Charlotte—

'Charlotte, did you ever finish your cushion-cover?' asked
Adelaide.

'I can't imagine what you're talking about,' said Charlotte.
'What cushion-cover?'

'In petit point, the one you took down to Cotton Hall ages
and ages ago.'

'Of course I finished it,' said Charlotte. 'It's on the drawing-
room sofa. Whatever made you think of it?'

'I've just found the purse *I* never finished,' confessed Addie.
'Do you suppose Clara ever finished her patchwork?'

'Probably,' said Charlotte. 'She usen't to take it to Broadstairs.'

'What a long time ago it was!' sighed Addie. 'It seems like
another life ...'

'It *was* another life,' said Charlotte, 'which I for one don't
regret in the least. Those awful summer visits we used to pay
Papa in that awful house!'

'The children enjoyed them,' recalled Adelaide, 'though I remember Alan being thrashed for putting the doll I gave Alice
onto old Ham's bonfire ...'

'He'd hardly thank you for reminding him of it,' said
Charlotte, 'now he's such an important official in the Treasury ...'

'My dear, of course I shouldn't remind him of it, I'm far too
frightened of him!' laughed Addie. 'But we had nice times at
Menton too; I'm quite sorry now we just go to Bournemouth! By
the way, dear, how is Timothy getting on? Do you hear from
him often?'

She put the question quite without malice—Adelaide was
never malicious—but Charlotte had to press a handkerchief to
her lips before she could answer with proper lightness.

'Oh, often!' lied Charlotte.

'Arthur,' said Charlotte to her husband in bed that night, 'I
want you to do something for me.'

They had been married more than thirty years. Out of a deep
slumber—

'Timothy?' asked Arthur Stacey.

'Yes. How can I help worrying about him? What occurs to me
is perhaps the reason he stays away is because he hasn't been as

75

successful as he hoped. I want you to go and look for him and find him and tell him that even if he's still just an extra no one at home will think any the worse of him but just admire his perseverance ... And say,' suddenly choked Charlotte, 'his mother wants to see him.'

'Of course I'll go, if you ask me,' said Arthur Stacey, 'but it'll be like looking for a needle in a haystack. Where do I start?'

'In Manchester,' said Charlotte. 'That was where his last post card came from.' (A highly romanticized view of the Ship Canal with *Doing fine, love, Timothy* scrawled on the back.) 'I've a feeling that if you went up to Manchester you might find him ...'

Arthur Stacey himself didn't think so for a moment. But he was truly fond of his wife, and her treasuring of that post card so touched him, the next week-end—he was indeed up to his eyes in work—he took train for Manchester and booked himself in for the night at the Grand Hotel.

In the proletarian, egalitarian city of Manchester one of its two theatres was offering *A Royal Divorce*, the other *Hearts and Crowns*. Arthur Stacey attended a matinée of the one, an evening performance of the other, unsurprised that on the playbill of neither appeared the name of Roger Trevannion. He sat doggedly, however, through both performances, to make sure Timothy didn't appear even as Lackey or Shepherd—*Hearts and Crowns* including a pastoral interlude at Le Petit Trianon. Both entertainments in fact bored him extremely; indeed whilst he sat through them half his mind was on a coming interview (actually on the Monday morning) with the Mayor of one of London's most important boroughs half-persuaded to set about re-building one of London's most notorious slums. Arthur Stacey was going to need his sleep, before tackling the old tortoise; but meanwhile, as the trams still clanged, as Manchester wasn't yet a-bed, strayed into a music-hall.

Where indeed was more stir of life and animation than in either theatre, as they welcomed their favourite comedian.

The however unlikely sometimes happens. Timothy had shot up into stardom, not indeed on the legitimate stage, but on the music-halls. At last he'd learnt his lesson; his genius was for the comic: and in an act of his own devising—Our Wullie in London—was convulsing full houses as he gormlessly wandered round the metropolis enquiring where the elephant was at Piccadilly Circus or why there wasn't so much as a fox-terrier on the Isle of Dogs. It was a simple performance enough, but it pleased—especially the climax, when after describing how he'd had his pocket picked, and was in search of a pawnbroker, what, he asked his audience, was he to look for?

'Balls!' roared the audience.

'Right first go,' agreed Timothy. 'But d'you know, they looked so like balloons to I, I thought here goes with my—'

'Prick!' roared the audience.

'—when a nice young woman came by and asked what was that I'd got hanging out.' (Pause.) 'I thought she meant my shirt. "Why, it's limp as an old dish-clout," says she. "Come back with me and I'll put a bit of starch in it. I'm quite famous for my—" Now what was the word she used? It rhymed with hunt, or punt, or runt—'

'Cunt!' roared the audience.

'*Oh what a rogue and peasant slave am I!*' often thought Timothy. But with applause ringing in his ears, and now a salary of ten pounds a week, and more than ever cherished by landladies and their daughters, managed to swallow his pride.

He also, in this new avatar, adopted a third *nom de théâtre*: Matty Topper. He didn't know why, it just came into his head as having the right music-hall ring.

Arthur Stacey settled into his seat without much expectation of enjoyment. But he was both tired in body and oppressed in mind, and anything was better at that moment than an hotel bedroom.

'Then they looked so like balloons,' pattered the red-nosed comedian on stage, 'I thought here goes with my—'

'Prick!' roared the audience.

The comedian's nose, besides being red, was also snub. His build was short and stocky. Arthur Stacey stared at first incredulously, then with dawning recognition; and by the time the audience was yelling 'Cunt!' was certain.

It was the most painful moment of his life. He was by no means a prude; in theory perfectly recognized that ever since the days of bear-baiting—ever since the days of *panem et circenses*—a coarse mob required coarse entertainment; and that indeed with cock-fighting still going on, and Staffordshire bull-dogs being pitted against each other to fight to the death, and terriers making havoc among a sack of rats, the entertainment he now witnessed was by comparison civilized. In theory, Arthur Stacey might have found the saga of Our Wullie dirty but at least harmless; but that it was his own son, flesh of his flesh, blood of his blood, who led the dirty laughter offended every instinct.

After the last clamour of ribald applause—for Our Wullie's turn crowned the first part of the evening—the house rose to push its way to the bars. Arthur Stacey however after some moments' reflection went round to the stage door.

'I should like a word,' said Arthur Stacey, 'with Roger Trevannion.'

The door-keeper shook his head.

'No one of that name here, sir—unless it's one of the gents in the male voice quartet?'

'I mean the comedian who has just finished his turn.'

'Ah! *That*'s Matty Topper,' said the door man. 'Ain't he a caution? Second door on the left.'

Arthur Stacey penetrated a sordid corridor. On the second door on the left—Timothy had indeed risen in his profession—was pinned a card with MATTY TOPPER on it. Arthur Stacey went in without knocking and found Timothy seated before his make-up table in the act of applying a liberal dollop of cold cream to his sweating countenance.

'Put it down,' said Timothy—between sweat and cold cream temporarily blinded. '"*I asked for porter, boy, you bring me ale!*"—quote, Mrs Siddons—but either'll do. Just put it down.'

In the silence that followed he applied a towel and blinked.

'Why, what a surprise, Papa!' said Timothy. 'Won't you sit down? Never mind the kippers, shove 'em on the floor.'

The only other seating accommodation was indeed a backless chair with a plate of picked-over herring bones on it. (Even at that moment of surprise, and something like dismay, Timothy was annoyed that his father should have seen it, as productive of a wrong impression. He intended to sup later, in some luxury, just needed something to keep him going before his second turn.) Arthur Stacey however refused the invitation. He meant to stay as short a time as possible, and what he had to say could just as well be said on his feet.

'I see now,' he opened drily, 'why you've taken yet another name; also why we haven't heard from you.'

'So you've been in front? I admit it isn't quite up to the Bard,' said Timothy, 'or the sort of thing Mamma would appreciate.'

'Nor did I appreciate it,' said Arthur Stacey. 'To speak frankly, I felt thoroughly ashamed of you.'

' "Sticks and stones may break my bones, hard words can never harm me!" ' giggled Timothy.

'Stop clowning,' said his father. 'Your mother is worrying herself sick. What am I to tell her now?'

'That I'm about the highest paid comic on the Northern circuit,' said Timothy.

'For myself, I would sooner find you sweeping mud on a crossing,' said Arthur Stacey. 'Do I understand you intend to continue ... clowning?'

'Well, I'm booked solid for the next year,' said Timothy happily, 'and I don't expect any falling off after that. The answer, my dear Papa, is yes, I do.'

Arthur Stacey believed him. He could even, in a way, appreciate Timothy's point of view. He didn't waste time arguing, but considered the situation with all his usual practicality of mind. From a previous conversation with Charlotte came back the word Australia.

'Then what we have to think of is some way to allay your mother's anxiety and at the same time ensure she never sees or hears of you again. The best that occurs to me is that you should write her a letter saying you've decided to emigrate to Australia and will have left before she gets it in order to spare the pain of parting.'

Timothy began to make himself up again. Actually an hour or more would elapse before he went on to crown the second half of the programme, but he was more at ease with something to do with his hands.

'I take your point,' he said. 'A son emigrating to Australia is at least respectable—now that we've stopped exporting convicts. Am I to raise cattle, or run sheep?'

'Whichever your imagination suggests,' said Arthur Stacey.

'Only Mamma would never believe it of me,' pointed out

79

Timothy. 'What about my carrying the torch of Shakespeare to the Antipodes in rep.?'

'I knew I only had to leave it to your imagination,' said Arthur Stacey.

'Of course it would need capital,' meditated Timothy. 'If I also take it I'm to be cut off without a shilling, what about coming across with a thousand or two now?'

For a moment Arthur Stacey, jingling the sixpence on his watch-chain, digested the impudence and opportunism of the proposal almost with admiration. For a moment it was in his mind to offer Timothy even five thousand, on the condition of his never being seen or heard of again. But he was shrewd enough to realize that to do so would be to invite perpetual blackmail.

'I am not so rich a man as you seem to suppose,' said he. 'It would be robbing your mother and brothers. I'm afraid your imaginary touring company must make do with equally imaginary capital. But if you'll write such a letter as I propose, I'll be obliged to you.'

Timothy (all the while applying grease-paint) meditated again. It occurred to him that if he obliged his father now, when the time came he might find he hadn't been cut off without a shilling after all ...

'Of course I'll do whatever you wish, Papa,' said he filially. 'Can you bring yourself to shake hands with me?'

Arthur Stacey indeed shook hands with his son—even warmly; but once outside the music-hall found his own so sticky with cold cream and grease-paint, when he got back to the Grand Hotel had to rouse a sleepy Boots to fetch him a can of hot water. Like his brother-in-law, Arthur Stacey rarely used bad language, but he swore at the Boots.

'I'm sorry,' said Arthur Stacey heavily, upon his return to London. 'I didn't find him.'

'But you've only been gone a day!' accused Charlotte.

'With this new development on my plate, how could I be away longer?' argued her husband.

'I should have thought your son more important to you than bricks and mortar,' said Charlotte bitterly.

Arthur Stacey, who had first been bored by two second-rate theatrical performances, then distressed to the core by his experience in a music-hall, then undergone an uncomfortable night in an hotel bedroom, felt a deep sense of injury; but being for obvious reasons unable to justify himself, was silent. So was Charlotte silent. Almost for the first time in their married life, they were at odds—each as unhappy as the other that it should be so, but still at odds, and Arthur unfortunately lost his temper with a Borough Surveyor.

Then suddenly, after a week, the cloud lifted.

'Read that!' cried Charlotte joyfully. 'Timothy's written at last!—and with such news! He's taking a touring company in Shakespeare to Australia and didn't tell me before he left because he felt the parting would be too painful! Just read his letter!'

Arthur Stacey had to admit that Timothy had done the thing in style. The letter-head—a bit over-inked, obviously the work of some jobbing printer—announced a travelling Shakespearean Company, Manager Roger Trevannion, late of the Lyceum ...

'Dearest Mamma,' had written Timothy beneath. 'I'm off—by this time will have gone—to Australia. I didn't tell you beforehand because the parting would have been too painful, but I know you will wish us all success. We have engagements already in Perth, Adelaide and Wagga-Wagga.' (Here Arthur Stacey felt Timothy's sense of humour had slightly got the better of him, and the next sentence confirmed it.) 'What a joy to carry the torch of culture to Wagga-Wagga! Now with our costumes and scenery to be shipped I've only a moment to say, dear Mamma, I remain ever your affectionate son Timothy.'

'It was no wonder you couldn't find him!' said Charlotte generously. 'He must have been practically on board ship already!'

'So he must,' agreed Arthur Stacey.

It was on the tip of Charlotte's tongue to say that if only he'd gone north a few days sooner ... But she was a wise woman, and refrained. Instead—

'If I've been rather horrid to you this last week, I'm sorry, dear,' she apologized.

'You were worried and disappointed,' said Arthur Stacey kindly. 'For the matter of that, so was I. Now we can both think of him with, er, pride.'

* * *

81

'If I was a bit curt with you the other day,' apologized Arthur Stacey to the Borough Surveyor, 'you must forgive me. I'd just seen my eldest son off to Australia.'

'Think nothing of it,' said the Borough Surveyor. 'It's always a wrench—though I think harder on their mothers. *My* son— my only son—is in Canada.'

Then they got down to bricks and mortar.

Undoubtedly Timothy was doing things in style. Some months later there arrived a letter on the headed note-paper post-marked Adelaide, reporting general enthusiasm and capacity audiences even in the outback, and Timothy himself in excellent health save for a touch of sunstroke easily overcome by imbibing milk and soda water. How the deuce had he managed it, wondered Arthur Stacey? Obviously, he answered himself, by employing the good offices of some genuinely Antipodes-bound Mancunian; Timothy was obviously finding it a good joke, pretending to be in Australia. 'Tell Aunt Addie,' he wrote (possibly from a bar alongside the Ship Canal), 'that the fair city that bears her name does her every credit!'

Arthur Stacey wondered how long he'd be able to keep it up. But Timothy had supplied his alter ego with half-a-dozen more such missives, all, such was his alter ego's conscientious-ness, punctually dispatched at three-month intervals. When they ceased to arrive, oddly enough, it was because Timothy was actually in Australia himself.

North Country audiences are notoriously loyal: for years the saga of Our Wullie in London continued to delight them. But there came a day when instead of yelling balls or prick or cunt they brutally yelled for something fresh. It was a piece of luck for Timothy that a London company adventuring to the Antipodes in a repertory of Shakespeare was looking for a clown: up to London went Timothy, and on the strength of having under-studied (or having been about to understudy, he left the point vague) Young Gobbo at the Lyceum, was hired.

He quitted Manchester with regret. It had been a kindly nurse to him. However fair a city Adelaide, it never compared with Timothy to Manchester.

For a while he did well enough, in the parts of Young Gobbo and Dogberry and First Gravedigger; only once actu-ally in Australia his imagination failed him, and it was just as well that Charlotte didn't live much longer.

She died at sixty—still not a bad age to attain to, considering how long she'd had cancer. Charlotte had never spoken a word to anyone, least of all to her husband, of the gnawing pain that racked her breast, and had consulted no doctor, suspecting all too well what a doctor would suggest. Rather than be cut, Charlotte preferred to endure.

Arthur Stacey survived her a decade, and on his death left a substantial fortune to be divided between his two younger sons, the eldest having been cut off without a shilling indeed.

It was the senior of the younger sons who naturally inherited his father's rather handsome watch-chain. Why an old sixpence dangled there he couldn't image: he had it taken off, kept it for a while in his stud-box, then somehow it disappeared.

But this is to look ahead. It wasn't Benny's going off that killed John Henry, but simply extreme old age.

Chapter Thirteen

HE WAS IN his ninety-second year and the end came gently
enough; one morning, after he'd stumbled twice getting out
of bed, he acknowledged that he might as well stay there.
There was nothing wrong with him (except extreme old age),
but both Hilda and Flora perceived the end near, and again
Flora telegraphed Harry. But even the ominous words, FEAR
FATHER NEARING HIS END, failed to impress the latter with
any sense of urgency, after the false alarm over Benny, and he
merely telegraphed back KEEP INFORMED. Then it was Flora who
grimly delayed, and within a fortnight out John Henry went like
a snuffed candle, his death-bed unattended by any of his kin from
London. Not that he seemed to notice their absence; he didn't
seem to notice even Meg on her knees by his pillow, nor Mr
Price reciting appropriate prayers. At the very last, as he grip-
ped Hilda's hand, it was only Benjamin he asked for; and as the
boy stood with incredulous eyes before his first sight of death—
not on any battlefield but in the familiar bedchamber—

'Now th'art the master of Cotton Hall!' literally croaked John
Henry.

His Will wasn't disputed. Harry and George, both men of law,
knew what it could cost to dispute a Will—and with small hope
of success, for the Ipswich solicitor knew his business. Thus the
family gathering for John Henry's funeral—though they hadn't
been at his death-bed all came to his funeral—was in rather a
low key.

'They manage these things better in France,' remarked
Arthur Stacey. 'Under the Code Napoleon it wouldn't have
been possible ...'

'Then I'm sure I wish we'd all been born French!' cried

84

Clara—so outrageous a sentiment as to be forgivable only because she was in a high state of nervous tension, and which Addie attempted to rationalize by observing that if they *had* been born French at least they'd have got the new fashions much sooner. George regarded his wife with disapproval, Harry his with affection. So did Flora regard Addie with affection; there were moments when her incurable frivolity lessened tension all round.

'All the same, house and land to go to a little by-blow!' exclaimed George uncontrollably.

'Papa and Hilda were married, in church, at least two years before his birth,' reminded Flora. 'And weren't you all at the christening?'

'Touché,' said Arthur Stacey. 'We were indeed. The term by-blow, George, is inappropriate.'

'I retract it,' said George, still sulkily. 'He's my half-brother born in wedlock. All the same—'

It was at this point that Hilda, red-eyed and swathed in widow's weeds, came in from the kitchen. Fat as she was, in widow's weeds she looked quite enormous—a monument of woe. Her hands however smelt of onion, from which she'd been preparing a special sauce to go with the saddle of lamb destined for the funeral party's lunch.

'Benny I'm sorry to say won't be with us,' she apologized, 'taking the head of the table as he ought ...'

'He shows tact,' said Arthur Stacey.

Hilda looked pleased.

'I'm sure it's kind of you to say so,' said she. '*I* gave him a right good scolding. But as soon as he'd flung in the first clod, he went off fishing ...'

Even without the heir present it was a sumptuous meal she set before them: first soles, then the saddle of lamb with every trimming, then a junket awash with cream, then filberts and port for the men and for the ladies a little delicacy of her own invention—prunes soaked in sloe gin and topped with more cream again. Hilda gave John Henry a good send-off, and after lunch the party from London, in the train, slept most of the way.

When John Henry's affairs were sorted out, moreover, it transpired that Cotton Hall was almost the only substantial property he had to leave. He'd indeed made a second fortune in railway shares, but to boom had succeeded collapse, and the fairy gold turned to withered leaves; moreover the cost of living steadily rising, the income from his first, more prudently invested fortune, now barely sufficed to run Cotton Hall. However all this was the Ipswich solicitor's headache, not Harry's, and he was thankful indeed he'd refused to act as executor; moreover it is always less disagreeable to be cut off without a sixpence if only sixpences, so to speak, are at stake—a feeling shared particularly by George and George's wife.

'But how dreadful for poor Hilda!' exclaimed the latter, making an elaborate show of sympathy for the widow. 'One only hopes *she*'s not too disappointed!'

In fact Hilda, once reassured that there'd always be enough money to pay the servants and tradespeople and odd job men— her mind reached no further—showed as much philosophy as Harry; and as for young Benny, he was as disinterested as a codling. The only point that troubled Harry was that the separate provision made for Flora, of a hundred and fifty pounds a year, was obviously incapable of being honoured, and out of his own substantial income he proposed to allow her, instead, the fifty.

'To spend on rich dresses?' asked Hilda, with a rare spark of irony. 'Miss Flo shall have a home here at Cotton Hall till her dying day!'

It was a lot Flora was ready to accept. Cotton Hall was the best place for her.

That he was now, in theory at least, Cotton Hall's master made singularly little difference to Benny's way of life; in fact no difference at all. His occupation, so far as he had one, was to go fishing. Sometimes he and the Strowgers sailed as far as Yarmouth to see the start of a yacht race, and once a gentleman-yachtsman short-handed shanghai'd Benny aboard to help get the sails up, and as Benny tumbled back into the Strowgers' dinghy called out to know where he was to be got hold of again.

'At Cotton Hall!' guffawed Jemmy Strowger. 'You've picked up the young master of Cotton Hall!'

'But I'll come and crew for you any time you want!' yelled Benny.

After which he thought less of fishing than of yacht racing; but never had to run away in pursuit of the big boats, for the gentleman-yachtsman (having taken his bearings) paid a call at

Cotton Hall, with the result—for he turned out to be a local grandee, Sir Roger Wynstan—that Benny crewed for him thereafter with Hilda's full permission.

It was about this time that the Harry Braithwaites came into money. Addie's Indian uncle survived even a third childless marriage (the regrettable fact being that somewhere in the orient he'd picked up a not-to-be-named disease that rendered him impotent), and before he himself passed on remembered he had a niece. Addie inherited a Nabob's fortune, and the Harry Braithwaites now began going to the Isle of Wight for Cowes Week. Didn't they deserve, said Addie, a little pleasure, after their long, hard-working lives?

Chapter Fourteen

CERTAINLY HARRY BRAITHWAITE had worked hard all his life, and at just over sixty was still in harness—indeed was more in demand than ever, not only in Probate but in divorce cases, which though considered slightly *infra dig* were nonetheless rewarding. So had Addie worked hard, in her own line. The boys could look after themselves, and did; Alan, after Winchester and Balliol, was rising steadily in the Treasury; of his younger brothers, similarly advantaged, one had opted for the Foreign Office and the other for Marine Insurance—all far more satisfactory careers, considered Addie, than that of their cousin Tim Stacey with his touring company. But Sybil, the only daughter, was Adelaide's cross, she having unfortunately turned out to resemble her Aunt Flora.

It was a real tragedy to Adelaide. To dress a pretty daughter she'd willingly have given up, if necessary, her own Paris frocks; fortunately it wasn't necessary, expecially as she looked so *chic* in them, whereas Sybil in a frock from Paris might as well have been wearing the product of some little local dressmaker paid no more than a guinea to run it up. She was tall but angular. The now fashionable bustle that swayed so elegantly behind her mother's rump made Sybil—the unkind quip was Alan's—look like a camel with its hump in the wrong place. There was indeed something camel-like about her altogether, with her long thin face bobbing above a long thin neck and her gawky unco-ordinated movements; she had even, like a camel, uncommonly large feet.

The jest was all the unkinder on Alan's part because Sybil still loved him better than anyone in the world. The play of the Tribe had marked her for life: it was in fact her secret dream that he would never marry but one day ask her to come and keep house for him, and thus the fact that she attracted no suitors—to her mother a source of angry grief—was to Sybil a source of comfort, for she knew well what pressure would have been brought to bear on her, after so many fruitless seasons, to accept even a widower if of sufficient means, and she wanted to be at liberty, when the happy time came, to devote herself entirely to her brother.

Of course in her first seasons Addie had given dances for her, and of course Sybil was invited back, and the hours Addie spent sitting among the chaperones on a gilt rout-seat with Sybil all too often sitting beside her were the most painful of her life. It wasn't only that Sybil's appearance was unattractive, she made no effort to attract; other girls so unfortunately circumstanced at least looked bright, as though they expected a partner; some even developed a whole repertory of mime, fanning themselves and uttering little gasps as though quite worn out with dancing and only too glad to sit down!—and though this deceived no one at least their chaperones could pretend too, and look solicitous and beg them not to over-exert themselves; the playing of such little tragi-comedies was at least an occupation. But Sybil simply sat, and when she did dance (with a son of the house put on duty by her hostess) seemed almost to encourage her partner to restore her to mother at once instead of taking her down to supper.

Such hours were a real purgatory to Adelaide. It was one thing to have to stay up till two in the morning because a daughter was so pretty and popular even the extras on her programme were booked, but quite another to sit counting the hours until they could decently leave, and often only a sense of duty and whalebone corsets sustained her through the ordeal.

'Why don't you face the fact, mother,' once said Alan, 'that Sybil doesn't like dances and will never be any good at them?'

'It's still my duty to give her a chance,' said Adelaide. 'How else is she to find a husband?'

'Perhaps she doesn't want one,' said Alan—more truly than he knew, but without any awareness of the reason.

'Nonsense,' said his mother. 'Of course every girl wants a husband!'

It was an additional source of bitterness that Alice, the daughter of George and Clara, had married at nineteen. To a nobody, of course, to an obscure doctor practising at Broadstairs; but at least she'd married ...

'I shall have to try musical evenings,' thought Addie.

With her usual cleverness she made quite a success of them. They indeed attracted older and older guests, but this had the advantage of making Sybil, approaching thirty, seem almost a slip of a girl, as she politely handed round refreshments and sometimes turned the pages for an accompanist. It was a pity she always looked so bored, but at least Addie could sit comfortably in one of her own easy chairs instead of on a gilt rout-seat.

Her years of purgatory were ended by two unrelated events. The first was Alan's becoming engaged to the daughter of his Treasury chief. (Like his father, he chose a wife for other qualities besides her looks, and though Addie declared he'd quite lost his head over dear Mabel, the odds were he might have kept it had she been the daughter, say, of a linen-draper.) As it was, however, the young people presented an idyllic picture enough—'Edwin and Angelina!' Addie called them— and Alan's happiness was to be made complete in the June after Addie in desperation hired a string quartet.

To Sybil it was a blow almost beyond bearing, as her always hopeless dream finally dissolved before Mabel's gay, practical talk of drawing-room furniture, while Mabel longed (she said) to have Sybil for an own, own sister, and in particular for a bridesmaid, but turned the knife in the wound. In the unwanted rôle of own, own sister she submitted to Mabel's pecks on the cheek, but against the rôle of bridesmaid stubbornly set her face.

'My darling, of course you must be a bridesmaid!' protested Addie. 'It will look so odd, if you aren't!'

'It'll look much odder if I am,' said Sybil bleakly; and indeed when Adelaide learned that all the other attendants were to be chosen from among Mabel's little nieces, she inclined to agree. Amongst that juvenile train Sybil would have been almost a figure of fun, with her gangling height and awkward stride! So she was spared the ordeal of appearing at St George's Hanover Square in shell-pink satin with a wreath of rosebuds in her hair.

'I'm sorry you're not going to stand by me,' Alan told her, the day before the wedding. (He wasn't really; he too recognized how out of place Sybil would look among the rosebuds.)

'You'll still have my every good wish,' said Sybil through stiff lips. She had to keep them stiff, or they would have trembled. Then—

'Oh, Alan,' she added uncontrollably, 'have you quite, quite forgotten Mato-Topa?'

'Mato who?' asked Alan.

'Mato-Topa, the Grand Panjandrum of the Tribe.'

He had to think for more than a moment.

'What, that old game we used to play as children?'

'When I was your Handmaid ...'

'I remember being thrashed for something to do with a bonfire,' said Alan, 'but that's about all ...'

The wedding was one of the events of the season, and all agreed that Mabel's train of six little girls was the prettiest thing ever seen.

The second event that ended Adelaide's purgatory was the acceptance by fashion of the Pre-Raphaelites. Hitherto the Pre-Raphaelite style of dress had merely furnished jokes in *Punch*, by which no one was more amused than Addie. Now, after a famous actress appeared (not on stage) in sage-green serge embroidered with water-lilies, and a famous beauty in blue embroidered with peacock feathers, neither wearing any bustle at all, Pre-Raphaelitism became not only acceptable but the vogue; and Addie, seeing a chance to take advantage of her daughter's lanky height at last, changed her tune; and Sybil, passive as a lay-figure, appeared at a musical evening in yellow linen embroidered with wheat-sheaves.

And at the musical evenings her new habiliments worked wonders for her. Though no one likened her to a Holbein, she was more than once likened to a Burne-Jones. In linens of various hues, suitably embroidered, Sybil became quite admired, and a wealthy amateur of the arts actually proposed.

'My dearest girl, do, do accept him!' urged Adelaide. ('Sad as your father and I will be to lose our only daughter!' she threw in conventionally.) 'Only think, he has a villa at Florence! And though he's not particularly handsome, one can't ask for everything!'

Leopold Vanek was in fact very far from handsome. His short, square face, always rather blue about the jowls, and deeply-bistred eye-sockets, indeed gave him the look of wearing a Guy Fawkes mask. But to her mother's profound relief Sybil accepted him, and there was another wedding at St George's Hanover Square. It wasn't such a gala affair as Alan's: though Mr Vanek produced as best man a Lord Edward S——, few other of his friends came to fill the pews. However the Braithwaites and Staceys turned out in force, so that the church didn't look embarrassingly empty.

The honeymoon was spent in Italy—where else? But Mr Vanek, carrying his bride to his Italian villa, intended to stay there more than the conventional month. He intended to stay there for good. Though genuinely attracted to Sybil in her guise as a Pre-Raphaelite, his object in marrying her had been to provide himself with a wife before a certain scandal broke.

The villa in Florence—or Fiesole, as both its native and English inhabitants preferred to call it—was large, and most beautifully situated, the view from every window superb. And with superb views Sybil had to be content—and was content. That her husband made no physical demands on her was purely a relief. They shared the same bedroom because not to have done so would have caused talk, but Leopold was always very thoughtful in letting Sybil undress and get into bed first while he himself disrobed in a dressing-room, and though his snoring at first kept her awake, in time she grew used to it. They became in their way as attached a couple as Harry and Adelaide, as Arthur Stacey and Charlotte, and if no children (naturally) blessed their union, neither regretted it. A *mariage blanc* was in fact the very thing for Sybil.

With the years Mr and Mrs Vanek became quite leaders of Florentine society, lavish with their wealth in support of art exhibitions and concerts and amateur dramatics. It was a coterie life, which again suited Sybil, as making no call on any deep emotion.

Her daughter off her hands at last, Addie, as well as her husband, certainly deserved a little relaxation at Cowes; and as an unexpected result a quite new type of visitor descended on Cotton Hall.

Chapter Fifteen

COWES WEEK! Where all the nicest and prettiest people in England (vide a gossip column of 188–), assembled as at a family party—where to be accepted on the lawn of the Royal Yacht Squadron was almost better than being presented at Court! If there was ever a heaven on earth, it was at Cowes in the late eighteen hundreds.

The Braithwaites of course never set foot on the Royal Yacht Squadron's sacred lawn except by special invitation; but Harry's particularly skilful handling of a rather tricky divorce case made him persona grata with one of the Squadron's senior members—whose name, thanks to Harry's skilful handling, was never mentioned in court at all—and Addie in white piqué always looked her best, and once received the honour of a compliment from a very important personage indeed.

'Vot a nice hat you're wearing!' said the very important personage, in a strong Teutonic accent.

There were naturally no humming-birds on it, nor marabout: it was a plain white straw but with a rather dashing navy blue bow—not too juvenile: *chic*. Addie always knew how to dress. She knew too how to drop a curtsey—not too deeply, but with proper respect; and after this incident the Braithwaites were accepted into the very seventh heaven of heavens, the holy of holies: the circle of wicker chairs surrounding the tubby presence of the very important person indeed—H.R.H., no less.

He always liked having good-looking women about him, especially when out of range of the vigilant eye of his august Mamma, and Addie was still very good-looking indeed, moreover got her clothes from Paris. She was stylish, and H.R.H. liked style too. He had also heard, from the Senior member, of her husband's peculiarly skilful handling of the particularly

93

tricky divorce case, and felt he might prove a useful acquaintance—not for himself, of course, but if any of his friends should find themselves similarly circumstanced. So Harry and Addie Braithwaite were accepted into the Holy of Holies, with H.R.H. for its Mato-Topa.

He didn't, as had Alan, demand sacrifices, except of time and attention. (The idea of requiring Addie to cast her hat into the sea, for instance, never for a moment entered his mind, nor did he ever designate a particular letter with which all sentences had infallibly to begin. But the result was much the same, as all hung on his words and agreed with everything he said, even, or especially, when he tended to self-pity.)

'All of these great houses I have to go to for the shooting!' complained H.R.H., as his stay at Cowes neared its end. 'Vot boredom, you can't conceive! How I wish there was some quiet little place in the country to go to for the week-end without ceremony, just with a few friends!'

All present knew that he meant with one especial lady-friend of whom neither his august Mamma nor the châtelaines of the great houses approved; but the show of sympathy (for one deprived of simple rural pleasures) was rather on the surface, among the circle of basket-chairs, for all their occupants knew that H.R.H. managed to meet the current object of his affections at least once a week in London. Still, his wish to take her with him into the country was so—well, so *boyish*, even the most cynical heart was touched.

The Harry Braithwaites were still what the sea-going fraternity rather contemptuously referred to as dry-land sailors. Thanks to the Nabob's fortune they could well have afforded at least a smallish yacht themselves, but Harry Braithwaite was too prudent to engage in any such extravagance, and Adelaide acknowledged that if accepted on the Squadron lawn they didn't need one. (It was the City men who needed yachts, to be accepted—and perhaps not even then!) However they always watched the end of a race with intelligent interest, if it finished within eyeshot of the sacred lawn.

On a certain occasion the race wasn't a particularly important one, for smaller craft entered from Yarmouth and Felixstowe and Poole Harbour. The R.Y.S. regarded their endeavours benevolently, but without the excitement the big boats would have aroused. One of the smaller craft's owners, however, had apparently the right to tread holy grass, and after triumphantly dropping anchor—for he'd come in first—had himself rowed in a dinghy to the sacred steps.

'Tie up, Benny,' he called, 'and come ashore with me!'

At the moment, naturally, neither Harry nor Adelaide made any connection with the lad who'd given Harry so much trouble by going for a drummer-boy. But Sir Roger Wynstan was good-natured enough to introduce to them, as the first persons he encountered, Benny Braithwaite who'd been crewing for him.

'Properly the Squire of Cotton Hall in Suffolk,' he added, with a grin, 'but a first rate deck-hand all the same!'

For another moment neither Harry nor Adelaide quite took it in. Then Addie—always swifter than her husband to appreciate any possibly advantageous situation—threw up her hands in delighted surprise.

'Benny Braithwaite? But he's a relation of ours!' cried she. 'He's my husband's nephew!'

She should properly have said, half-brother, but as she glanced from Harry's elderly, portly form to the round innocent face and gangling limbs of young Benny, she felt the true relationship too improbable for a stranger's acceptance. So she substituted nephew, and Harry didn't correct her. Benny for his part was simply flummoxed, for the lady in the smart hat, whom he never remembered having set eyes on, now looked as though she were going to kiss him, and despite his patron's adjurations he climbed back into the dinghy and rowed off.

'He's as shy as a coot,' apologized Sir Roger. 'Cotton Hall's quite at the back of beyond ...'

'Don't we know it!' exclaimed Addie. 'Do tell us how they all are there? My husband's so busy, we scarcely ever get down—do we, Harry?'

'Very rarely indeed,' said Harry, rather accurately re-membering the last occasion: the day of John Henry's funeral.

'And how are they all?' repeated Addie, with genuine curiosity.

'To tell you the truth,' said Sir Roger, 'I've only once set foot inside the place myself. Was it always so rum?'

'No, that was my father-in-law's doing,' said Addie. 'He was an eccentric of eccentrics! You met his widow?'

'An enormously stout dowager?'

'I'm sure she would be!' said Addie. Then, rather to her credit, she remembered Flora. 'And did you meet Miss Braithwaite too?'

'The old lady everyone calls Miss Flo?'

It gave Addie quite a shock to hear her sister-in-law referred to as an old lady—Flora at least seven years her junior. *'But that's what comes of living all one's life at the back of beyond!'* pitied Addie.

'One day soon we must go and look them up again,' said she, 'but how very fortunate for Benny that you've taken him by the hand, for otherwise I dare say he'd be turning into a complete Tony Lumpkin!'

'Oh, I haven't done anything for him,' said Sir Roger modestly. 'He just comes crewing for me ...'

'You make me feel how remiss we've been,' said Adelaide gravely. 'Promise, promise to bring him ashore tomorrow!'

'Now why on earth,' asked her husband, when Sir Roger, the promise readily given, had made off to clean himself, 'did you say that? The last thing I want is ever to set eyes on the infernal boy again—*or* on Cotton Hall!'

Addie for the moment made no reply; but an audacious plan was forming in her mind.

Next day, true to his word, Sir Roger hauled Benny ashore by the scruff of his neck, and Adelaide was very gracious to him. All the pretty ladies in their basket chairs were gracious to him; he'd grown into a big-limbed, hardy-looking lad, brown eyed under a shock of flaxen hair—and then his manners had such an engaging simplicity! (The ladies didn't pull him about as the girls in the Ipswich brothel had done, but he nevertheless accepted their overtures with apprehension: if he hadn't been sponsored by Sir Roger, his manners might have been found downright awkward.) Addie wasn't bold enough actually to present him to H.R.H., but managed, by strolling now and then past the Holy of Holies on Benny's arm, so that H.R.H. should at least notice him; and indeed, after Benny had departed, H.R.H. beckoned her over to him with a chuckle.

'Von doesn't often see you cradle-snatching,' said he, with that rather crude joviality all his entourage found so endearing.

'He's my husband's little nephew, sir,' said Addie, with a *moue*.

(If she'd been younger she'd have pouted, but being in all things discreet, she just made a *moue*.)

'And a very handsome little nephew too!' said H.R.H. 'Vere does he come from?'

'Cotton Hall, in Suffolk—the old family place,' explained Adelaide, 'that my husband gave up when we hadn't any use for it. It's the most ridiculous old place—though partly, of course, quite historic—and quite at the back of beyond!' She paused, as though struck by a sudden thought. 'If you ever really do, sir, want somewhere to spend a quiet week-end, Cotton Hall is the very place! And of course if there's anyone special you'd like to invite—?'

H.R.H. was no fool. He knew just as well as Addie what prestige would accrue to her from such a visit. At the same time the idea of back-of-beyond, off-the-map, so to speak, retreat strongly appealed to him.

'November, perhaps?' reflected H.R.H.

'Whenever you say, sir!'

The royal memory was as good as a pocket engagement-book.

'On the third, opening of Parliament,' he checked. 'On the fourth, Lord Mayor's Banquet, on the fifth, a Drawing Room: the week-end of the ninth to tenth, perhaps? My Groom of the Chambers will send you a list.'

It wasn't however until they were in bed that night, in their narrow but expensive lodgings—the indigenous population of Cowes made a very good thing out of their lettings during Cowes Week—that Adelaide made her husband privy to her wonderful plan.

'Harry.'

'Well, what is it?' mumbled Harry, who wanted to go to sleep.

'Haven't you often heard H.R.H. say how he longed for some quiet little retreat in the country where he could spend the week-end with just a few friends? I'm sure nowhere could be quieter than Cotton Hall ...'

'You're mad,' said Harry. 'Go to sleep.'

'I am not mad,' said Adelaide, on the contrary sitting up. 'Of course Hilda would have to be got round first—but just think what it would mean for her as well, to have H.R.H. at Cotton Hall! And of course there'd need to be a good deal of preparation—'

'I imagine H.R.H.'s idea of a quiet week-end with just a few friends,' said Harry, 'includes a seven course dinner and a Hungarian Band.'

'In the minstrels' gallery!' cried Adelaide. 'Of course! Don't you see it's simply *meant*? And as for the catering there are cooks in London who can be hired to see to everything!'

'And have you thought what it would cost?'

'Of course, hundreds,' said Addie impatiently, 'but wouldn't it be worth it?'

Half asleep as he was, Harry remembered that it was his wife's nabob-inherited money that would pay, and though what was hers, before the Married Woman's Property Act, was his, he'd always allowed her a say in the spending of it ...

'Anyway, H.R.H. has accepted!' gloated Addie.

Which was how there came to be a very different type of visitor at Cotton Hall.

Chapter Sixteen

OF COURSE THERE needed to be a great deal of preparation. Addie went down to Cotton Hall immediately Cowes Week was over.

The ladies there received her unexpected visit with at first surprise, but when she described meeting Benny at Cowes under the wing of Sir Roger, in their simplicity found it only natural that she should come to tell them about it. They were pleased to see her: Hilda recalled her as always being very good-natured, and Flora remembered that long-ago invitation to spend a fortnight in Town ...

'And my goodness, you don't look a day older!' complimented Hilda. 'However do you manage it?'

Actually Adelaide managed it by the discreet use of rouge—and why not? If only Flora would wear a little rouge, thought Addie! For Flora's appearance shocked her. Sir Roger had called her an old lady—but then Sir Roger was young: now even to Addie's eyes she looked an old woman. She still held herself erect, but so stiffly! Nor could any amount of rouge, thought Addie (changing her mind), have done anything for those long, lank, narrow cheeks. Her high narrow forehead moreover was beginning to show brown patches about the temples, from which the hairline receded more steeply than ever ...

By comparison, Hilda was blooming. She might be—she was—enormously stout, but it was a wholesome bulk of flesh, and she hadn't a grey hair. The fluff of down that had always distinguished her complexion showed signs of thickening, on the upper lip, into a slight moustache, but not disagreeably, rather jollily. If Flora looked older than her age, Hilda looked younger.

Naturally there was also family news to be exchanged, and Hilda was particularly glad to be able to tell of Meg's marriage to Mr Price and of the golden opinions she was winning at the Vicarage; to which Addie (who had practically no recollection of Meg whatever) replied that of course a vicarage was the perfect place for her. Addie then told of Sybil's and Alan's marriages and received congratulations in turn; but what she had to relate of Harry Braithwaite's continuing success at the Bar, and of Arthur Stacey's continuing success in building squares and crescents, meant nothing to Hilda compared with Benny's having been introduced (after Addie explained what an honour it was), onto the Royal Yacht Squadron lawn.

'I always knew Sir Roger would be his friend!' declared Hilda. 'Sir Roger values Benny at his true worth!'

'Indeed he does,' smiled Adelaide. 'He says he's the best deck-hand in all East Anglia!'

'And named him to all those grand folks as the master of Cotton Hall?'

'Indeed he did,' said Addie, suppressing a memory of Sir Roger's grin.

'I only wish his Da had known of it!' sighed Hilda. 'It 'ud have given him rare pleasure!'

Neither she nor Flora suspected any ulterior motive in Adelaide's visit, but since she intended to return to London the same day, it couldn't be long in coming out.

'Dear Hilda, dear Flora,' cooed Addie, 'I wonder whether Harry and I could just *borrow* Cotton Hall, for a little week-end house party in November?'

'November? That's an odd time for folks to be coming into the country,' said Hilda. 'But why not? I'm sure a little stir of life wouldn't come amiss! How many would you be?'

'Oh, just five or six,' said Addie. 'I'm so glad you agree! And of course I'll be here in advance to help with all arrangements. There might,' she added carelessly, 'be someone rather important coming ...'

Hilda thought she meant Sir Roger, on whose behalf she was ready to have any number of geese and turkeys plucked. She had no idea what upheavals were to take place, before H.R.H. could spend a quiet week-end in the country.

'Hilda's quite delighted!' reported Addie to her husband. (She didn't reveal that Hilda didn't yet know how highly she was to be honoured.)

'Then you mean to go through with the thing?' said Harry Braithwaite, with marked lack of enthusiasm.

'Of course I do!' said Addie. 'It will be the triumph of my life!'

'Which I'm afraid I shan't be there to witness,' said Harry. 'I'm up to my eyes in work.'

'*Harry!*'

'Very many ladies entertain H.R.H. in their husbands' absence,' said Harry. '*He* won't notice anything odd. You must take the triumph on your own shoulders, my dear, along with the bills.'

However when she thought about it Addie wasn't altogether displeased. There was always a—not a censoriousness, but a so to speak moral strictness about Harry, that might strike a jarring note in the far from strait-laced little house-party she envisaged.

'Just imagine!' exclaimed Margaret to Mr Price, 'there's to be a house-party at Cotton Hall!'

She hadn't been present when Adelaide paid her exploratory visit, but naturally Hilda reported all about it next day, and it seemed to Margaret too a pleasant thing that the old house should have a little stir of life in it.

'A house-party?' repeated Mr Price more cautiously. 'Who on earth will be the guests?'

'Friends of Aunt Adelaide's,' explained Margaret, 'and of course Sir Roger who's always been so good to Benny. Sir Roger took Benny ashore on the lawn of the Royal Yacht Squadron at Cowes!'

'I've read of it as a semi-sacred spot,' said Mr Price humorously. 'If that's where your Aunt Adelaide makes her friends I doubt whether you and I, my dear, will have much part in the festivities. People of fashion,' explained Mr Price, with the air of one perfectly familiar with the *beau monde* (though where he'd read about Cowes was actually in an article about Famous Lawns in the *Gardening Weekly*), 'I believe often enjoy a little excursion into rural surroundings, but strictly *en intimité*.'

'How beautifully you speak French,' admired Margaret, momentarily distracted. 'I noticed in Paris ...'

'So we'd better wait until we're bidden—and I only hope your mother won't be put to any great expense.'

Like Harry Braithwaite, Mr Price was a sensible man.

* * *

Adelaide didn't return to Cotton Hall until the beginning of October, by which time the Groom of the Chambers had sent her a guest list. It was brief: H.R.H., no doubt realizing that Cotton Hall wasn't on the scale of Blenheim, would be accompanied only by Lord and Lady X—and one particular friend. (And of course his valet and the particular friend's maid.) At the names of Lord and Lady X—Addie rather raised her eyebrows, they were so notorious for lending respectability to a dubious *mise en scène*. But she obviously couldn't expect Dukes and Duchesses, and was chiefly concerned as to where everyone was to sleep.

Cotton Hall had been used to accommodate any number of Braithwaites and Staceys, but the warren of nursery quarters wasn't suitable for non-family guests. H.R.H. of course rated the largest room, the connubial chamber once shared by John Henry and Hilda, and now occupied by Hilda alone; but even Addie flinched before the prospect of turning Hilda out of her own bed. The next largest was that once occupied by Flora and Charlotte, so that it had a double bed in it—the bed in which Flora had given birth to Meg—moreover a little dressing-room alongside perfectly adapted to any solitary female guest. Addie fancied H.R.H. would be perfectly comfortable there—only it was Flora's room.

'Would you very much mind, Flo,' suggested Addie, 'for once moving up into the old nurseries? I'm sure I'll keep you company there myself!'

'Why not use the room George and Clara used to have?' objected Flora.

'Because that's where I'll have to put Lord and Lady X—,' explained Addie.

'I'd no idea you had such important friends,' remarked Flora.

Addie smiled a secret smile.

'My dear, the X—s aren't particularly important!' (Nor were they; they were useful hangers-on to H.R.H.'s non-court circle.) 'They've still got to sleep somewhere!'

'And where will Sir Roger sleep?' asked Flora.

'Sir Roger?' repeated Addie, surprised. '*He* won't be sleeping here at all. Of course he'll come over from Yarmouth—'

'But we thought—Hilda and I—it was for Sir Roger you were getting up the party?'

Addie then saw she had better clear up all misunderstandings at once.

'No, dear Flora,' said she. 'Hold your breath and don't faint; the very important person who is coming to honour our little house-party is H.R.H. himself. His Royal Highness,' glossed Adelaide, 'the Prince of Wales!'

Rather to her disappointment, Flora didn't faint, and only for a moment looked astonished before drily observing that the Braithwaites were going up in the world indeed.

'Incognito, of course,' went on Adelaide. 'But what a feather in my cap all the same!'

'Even if he's incognito?' said Flora.

'Of course every one who matters will know—that is, everyone in his own set. You can't imagine how I'm going to be envied!'

'I don't think Hilda and I are much to be envied,' said Flora, 'having the house turned upside down over our heads.'

'My dear, Hilda's perfectly delighted already!—and when I let her into the secret, as I shall this very day, she'll be more delighted still!' declared Addie.

And Hilda was delighted—though without going quite into the ecstasies Addie had expected. Proud as she was of Cotton Hall, she saw nothing extraordinary in even the highest in the land looking forward to paying it a visit. ('Didn't Sir Roger himself tell me it was remarkable?' recalled Hilda.) The idea of seeing fine ladies in beautiful dresses, also promised by Adelaide, appealed to her. Her only trouble came when Addie explained what 'incognito' meant.

'You mean even Queen Victoria won't know where he is?' asked Hilda.

Addie was for a moment taken aback. In H.R.H.'s particular set his august mamma was never referred to save, indeed, as his august mamma, or the old lady at Balmoral, they being too polite, if not well-bred, to employ Kipling's sobriquet of the Widow of Windsor. But Hilda, less sophisticated, said Queen Victoria flat out, and it was a moment before Addie could laugh.

'She will and she won't,' lied Addie. 'You needn't fear being beheaded on Tower Hill!'

'I'd not like him to come here *without* her knowing,' persisted Hilda.

'All sons, even if they're Princes of the Blood, must get off their mother's apron-strings now and again!' said Addie.

'Which were the very words John Henry once spoke to me,' recalled Hilda. 'Tell him he may come and be welcome! Where shall us put him?'

Addie seized her opportunity.

'Well, of course Flora's room has the prettiest view—' she began, when in lounged Benny (as usual dripping wet; he'd been fishing) to distract his mother's attention.

'Oh, Benny, come and hear what grand company we're to entertain!' cried she. 'The very highest in the land!'

Benny ducked his head to Adelaide, at the same time throwing her a look of deep suspicion.

'H.R.H. himself!' smiled Addie. 'Can you believe it!'

'What, that fat old bustard on the lawn?' said Benny disloyally. 'Why, is it for him all this fuss is about? I thought it was for Sir Roger.'

'Of course Sir Roger will come over from Yarmouth,' said Addie impatiently. 'Now we really must settle where everyone's to sleep. If Flora would give up her room to H.R.H.—'

'Why should Aunt Flora be put out?'

'Because she's a loyal subject!' said Hilda.

It was an aspect of the matter Addie hadn't thought of. Nor did it all weigh with Flora. It was for simple Hilda's sake that she now reluctantly nodded agreement.

'Then Aunt Flora can have mine,' said Benny, 'because I'm going fishing with the Strowgers.'

Not even Flora's disloyalty (had she proved herself disloyal) could have shocked Hilda more.

'Benny! When for once we're going to entertain grand company don't you want to show yourself the master of Cotton Hall?'

'No. I don't like grand company,' said Benny stubbornly. 'I'd rather have the Strowgers.'

'But your own friend Sir Roger's going to be here!' protested Hilda.

'It's all right for him,' said Benny. 'He's used to it.'

'And fine ladies, Addie says, wearing beautiful dresses!'

'I don't like fine ladies either,' said Benny, more positively still. 'All they do is flap and squawk like a gaggle of geese.' (It was a hard judgment, of the habituées of the Royal Yacht

Squadron lawn, though their voices were admittedly high-pitched.)

'But you had a *succès fou* among them!' cried Addie.

'And don't mean to be made a fool of again,' said Benny.

'You silly boy, I meant they were all quite delighted with you!' said Addie.

'Aye; as they'd have been delighted with a strange fish Sir Roger'd brought ashore,' retorted Benny with unexpected shrewdness. 'I'm sorry to disappoint you, Mammy, but count me out.'

It took Hilda longer to reconcile herself to the prospect of the Master of Cotton Hall's not being present than it did Adelaide. In fact Adelaide had always felt Benny might be rather in the way, he so rustic in his manners—the dear boy!—and so unused to the ways of society. She would have pressed his hand, but that he rather drew back, so she pressed Hilda's instead.

'Dear Hilda, why *should* Benny be bored by a party of so much older people? Why not let him have his way?' ('I mean to,' muttered Benny.) 'I'm sure you and I and Flora can manage everything perfectly—Benny's room for Flora—*I* don't in the least mind sleeping in the nurseries—solves all problems!'

Hilda still wasn't quite contented. She made several more attempts to make Benny change his mind, pointing out, amongst other inducements, how much old John Henry would have liked to see his heir doing the honours of Cotton Hall, and Benny listened with tolerable patience. Then—

'I ran off once,' said he.

Upon which Hilda ceased her persuasions, and packed Benny such a hamper to take along with him, it almost sank the Strowgers' dinghy.

So were the Prices counted out, as Mr Price had suspected they would. 'Darling Hilda,' said Addie, 'though Margaret *is* your daughter—in a sense the daughter of the house!—why put her to the expense of buying an evening gown she'll probably never wear again?'

'And of course Aunt Adelaide is quite right,' said Margaret, again reporting to her husband. 'What do *I* want with a grand evening gown?'

'There's your wedding-dress,' said Mr Price, 'that you've never worn since ...'

'By now it's out of fashion,' smiled Meg. 'Besides,' she added shyly, 'it's too precious to me to wear amongst strangers ...'

'Dear Squirrel, you're the best wife a man ever had!' said Mr Price fondly.

Fondly, not passionately. Remarkably for a country parson and his spouse, no children had blessed their union; but so devoted were they to one another, neither missed the patter of little feet.

Chapter Seventeen

AT LAST THE great day approached. When Addie promised beautiful ladies in evening dresses she wasn't thinking only of Lady X— and H.R.H.'s particular friend; she expected quite a number of beautiful ladies, since after a simple little dinner she planned a simple little impromptu dance. (It couldn't be quite impromptu, of course, because the Blue Hungarian Band needed hiring a month in advance.) The fact was that H.R.H.'s proposed visit to Cotton Hall, and even the exact date of it, had become rather widely known, at least amongst his particular set. (Of course it became rather widely known; otherwise, from Adelaide's point of view, there'd have been no point in it.) Quite a number of H.R.H.'s intimates discovered that they too would be paying visits in Suffolk at the same time; others, *faute de mieux*, put up at the Crown. ('My dear,' they told each other, 'it's going to be just like Cowes Week—all of us in dreadful little lodgings!') So Addie could count on a dozen couples at least, of which six were invited to the preliminary dinner.

H.R.H. wasn't expected till the afternoon; indeed his week-end visit had been curtailed to but one night's stay, the Saturday, but such are the hazards of entertaining the great, and Addie took the disappointment like the woman of the world she was, philosophically. 'Really I'm quite glad,' she told Flora, 'for to employ those London people two whole days would have quite ruined me!'

But if Addie wasn't ruined the peace of Cotton Hall was, as on the Saturday morning there descended from London what hampers and ice-boxes, what baskets of hot-house fruit and cases of champagne, convoyed by what chefs and scullions and waiters! They took over like an invading army, spreading alarm and dismay among the indigenes. (Cook, declaring it plain to be seen she was to be treated as no more than a scullery maid, gave notice at once.) But like an army too the invaders went about their work with military precision; they were the best-trained staff in London, master-minded by a real genius for organization. To take one point alone: the whole caravanserai, boxes and all, upon arriving at Ipswich was met by a station omnibus to take them to Cotton Hall, which same vehicle was engaged to take them back in the early hours of Sunday morning in time to catch the first up train. How was it done? Merely by looking into the facilities offered by the L.N.E.R., which included station omnibuses for parties over twelve, and though it was perhaps chiefly choirs the L.N.E.R. were thinking of—

'If they've got to be singing,' offered the master-mind, 'my head chef's a real basso profundo. What do they want— Handel's Largo?'

Whether or not to the strains of Handel's Largo the kitchen-party arrived in good time; but not so (to look ahead some twelve hours) the Blue Hungarian Band, which mistakenly stayed on the train till it reached Yarmouth, and only by the hazard of encountering Sir Roger (collecting a pair of guns from Purdey's) got to Cotton Hall at all, in his shooting-brake.

H.R.H. arrived about half-past five, followed some quarter-of-an-hour later by the most beautiful woman Flora had ever seen.

She was very tall, for a woman, with rich auburn hair, sapphire eyes and a classic profile. Her furs were sables, and the plain travelling suit beneath them of quite miraculous cut. She didn't speak much—but then why should she? Like Griselda Grantley, or rather the Marchioness of Hartletop, she amply satisfied the demands of society merely by her appearance and her smile. But her manners weren't proud at all, and she accepted to be put into the little dressing-room without the least complaint, and Lord and Lady X—, in the bedroom once shared by George and Clara, were equally content.

So now all were assembled, and Addie's triumph was complete.

'I'm afraid you'll find it a very simple little dinner,' she apologized, as H.R.H. armed her to the dining-table, 'but I hope you'll enjoy our local soles!'

The soles were of course preceded by soup—*bisque d'homard*—

and *canapés à la caviare*, followed by pheasant or partridge, then saddle of lamb, then a sorbet (to refresh the stomach), then by such knick-knacks as an ice-pudding, *petits fours* and savoury mushrooms on toast.

'A very nice little dinner indeed!' complimented H.R.H. 'And now I hope a little music?'

Music there was, but only thanks to Sir Roger, who having to drive a shooting-brake instead of his trap never got to the dinner at all. As it was, the Blue Hungarian Band scrambled into their Blue Hungarian habiliments just in time, and up in the minstrels' gallery (despite having been stuffed into the shooting-brake like so much game after a good day's sport) gallantly rose to the occasion, and as H.R.H. entered the big hall launched into the strains of the Blue Danube waltz.

'*Oh Danube so blue, so blue, so blue!*' called the violins, '*Oh Danube so blue, so blue, so blue ...*'

H.R.H. put his arm round the waist of the most beautiful lady, and they opened the ball.

Of course it wasn't really a ball: it was just a little country-house hop—no more than a dozen couples. But all the men were in white tails, and all the ladies in silks and satins and long white gloves and a great many jewels—though without tiaras, it having been agreed that for a little country-house hop tiaras would be inappropriate. So they all wore flowers in their hair instead, though owing to the time of year the flowers were mostly artificial. Addie with her usual discretion wore a spray of purple lilac to complement her lavender satin, but the most beautiful lady of all wore a single fresh white gardenia—symbol, no doubt, H.R.H. whispered in her ear, of a blameless life?

It wasn't really a ball; but as the couples twirled and reversed, and the Blue Hungarians played and played, it was as much like a ball as John Henry could have imagined.

Hilda and Flora quitted the festive scene rather early, leaving Adelaide to perform all hostess duties. To H.R.H. in fact she was the only hostess, he having taken Hilda for some invaluable old retainer needing to be kept sweet. He regarded her with his usual amiability, however—what a blooming complexion she had, how ridiculous, almost engaging, that rudimentary moustache!—and at a hint from Addie had offered his arm to her for a polka with perfect willingness.

'And d'you know what, Miss Flo?' giggled Hilda, as she and Flora retired. 'He pinched my behind!'

No one at all had invited Flora to dance. She'd sat silent at the dinner-table, then in silence under the minstrels' gallery, accepting now and again a glass of champagne from one of the strange, smiling waiters. More than one glass indeed had Flora accepted, before Hilda decided it was time they withdrew, and her foot, following Hilda's upstairs, now and then stumbled ...

'Why, Miss Flo, I believe you're tiddly!' giggled Hilda. 'I'm sure *I* am!'

They were all tiddly, that night at Cotton Hall. They began—all adults as they were—to play hide-and-seek, chasing each other through Cotton Hall's back passages, finding themselves in laundry-rooms and pantries, surprising the Blue Hungarian Band in the closet where they were resuming their normal habiliments, until Addie observed that the door of H.R.H.'s bedroom, as well as that of the little dressing-room next to it, was firmly shut. (It was so nice he didn't feel he must stand on ceremony!) Then she sent them all home, and with aching head but happy heart toiled up to the nurseries.

Next morning all was decorum again. H.R.H., with proper compliments, left for Balmoral; the beautiful lady returned to London, and the other figurantes dispersed like visions in a dream. It took somewhat longer for the house to be put to rights: there were sheets to be changed, ash-trays full of cigar-butts to be emptied, a quite enormous number of champagne corks to be collected from here and there in the big hall, which tasks were rather sulkily performed by Cotton Hall's usual servants, whose sulkiness was increased by the fact that everything left over from dinner had been scoffed up by the Londoners. Still a scratch luncheon was served before Addie too quitted the scene, with renewed thanks to Hilda and the promise—who knew? of a signed photograph from H.R.H. himself.

This brief entertainment cost the Braithwaites several hundred pounds, but Addie had no regrets, expecting as she did to be henceforward persona grata in H.R.H.'s particular set. It didn't so happen, however, H.R.H. being under the impression that a signed photograph paid off all social debts; and Addie was quite in the right to keep it for herself, framed in silver on top of the piano in Belgrave Square.

Neither Benny nor Sir Roger profited much either: the first because he'd gone off fishing, so it was his own fault, the second because he'd selflessly fetched the Blue Hungarian Band in his shooting-brake, so missing the dinner, at which he'd hoped to interest H.R.H. in the possibility of more racing from Yarmouth; even a Yarmouth Regatta? Not of course to equal the Regatta at Cowes, but almost as prestigious for smaller craft? Between soup and savoury Sir Roger had meant to put in several words for the smaller craft; only he never had the opportunity. In fact he got nothing to eat at all; by the time he arrived with the Blue Hungarian Band, the table had been cleared.

The invasion over, Cotton Hall subsided once more into its usual lethargy. Benny went fishing, and crewed for Sir Roger, but never again set foot ashore at Cowes.

'For what came of it,' said Benny to his patron, 'but my Aunt turning Cotton Hall upside down all for the sake of an old bustard—'

('H.R.H.,' corrected Sir Roger.)

'—and us coming nigh to losing a good cook? Cook told me about it herself: she walked straight out of the kitchen as soon as that London chap came in and went straight upstairs and packed her box and sat on it all day waiting for the carrier to come and fetch it, and when he didn't because the knife-boy couldn't find him dragged it herself down the back stairs in the hopes of getting a lift with it on your shooting-brake with the Blue Hungarian Band.'

'Good God!' exclaimed Sir Roger, in retrospective alarm.

'Not as far as Ipswich,' explained Benny, 'just as far as Yoxford, where she lives. She didn't know then about the omnibus. But you were so late getting off she went back for a lie down and fell asleep, and when she waked in the morning and saw all the London folk had cleared off, she changed her mind.'

'And dragged her box all the way back again?' said Sir Roger, fascinated.

'No, she couldn't do that,' said Benny. 'It was too heavy. She had to unpack all her things and carry them back piecemeal and dropped her best pair of corsets in a slop-pail left halfway. She says they'll never be the same again. And the knife-boy, when he couldn't find the carrier, spent all day following the shooters, so

Cook gave him *his* notice anyway, and the new one's no more good at boots and shoes than a wet herring.'

'Bless my soul!' said Sir Roger. 'One had no idea what dramas were going on in the wings!'

'Fine people never know anything about anything,' said Benny obscurely, 'so long as their dinner's cooked on time.'

'If it's any consolation to you,' said Sir Roger, 'it was a very successful dinner indeed.' (Which was handsome, he himself not having partaken of a course of it.)

'I remember a piece of Latin Mr Price taught me,' said Benny. '"*Quot homines,*"' he pronounced carefully, '"*tot sententiae.*" It means everyone his own taste. I've no doubt the grand dinner was to the old bustard's—H.R.H.'s—taste, and to my aunt's, who got round Mam and Aunt Flora; but such goings-on aren't to mine; and as master of Cotton Hall I mean never to allow 'em again.'

This was the first time Benny had spoken of himself, or probably even thought of himself, as the master of Cotton Hall; but henceforward, for a little while, its mastership seemed to mean more to him. He paid the chimney sweep himself, and talked of turning the croquet lawn into strawberry beds; but this domestic enthusiasm didn't last, and he was soon off crewing again for Sir Roger. But one thing was certain; no such goings-on ever took place again. The subsequent guests who in due course arrived at Cotton Hall were of a different stamp indeed.

Though defrauded of H.R.H.'s photograph, Hilda nevertheless had her own profit from his Jove-like descent. Naturally rumours of it spread all through the countryside, and several of the ladies of neighbouring squires for the first time drove up to pay carriage-calls, avid for inside information on the social habits of the great, and now Hilda got her own back on them for their long neglect. 'One hears Cotton Hall has been quite a centre of gaiety!' or, 'What a distinguished guest one hears you've been entertaining!' prompted the squires' ladies; bland behind her silver teapot Hilda murmured the magic word *incognito* and let it sink in, before adding that of course Benny had made some very nice friends at Cowes whom she was always happy to see—though of course strictly *incognito*! (Meg, who was present on one of these occasions, quite marvelled at Hilda's adroitness in at once arousing and baffling curiosity, though truth to tell Hilda, after so much champagne, recalled little more of the evening than a royal pinch on her behind, a memory which she naturally suppressed.) The squires' ladies went away disappointed, and didn't subsequently call again, but at least Hilda had seen them off, as she robustly expressed it, with their tails between their legs. In the village the visit was no more than a nine days' wonder, forgotten as soon as the herrings began to come in again at Yarmouth.

Chapter Eighteen

THE YEAR 1890 saw two deaths: of Harry Braithwaite, succumbing to a heart attack, and of Mr Price, less dramatically, from pneumonia. Addie mourned her husband sincerely, but found solace in the affection of sons and daughters-in-law and grandchildren. Frivolous as ever, even as a widowed matriarch she was always the first to put a paper cap on her head at Christmas dinners after pulling the first cracker.—('Pull it with me, Grandma!' clamoured the children. 'With me, with me, with me!')—and in her sixty-fourth year bought herself a sable jacket from Revillon Frères. ('How nice you are to hug, Grandma!' cried the grandchildren.) She was a little chagrined that Sybil and Mr Vanek, after returning to England for the funeral, returned immediately to Florence; but really they'd become so Italian in all their ways, as Addie said she hardly knew her own daughter—and certainly didn't miss her, perpetually engaged as she was with a flock of grandchildren.

Margaret had no such consolations. Mr Price's pre-deceasing her, he being so much the older, was only to be expected, and she accepted it, after the first period of rebellious grief—'But why so soon, O Lord, why so soon?'—with resignation and without extravagant mourning, and his obituary in *The Times* read simply *Francis Price, priest, in his fifty-second year, beloved husband of Margaret Braithwaite.* It however naturally caught the eye of Clara, who always read *The Times* death column from end to end, and upon her reporting it to Addie the latter after a pause for recollection confirmed that it was indeed their niece who had been widowed. '*I* never even knew she was married!' complained Clara. 'I certainly told Charlotte,' said Addie vaguely. 'How thoughtful of you to let me know, dear! I'm sure you're as good as a vulture to us!'

From which it will be seen that Adelaide's antipathy for her sister-in-law Clara hadn't diminished with the years.

Mr Price had insured his life so carefully, Margaret was secure of a modest income, and until a new incumbent was inducted the Church Commissioners invited her to go on occupying the Vicarage; nor did the Church Commissioners seem to feel any urgency about the spiritual welfare of so minute a parish. (A neighbouring clergyman did duty every other Sunday, at Evensong.) Thus Margaret—as has been said, the Prices never had children—was left equally without hopes or fears for the future. She had however a secret dream.

Sir Roger Wynstan, with a new and larger yacht, had begun to undertake more adventurous voyages—to the Bermudas, to the Antilles—and always took Benny with him, and thus for much of the year Cotton Hall was occupied only by Hilda and Flora—the one a middle-aged woman, the other already, in Sir Roger's term, an old lady. But though the elder, Flora was by far the more active; she had taken to gardening, and was rarely to be seen during the daylight hours without an old sun-bonnet on her head and hands grimed with compost, for she never wore gloves; she found satisfaction in thrusting her long bony fingers deep into the soil, down among the roots. (Bedding out was her particular pleasure.) The lodge like a Swiss chalet became her personal tool-shed: to the other, the one shaped like a bee-hive, the path became quite over-grown, and if now and then a tile fell off the roof it fell unnoticed into the surrounding bushes, for the Cotton Hall gardens were no better kept than in the days of Old Ham. He was dead too, and a replacement merely moved the grass and kept a bonfire smouldering, and but for Flora there would hardly have been a sprig of alyssum or head of lettuce in sight. But Hilda's ever-increasing bulk confined her first to an easy-chair, then to her bed.

Hilda had grown quite enormous, the once wholesome bulk of her flesh now dropsically swollen. Her limbs were like bolsters, her cheeks like two pincushions; above them her small light eyes brightened only in expectation of a next meal. In vain Margaret tried to get her to diet a little, and equally in vain tried to enlist Flora's help. 'Except for seeing Benny now and then, food is her only pleasure,' said Flora. 'Why deprive her of it?'

Margaret was silenced—partly because Flora's first words had struck home. Naturally Benny was Hilda's favourite, and

Margaret loved him dearly herself, as she always had done; but that her constant attendance on Hilda, now almost immobile, was merely taken for granted a little wounded her. However such was her sweet disposition, she forgave both Hilda her indifference and Flora for underlining it.

Flora out and about in all weathers, Hilda even on the finest days in bed, Cotton Hall for much of the year was to all intents and purposes empty as a worm-eaten nut.

It seemed to Margaret a pity.

Two years in fact passed before Mr Price was permanently replaced by a new incumbent already furnished with a wife and small children and Margaret could remain at the Vicarage no longer. Mr and Mrs Ruddock warmly invited her to stay on as long as she liked—'As an unpaid curate!' said Mr Ruddock humorously—but the wife's warmth was slightly less than the husband's, and with her usual good sense, and though the parish was her life, Margaret knew it wouldn't do; and then it was that she made Hilda and Flora privy to her secret dream.

'Of course there can't be nunneries now,' opened Margaret, 'at least not in the Church of England, but don't you think, Mamma, Aunt Flora, some quiet place of retreat for Anglican ladies might fill a real need? There wouldn't be a chapel even, just regular prayers, and perhaps helpful talks by a clergyman, or visiting missionaries ...'

'You mean here at Cotton Hall?' asked Hilda, sitting up in bed.

'Yes, I do,' said Margaret boldly. 'It seems such a waste, this big house with only you and Aunt Flora in it—for Benny's hardly here at all. Of course you'd both stay, and I'd move in too, and be able to take better care of you, and if we used the nursery quarters I'm sure there'd be room for say half-a-dozen ladies as well.'

'And who would take care of *them*?' asked Flora.

'They'd take care of themselves,' said Margaret. '"Who sweeps a chamber for Thy sake, makes that and the deed divine."'

Evidently she had the whole plan worked out. (It was probably Mr Ruddock who'd give the helpful talks.) And when Flora considered it, she began to find it not at all a bad one. She and Hilda growing older, it would indeed be a comfort to have

Margaret under the same roof, and Hilda agreed. 'Though I'm not sure I'll like holy-bolies all over the place,' said Hilda warily, 'but if Meg's set her heart on it, and will come and live here too, I've no objection.'

Nor had Benny any objection, when fortunately just at that juncture he reappeared from a West Indian cruise, he being as fond of Margaret as she was of him.

'As my sister, and after her sad loss, Meg's just as much right to the place as I have,' said good-natured Benny. (Though in fact she wasn't his sister any more than she was Hilda's daughter.) 'And if there's no room for me, I can always have a berth with Sir Roger.'

'Of course there'll always be room for you!' cried Hilda. 'Meg speaks of half-a-dozen, but it's my belief she won't find even two or three willing to come and sweep and pray!'

The event proved her mistaken; and a new sort of guest altogether began to arrive at Cotton Hall.

Margaret herself was surprised by the response to a short advertisement in the *Church Times* and another in *The Lady*. All over the country, it seemed, pious gentlewomen were seeking a refuge from the day and age; were not even leaders of Society in London becoming concerned at its increasing materialism? Margaret could pick and choose, and chose mostly widows, like herself, except for one failed sculptress whose plight with a marble Mother and Child on her hands more than commonly touched her. It had been her original plan that each guest should stay only a few weeks, but many, finding a haven at last, and for the very moderate payment Margaret asked of them, stayed on and on. It helped that they were all of much the same age and standing—that is, over forty, and middle or upper-middle-class; the only deviation besides the failed sculptress from Bloomsbury was a failed 'cello-player from Bath; in general all shared the same background, and this made for a comfortable homogeneity; and so Cotton Hall throve.

It was so strictly Church of England, there was never a chapel, but the big hall did almost as well: each morning Margaret led prayers there, with hymns and the Collect for the day and a reading from the New Testament, and each evening there were more hymns and a reading from *Paradise Lost* or *The Pilgrim's Progress*. (In between every one was supposed to pray as the spirit moved them. Most just repeated to themselves 'Our Father', or even simpler, more childish petitions learnt at a mother's knee: they didn't pray as Saint Teresa of Avila had prayed; but if their prayers didn't rise to Heaven with the holy beauty of altar candles, they had the modest trustfulness of night-lights.) Some weaker spirits, tired of sweeping to the glory of God and preparing their own meals, fell by the way—the sculptress fled back to Bloomsbury and the 'cellist to Bath—but both were swiftly replaced, and most not only stayed the course but stayed permanently.

Benny's room was sacred, as was Hilda's, now shared by Margaret, but Flora's in time had to be divided into three, she herself retreating to a small nondescript chamber behind the stair to the minstrels' gallery. Above each cubicle door a poker-work text urged the occupant to WORK AND PRAY, or reminded LABORARE EST ORARE; from each the occupant issued punctually at six-fifteen, so that before early prayers at half-past seven all domestic duties were accomplished; and if one or two of the weaker sisters took the opportunity to make themselves a cup of tea, Margaret looked the other way; and then how gladly, how rejoicingly, all lifted their voices in the morning hymn!

'Lord behold us with Thy blessing
Once again assembled here!'

Though they were all new to religious life who assembled at Cotton Hall, once so assembled they formed themselves into a community; so Cotton Hall throve.

And amongst this innocent flock Hilda and Flora throve too. The big house was indeed swept and garnished as to the glory of God, a particular comfort now that servants' wages were harder to find, while the meals, if leaning chiefly on dairy produce, were at least adequate. Only Hilda's stomach absolutely refused to accommodate itself to a vegetarian diet, and for her Margaret cooked a pork or mutton chop each day. As for Flora, a vegetarian diet suited her very well, especially as it gave purpose to her gardening. Several members of the community, gardeners themselves, willingly took over the flower beds, and even attempted to introduce a herbaceous border into what had once been the moat; Flora concentrated on vegetables. With what appreciation were her first new peas greeted, with what enthusiasm her tomatoes and lettuces and cucumbers! Flora at this time was almost happy.

So was the new incumbent Mr Ruddock made happy. It was indeed he who gave the occasional helpful talks, and by comparison with the rest of his parishioners found the ladies of Cotton Hall a pleasant change. ('Concerning the Ark,' once probed a Strowger—Mr Ruddock having attempted a helpful talk in the Church Hall—'hadn't they pumps?') Mr Ruddock found the ladies a pleasant change.

Naturally the news of Cotton Hall's transformation into a house of retreat for Anglican gentlewomen got back to the rest of the family. Both Adelaide and Charlotte took *The Lady*, and as Clara had picked up the name Braithwaite from *The Times* obituary column so both picked up the name Cotton Hall, and raised eyebrows together over such a ridiculous folly. But when a second advertisement appeared—'*Cotton Hall: please, no further applications*'—they took the matter more seriously.

'What on earth can Hilda be thinking of?' wondered Charlotte.

'It's none of Hilda's doing,' said Adelaide shrewdly. 'It's much more likely the daughter's—what was her name? Margaret?—who married the Vicar. Didn't Clara tell us he died two or three years ago? Now that she hasn't a parish to run she's taken up this new fad, and got round her mother and Flora.'

'But what on earth is her brother thinking of?' argued Charlotte. 'The boy you met at Cowes?'

'As one hears he's always off sailing with Sir Roger Wynstan, I suppose he doesn't much care what becomes of the place,' said Addie. 'That will come later, my dear, when he marries!'

She was unjust both to Margaret and Benny. Margaret's was no fad, but the fulfilment of a long-cherished dream, and Benny, when he eventually did marry, less than ever wanted to turn her out.

He'd loved Margaret ever since she crooned lullabies over his cradle, ever since she helped him with his lessons. Without any blood-tie between them, he loved Margaret on the perfectly rational grounds that she'd always been good to him, and so let her do what she liked with Cotton Hall.

They came even to have a joint banking account, upon which Margaret drew as necessary for the running of the establishment and Benny for his personal requirements. These were few, since crewing for Sir Roger he had all found and his tastes were simple: a cheque drawn for twenty pounds was a rarity with him: and as more and more ladies contributed their mites Margaret, with her own income from her husband's insurance to put into the kitty, was scarcely more spendthrift: so that when Hilda sometimes asked was John Henry's money holding out, could always give a reassuring answer.

Every now and then, between voyages, Benny dropped in and cast a benevolent eye over his patrimony—though he never thought of it as such, he had as little feeling for property as a codling—considerably fluttering the mild community with his handsome sailorish presence and loud sailorish voice. Now and then he actually attended evensong, when in his honour *For Those in Peril on the Sea* was added among the hymns, which (standing a head and a half higher than any one else) Benny bawled out with simple fervour. Naturally all the ladies adored him, and knitted sea-stockings and mufflers for him without end. But even ashore he usually preferred to berth with Sir Roger, whose house was always open to him, and where between one cruise and the next they spent their time studying Admiralty and hydrographic charts.

Thus there ensued another happy, halcyon time at Cotton Hall; only with so much praying going on around, Hilda couldn't help but be affected.

Chapter Nineteen

SHE WAS BY this time, as had been said, so enormously stout, she preferred to stay in bed all day. So unwieldly had she become, Margaret had sometimes to help her to turn over in it. But however distressed in the flesh, she became mentally more distressed still, especially as she began to draw shorter and shorter breaths.

Sometimes she could hardly draw breath at all, into the failing lungs under her enormous breasts, and one day when Margaret brought her up a pork chop, absolutely thrust it aside.

'There's apple sauce with it,' persuaded Margaret, 'and the kidney ...'

But still Hilda pushed fretfully at the tray, and Meg, taking it up again, began to be alarmed. Though she had often tried to persuade Hilda to eat less, to see her advice taken dismayed her.

'Is there anything else you'd like—a boiled egg?'

'Nothing,' whispered Hilda. 'Meg, I'm going to die.'

It was a moment Meg was fortunately well equipped to deal with. Now putting the tray with its mundane burden altogether aside, she sat down by Hilda's pillow and prepared to listen, soothe, and encourage.

'We must all die when our time comes,' said she gently, 'that is, when it's God's time to call us home.'

'Only one doesn't think about it,' whimpered Hilda.

'I believe you should perhaps think of it now,' said Margaret. 'Would you like to see Mr Ruddock? He's very kind and helpful.'

'Only he can't hear confession like the Romans do,' said Hilda. 'Fetch Flora, and leave us alone a bit ...'

Flora, summoned from the garden, came wiping her earthy

hands on her apron and with the old sun-bonnet still on her head; Margaret's voice, usually so quiet and controlled, had held an unusual note of urgency; but she sat down beside Hilda's pillow without fuss.

'I was just thinning the lettuces,' she observed, 'but Meg said you wanted to see me?'

'Blow the lettuces,' said Hilda—but faintly. 'I'm going to die.'

'For the matter of that, so am I,' said Flora. 'I'm getting on for sixty. Is that all you brought me in to tell me?'

'No,' said Hilda. 'You've got to listen, Miss Flo, and remember ... You're such a stringy old hen, I dare say it'll be years before *you* go, but I'm nigh on my death-bed—Meg as good as told me so, asking if I'd like to see Mr Ruddock!—and however can I face my maker with a mortal sin on my conscience?—even though it was so long ago?'

For a long moment Flora paused, remembering indeed. Then—

'Passing off Meg as yours and Papa's should rather be a sin on *my* conscience,' she said. 'But I never think of it.'

It was true. The night of Margaret's birth, the days of deception that followed, were so far from haunting Flora that only at rare intervals did she recall them, and then almost as an episode in someone else's past, not her own, to which the translation of Meg into Mrs Price had as it were put finis.

'Your Maker in Heaven will think only of how good you were to me,' resumed Flora, 'for what on earth should I have done without you?'

But Hilda shook her head impatiently.

'It's not that I mean. I'd sooner cut my tongue out than let Meg know she's a bastard. As to that she'd never guessed but that John Henry and I were wed before she was born—she was too little to take account of dates! It's not about Meg I mean, it's about Benny, him that's come into all the property. Didn't you ever suspect yourself he was none of your Da's getting?'

Obviously the time had come not for fair words but plain speech.

'Sergeant Butley?' asked Flora.

'To my shame!' cried Hilda, either hysterically or histrionically.

'Not at all,' said Flora. 'I think you were very sensible. Obviously no one local could have served you. Did he know,' she asked, with genuine curiosity, 'Benny was his son? Is that why he took him off?'

'Never!' cried Hilda. 'It was just sheer devilment. He knew no more, when he tumbled me, than the babe unborn. In proof of which, when he got up from me, "Now you can tell your ploughboy," said he, "how a soldier fucks!"'

'I think you were very sensible,' repeated Flora.

'But to deceive your Da!'

'Believing Benny was his son made him happier than anything in his life,' said Flora, 'and *he* never suspected.'

'But he'll know now,' pointed out Hilda. 'It's not only my Maker I'll have to face, it's John Henry—for doesn't Scripture tell how we're all going to meet up above? He'll know *now*—and that he left all his property away from his own flesh and blood?'

It crossed Flora's mind that if in some after life John Henry was aware of the circumstance, Heaven would indeed be another Hell for him. She herself believed in neither Heaven nor Hell; what she anticipated, and hoped for, was immediate extinction. It was one of the consequences of her heart having been broken.

'He'll give me right hell,' continued Hilda, as though meeting Flora's thought, 'and I can't face it, Miss Flo, though it's only lately I've thought of it. You can rejoice and be bold as brass when in good health, but not when you're dying ...'

She was obviously in extreme distress—her enormous bosom heaving, the tears starting to roll down her pincushion cheeks, a sight at once grotesque and pathetic.

'Then pull yourself together,' said Flora, 'and tell me what you want done.'

'I want to write a letter,' said Hilda, 'like my Last Will and Testament, to be read after my death—for I couldn't bear it known while I'm still alive—which I'll sign, and you can witness, confessing all, and then afterwards you can show it to the lawyers and my step-son Harry can come into his rights at last.'

Before the implications of such a proceeding Flora was momentarily too startled to speak; then she made the obvious objection.

'But Harry's dead,' pointed out Flora.

'Then his son can come into 'em,' said Hilda impatiently. 'His son Alan—he who once asked me for parboiled eggs!' she added, to Flora quite inexplicably. 'Ah, wasn't it all a long time ago!'

'Yes,' said Hilda briefly. 'Have you thought what it will mean to Benny?'

'Benny won't care,' said Hilda positively. 'He's never wanted Cotton Hall—look how he let Meg do what she liked with it! And he'll always have a berth, as he calls it, with Sir Roger. I dare say Benny will be glad to be rid of the place.'

There was much truth in this. It was only when Flora thought of Margaret that she raised another objection.

'And suppose Alan wants Cotton Hall? What will become of Margaret and the Community?'

'I can't be bothered with that,' said Hilda. 'Meg's not my daughter, she's yours!'

The composition and dictation of so important a letter occupied Hilda's last weeks rather agreeably. Sometimes she began 'To all whom it may concern, I being of sound mind,' sometimes, more personally, 'To my step-grandson Alan Braithwaite, hoping he may forgive and forget.' In a first version Sergeant Butley was given name and rank, in others dissolved into an anonymous lad-met-behind-a-hedge, or was fantasized into some grandee whose carriage had stopped outside the Crown, and who had mitigated the boredom of waiting while his horses baited by tumbling her equally behind a hedge. This was indeed Hilda's favourite gloss, but Flora rather firmly led her away from it by pointing out that the Crown had never had stabling, and refused to be witness. It was still a matter of chance whether Hilda pin-pointed Sergeant Butley or not, but due to the accident of her death almost immediately after she had signed, and Flora witnessed, the second version, her seducer remained anonymous. In any case Hilda came clean at last, and it is to be hoped met John Henry in heaven with a clear conscience.

Her funeral was very simple, in the church once her son-in-law's so to speak, now under the aegis of Mr Ruddock. Benny was unfortunately somewhere off the Antilles, but among the wreaths the most prominent was that ordered by Margaret for him *in absentia*. All the members of the community attended, and all from the village who had known her as John Henry's wife. There was no such feast as had marked John Henry's burying, just tea and hot scones (to cheer them up a little), for the ladies

124

of Cotton Hall, after partaking of which Flora went to her own room and took from her desk Hilda's farewell letter that was to make the twisted root straight at last.

Her obvious duty was to dispatch it at once to Alan Braithwaite. 'Tomorrow!' thought Flora.

She didn't often attend evensong, nor did she now. But she mounted into the minstrels' gallery and stood a little while looking down on the innocent flock below.

They were singing *Now the Day is Over*. Even with Margaret's strong lead in the alto, their voices raised rather quaveringly: at *shadows of the evening*, and the subsequent verses, sometimes failed almost entirely, until Margaret, singing her heart out, led them triumphantly into *Glory to the Father/Glory to the Son/and to Thee, blest Spirit/Whilst all Ages run ...*

Flora returned to her room and read Hilda's letter again.

When Alan Braithwaite received it, what would be the consequences?

In the first place, no doubt, a great deal of lawyers' work. Flora almost smiled, thinking of the dismay of the Ipswich solicitors, faced with so disconcerting a document. Was it even legal? She herself had witnessed Hilda's signature, but to what was practically a Last Will and Testament shouldn't there have been a second witness? No doubt a point could be stretched, thought Flora; again, it was a matter for solicitors; but in all probability wouldn't John Henry's original Will stand, that left Cotton Hall to Harry and the rest of his assets to be divided between Charlotte and George and herself? Remembering how much less he'd left than was expected, Flora doubted whether the proceeds would make much difference even to George's and Clara's way of life—and certainly not to the Staceys', while for herself all she asked was a home at Cotton Hall.

But Cotton Hall, bequeathed to Harry, would presumably— as Hilda presumed—have been bequeathed by him to his son Alan, and what would Alan, now with a wife and family of his own, want to do with it?

Come and occupy it in the summer—the summer visits of old repeating themselves?

But then what would become of the Community? Obviously they'd have to shift. Only where to—their whole existence dependent on a large, rent-free country house?

And if the Community disintegrated, it would break Margaret's heart.

As has been said, there were long periods when Flora completely forgot Margaret was her daughter. Hilda had needed to remind her of it ...

'I've never done much for her,' thought Flora.

Now she could.

For a moment, the letter in her hand, she was on the point of putting a match to it. What prevented her she hardly knew—a superstition of piety towards the dead? In the end she put it into its envelope, then into another, and locked it in her desk. The second envelope, of good stout manilla, happened to have contained seed packets, and still had Broccoli (sow in late spring) written on it, and Flora let the legend stand.

Thus Alan Braithwaite learned of his step-grandmother's death only after another obituary in *The Times*—'At Cotton Hall, peacefully in her forty-third year, Hilda, widow of John Henry Braithwaite, beloved mother of Margaret and Benjamin, R.I.P.'—had been punctually reported by Clara to Adelaide and Charlotte: both of whom took far more notice of it than they had of Mr Price's.

'Hilda *dead*? I can't believe it,' said Addie to Charlotte. 'She was years younger than I am.'

'Or than I am,' said Charlotte, the elder.

For a moment they regarded each other uneasily. There is always something dismaying about the death of anyone younger than oneself.

'I wonder what it was?' said Charlotte.

Neither dared pronounce the word 'cancer', but it was in both their minds.

'In any case it makes no difference to *us*,' said Charlotte.

'But it will to Benny,' said Adelaide. 'Now he'll be able to make a clean sweep and get all those old women out of Cotton Hall at last!'

It was still several days before she relayed the news to Alan, when he came with his wife to Sunday tea. (Adelaide's Sunday teas were an institution; she always had *pâté de foie* sandwiches.)

'How pretty Mabel looks in that hat!' said Adelaide. 'But Mabel would look pretty with a sugar-bag on her head! By the way, Hilda—your grandfather's second wife—has just died.'

There was a surprisingly long pause.

'What happens to Cotton Hall?' asked Alan.

'Why, nothing,' said Adelaide. 'It belongs to Benny. What a good-looking boy he was,' recalled Addie, with a rare lack of tact, 'when Sir Roger brought him ashore at Cowes!'

'I wasn't there,' said Alan. 'I was never with you and my father at Cowes week. Or at the famous house-party either.'

'Of course not, darling,' consoled Adelaide. 'You were too busy making your way at the Treasury. Your father's life work was over—and really it was rather a bore!'

Yet she couldn't help casting a secret smile at the big silver-framed photograph on the piano. What a triumph it had been, luring H.R.H. into the wilds of East Anglia!

'I think it's time we went home,' said Alan. 'On Sundays, Mabel always baths the children herself ...'

'When Nanny's out,' smiled Mabel. 'It's quite a treat for them!'

'I'm sure it is,' said Adelaide, who for her part had never bathed Alan in her life. 'My dearest boy,' she added suddenly, 'do you *mind* not having Cotton Hall?'

'Only because I knew father always felt it should have been his, and in due course would have left it me. That's all.'

'Hilda's dead,' said Charlotte Stacey to her husband. 'Clara saw it in *The Times*. How strange it seems, when she was so much younger even than Flora!'

'In my opinion Flora will outlive us all,' said Arthur Stacey. 'She's got your father's stamina.'

'I suppose she'll go on living at Cotton Hall?'

'I imagine so,' said Arthur Stacey. 'Do you want to go and see her?'

'I don't think so ... It's odd,' mused Charlotte, 'but I never think of her as my sister. Somehow after Papa remarried she seemed to grow completely away from us.' (Actually it wasn't after John Henry remarried; the breach stemmed from Alexander's betrayal.) 'She wouldn't even come and stay with Addie when Addie invited her. I can't think what we should find to say to each other.'

'Then leave well alone,' said Arthur Stacey.

He still wore John Henry's sixpence on his watch-chain, but

sometimes would have been hard put to tell how it had got there.

'"At Cotton Hall"!' cried Clara, chewing over the news with George. 'The impudence of the woman!'

'Where else should she have died? After all, it was her home,' said George moderately. 'Try to be more charitable, my dear.'

'Oh, certainly,' said Clara. 'Much as I always disliked the woman as an intriguer and schemer, I suppose mourning for three months?'

But no one else except Margaret went into mourning for Hilda.

It was perhaps remarkable that the pious ambience of Cotton Hall produced in Flora, suppressing Hilda's letter, no such feelings of guilt as had induced Hilda to dictate it. If Hilda had sinned, had not she too? But she was tougher than Hilda.

Chapter Twenty

HILDA'S DEMISE, the absence of her once so substantial presence, made remarkably little difference at Cotton Hall, except that Margaret had no longer to cook pork or mutton chops for her. Vegetarianism could reign unflawed. And what delicious young peas, crisp lettuces, succulent tomatoes Flora continued to produce! No one ever thought of *her* dying; she might be nearing sixty, but with age was simply becoming more distinguished and Holbein-looking than ever. (An artistic member of the Community quite longed to paint her portrait. But Flora would never consent to sit.) At the same time, because she'd always been there, to Margaret she seemed old as the hills.

'Did you ever wear a crinoline, Aunt Flora?' once asked Margaret.

Flora smiled.

'Indeed I did, my dear—about the time you were born.'

'They must have been terribly inconvenient?'

'In some ways yes, in others no,' said Flora.

'And that was when Cotton Hall used to be full of relations? I can just remember—or think I do. There was Aunt Charlotte and Aunt Adelaide and Aunt Clara—'

'Indeed there were,' said Flora briefly.

'But wasn't it a happy time,' pressed Margaret, 'when you were all here together?'

Flora, looking back to those long-ago days, remembered no particularly happy times at all. What she chiefly remembered was the constant fripping of Adelaide and Charlotte versus Clara and the disagreeableness of John Henry. But why destroy Margaret's illusion?

'A very happy time indeed,' said Flora.

'Of course all my cousins were grown up before I was big

enough to know them,' regretted Margaret. 'Wasn't there some kind of a family quarrel?'

'Call it a parting of the ways,' said Flora.

'Of course if they all *were* still coming here—I mean, now, my cousins and *their* families—I shouldn't have Cotton Hall for a retreat,' said Meg. 'But I've sometimes thought, Aunt Flora, would it be kind and help to patch things up if I asked some of them down on a sort of Visitor's Day?'

Like Arthur Stacey—

'Let well alone,' advised Flora.

Shawls had been as long out of fashion as crinolines: how many years had passed since Hilda peacocked to church in her fabled cashmere! It became an all-purpose comforter, used to wrap round her shoulders while she sat up in bed eating her perpetual meals off trays; then she'd found a flannel bed-jacket handier, and Meg put it aside in a bottom drawer. It was a pity; it had once been an Ipswich draper's pride, and John Henry paid good money for it. But now the moths had got at it.

Contrary to Addie's prognostications, Benny showed no desire to make a clean sweep; she was as wrong as Clara had been, foretelling he'd die young. Meg continued in possession of Cotton Hall undisturbed—Benny perfectly content to roam the seven seas with Sir Roger and only once a year drop anchor in a safe, tideless harbour. This was regularly in autumn, since however committed to sea-faring Sir Roger retained sufficient natural instincts always to come home for the shooting, which meant Benny was always home for the Harvest Festival, when he was wonderfully useful helping decorate the church and roaring out *All Is Safely Gathered In.* Though he was now over thirty, all the ladies still thought of him as a dear, good boy ...

All the same, the years hadn't passed without his falling into many a misadventure which Sir Roger got him out of.

There was an occasion in the Azores, for example, when having chivalrously punched a ponce in the face he was in the calaboose for two days, and Sir Roger had to bribe right and left to get him out. There was an occasion in Costa Rica when Benny so thrashed a man for thrashing a donkey the man (so he alleged) was crippled for life, and it cost Sir Roger twenty pounds to compensate him. Sir Roger began to feel that he possessed in Benny not only a first-class deck-hand, but also a large, unruly (however well-intentioned) mastiff. As will have been seen, Benny was always well-intentioned; but at a last scrape he got himself into, Sir Roger threw in his hand.

In the third or fourth autumn after Hilda's death punctually Sir Roger returned for the shooting-season. Margaret naturally heard of his arrival and confidently looked forward to Benny's appearance at Evensong preliminary to his trundling pumpkins round the font. But no Benny appeared, nor did any word come from Sir Roger in explanation; and at last, as the guns began to pop over the stubble-fields, Margaret made her way to where Sir Roger stood waiting behind a hedge.

'Keep away, damn you!' cried Sir Roger. 'Why, it's Mrs Price,' he added, hastily unloading. 'I was just going to look you up ...'

'To tell me where Benny is?' asked Margaret. 'Has the boat— I mean the yacht—had to go into dry dock somewhere?'

'She could certainly do with it,' agreed Sir Roger. 'Bottom needs scraping ...'

'And Benny's seeing to it?' said Meg. 'Then I suppose we must wait in patience—only Harvest Festival's next Sunday.'

Sir Roger looked down the barrel of his gun.

'As a matter of fact, Benny's not on this side of the water at all. That's what I was coming to tell you. He's still at San Domingo.'

'You mean you've left him behind?' cried Margaret.

'Say rather, he skipped ship,' said Sir Roger. 'When I was ready to sail, young Benny wasn't. But don't worry, we'll pick him up next time round. Don't worry in the least, Mrs Price; I'm only glad I met you. All well at Cotton Hall, I hope? I must re-load!'

'Aunt Flora!' cried Margaret, running upstairs so swiftly that her hat fell off her head. 'Aunt Flora! I've just seen Sir Roger—'

'Well, where's Benny?' asked Flora.

'Left behind at San Domingo.'

'Left behind?' repeated Flora incredulously.

'Sir Roger says he skipped ship, but I don't believe it. Benny would never skip ship! And isn't San Domingo where there's yellow fever? He must be ill, Sir Roger couldn't look me in the eye!' declared Margaret. 'It's my belief he's left him behind just so he can get back for the shooting!'

'Perhaps we'll have a letter,' said Flora soothingly.

But weeks passed and no reassuring missive arrived. 'He must be too ill to write!' cried Margaret—and at last, just as she'd have gone, had she been old enough, to look for Benny enlisted as a drummer-boy, she went to look for him in San Domingo.

She needed courage. Competently as she ran Cotton Hall, Margaret was for her age peculiarly inexperienced. Save on her honeymoon she had literally never set foot outside the parish, and all the circumstances of her life had combined to preserve an innate unworldliness. She went abroad an innocent indeed.

Actually it wasn't an entirely desperate a venture. Though even the enterprising Messrs Cook hadn't yet cast their shoe over the West Indies, a rival firm had; and on the steam yacht *Alberta*, for a hundred pounds all found (including guides to the caves at Santana), Margaret embarked, all the ladies of the Community headed by a Miss Pocock, a spinster of ample means contributing to her expenses. It was in fact the most romantic and exciting thing they'd ever done, sending Margaret to the West Indies in search of a long-lost brother, and she promised to keep a diary all the way.

Chapter Twenty-One

On board the SS Alberta,
10th Oct.

WELL, HERE I am, all unpacked, ready to take up my pen! The ship is beautifully clean, especially the brasswork, and what I believe Sir Roger would call 'well-found'. I share my cabin—how extraordinarily!—with a lady who once met Aunt Addie at a Mansion House reception! ! How we discovered this was equally surprising—I mentioning Uncle Harry as a connection, upon which she swiftly picked up his name as a barrister whom her late husband (in Somerset House) always had a special regard for. It is a small world indeed!

The Captain also is very pleasant—not in the least what one would call a 'sea-dog', but perfectly well-spoken and with a proper air of authority. Mrs Anstruther (my cabin-mate) and I both agree that we feel perfectly safe in his hands. Now there goes the gong for our evening meal, so no more now!

Friday the 11th.

How splendidly the great waves roll in! One never tires of watching them rushing towards us in great hills and valleys of green water all crested with white foam! I don't know why, but 'the body of heaven in its clearness' (Exodus xxiv 10) is the expression that comes into my mind, and how I wish all my dear friends at Cotton Hall were with me to share the wonderful experience!

Mrs Anstruther and I continue to find much in common: she, like me, truly venerates our dear Queen—she has attended a Drawing-room—but has reservations about her successor. (So had Margaret, after the goings-on at Cotton Hall when H.R.H. paid a quiet week-end visit, and it says much for her character that she refrained from trumping Mrs Anstruther's ace, of having been presented, by

133

revealing that the delinquent in question had once actually been her own mother's house guest.) *She is of course far more worldly than I am, but I am sure only from force of circumstances, for it turns out she is an Honourable.*

Among the other passengers our special cronies are two ladies travelling like ourselves alone—sisters, spinsters, taking the voyage to recruit their health after nursing a widowed mother through a long and trying illness. They come from Gloucestershire, and I understand are quite well-known breeders of Angora rabbits.

One fly in the ointment! In the cabin next to ours are a couple neither Mrs Anstruther nor I at all care for. To say they are 'in trade' is of course to say nothing against them, but it seems they come from Sheffield. The husband seems actually proud of it—he makes steel, he says, of the very highest quality, such as is used for surgical instruments. I can well understand his professional pride, but his manners are deplorable and we feel very sorry for his wife.

There is another married couple on board of whom at present the less said the better, for appearances may belie them. As Mrs Anstruther so rightly observes, there are more explanations than one for a high colour. Her husband, who was very fresh-complexioned, never touched anything but a little sherry. Our 'ship's company' is completed by two young men, friends, one apparently connected with a Marine Insurance Company, the other 'something in the City', and rather 'snobs'. Mrs Anstruther and I have little to do with either, we just say 'good morning', and that is all.

Oct. 12th.

Today our kind Captain came round asking 'any complaints?' 'Indeed no!' cried both I and Mrs Anstruther.

I sometimes wonder whether he has not some secret sorrow—a wife or child lost perhaps, while he was far from home? He looks so grave and preoccupied, his eyes have sometimes quite an absent look. But he always tries to appear cheerful and crack a joke. When I asked him was there any special polish his men used, to keep the brasses so bright, he said just elbow-grease! Verb sap!

He also assured me that yellow fever, in the Antilles, was quite a thing of the past, and indeed that its incidence there had always been exaggerated. Perhaps Benny has but broken a leg or arm? I try to think so.

I cannot tell you, my dear ones, how much I miss our morning gatherings for prayer. In fact I suggested to Mrs Anstruther and the Misses Cook that we might perhaps hold a little service of our own, in the

134

saloon, before anyone was about; but though the Misses Cook I believe would have agreed, Mrs Anstruther said it would make us too conspicuous. So I say my orisons by myself while she is still asleep, lovingly remembering all my friends at Cotton Hall!

Oct. 14th.

Even on Sunday, alas, there was no proper service. Though I understand ship's captains are empowered by maritime law at least to read the lessons, when I proposed it he asked to be excused. Perhaps he is a Nonconformist?

October 18th.

The Misses Cook have taught me to play whist (Mrs Anstruther was familiar with the game already), and in the evenings we make up a very pleasant 'four'. I must say that though I have never touched cards hitherto, I see no harm in it—unless that is one plays for money, which we would never dream of. There is also a bridge table, where they do play for money, and there the 'regulars' are the couple from Sheffield and the other married pair, of whom our suspicions have proved only too well-founded. They never appear on deck and take all meals in their cabin, from which their steward (whom one cannot help encountering, as it is just opposite ours) carries away at least one empty whisky bottle a day! 'At least they are not secret drinkers!' said Mrs Anstruther humorously. But they are obviously hardened ones, for when they appear in the evenings to play bridge their speech, far from being slurred, has an unnatural precision.

In short, we now form quite two camps! In the one is myself, Mrs Anstruther, and the two Misses Cook, in the other the persons from Sheffield, the X—s (as I shall call them) and the two young men, who have now joined the bridge-table, though not at bridge but in a round game called 'poker', which they play every night.

The Misses Cook are most interesting on the subject of Angora rabbits, which they breed of course not for the poulterer but to sell as pets and for the clippings and combings of their fur, which may be spun and then woven into the most delicate scarves or even shawls. Is there a hint here for us at Cotton Hall?

Oct. 26th.

My dear ones, last night quite a drama!

Of course we at our whist-table never cast a glance at the poker-players', but last night words rose so high, such dreadful accusations were made, it would have been hypocritical to pretend not to notice. After several

135

increasingly angry exchanges—'Very well, you've cleaned me out, you d—d sharpers!' cried the young man in Marine Insurance, throwing down his cards and rising from the table. Then he punched Mr X— on the jaw and rushed out on deck!

I naturally followed. I do not think I actually feared he was about to cast himself overboard (though Mrs Anstruther said afterwards she had never seen anyone move faster in her life, that was her partiality), but he surely needed someone at his side, and the other young man, believe it or not, was actually apologizing to Mr X—! In any case I cannot have been more than seconds behind him.

He was indeed leaning *over the rail when I caught up, but not* clambering *over it. In fact he was being quite dreadfully sick. I looked aside until he raised his head, then as he fumbled blindly in his pocket offered him a handkerchief of my own. He accepted it still blindly, then opened his eyes and becoming aware of my presence asked what the h—l I was doing there.*

'I came on deck for a breath of air,' said I. (A lie, but I hope a white one!)

'Then I'm afraid you've seen a very unpleasant sight,' said he, more courteously, before being sick again. This time however less rackingly, since I ventured to put a hand to his forehead to hold his head up, as one does with a child; after which he wiped his face with my handkerchief again, and seeing him more or less recovered, I had no hesitation in speaking my mind.

'I also saw a very unpleasant sight in the saloon,' I told him. Without pretending to misunderstand—

'You mean my punching that old card-sharper on the jaw?' said he. 'I'm sorry it was in front of ladies, but I only hope I knocked half his false teeth out!'

I paused. He was obviously in no softened mood; but I felt a word in season might still bear fruit for the future.

'The root of the trouble lies far deeper,' said I. 'Think, my dear boy: would your mother *like to know you were playing cards for money?'*

At that his face became quite contorted with emotion!

'I can't tell you,' he said. 'She's dead.'

The poor, poor boy! For a moment how I regretted my question! But for a moment only; the next he had laid his head on my shoulder and was sobbing his heart out in a flood of I hope healing tears!

We stayed on deck quite a long time. (No one from the saloon followed to see what was happening, which I thought strange, but Mrs Anstruther told me afterwards that while the poker-table dispersed in disarray she and the Misses Cook felt they could safely leave all in my hands.) As my young friend grew calmer, we began to pace up and down the deck while he told me all about his unhappy (fatherless as well as motherless) childhood, and of his attempts to make a career for himself as an artist, all frustrated by a guardian who insisted on putting him into Marine Insurance. We stayed so late, when we returned the saloon was empty and half the lights out, but of course Mrs Anstruther was waiting for me in our cabin. I briefly reported 'All's well,' and sought my bunk really in an extremity of fatigue.

Oct. 27th.

Mrs Anstruther and I have seriously debated whether to inform the Captain of this incident, which he did not himself witness and which apparently none of the stewards told him about. In the end we decided to say nothing—he has enough cares already—especially as Mr X— appeared to have suffered no more than a slight concussion. Indeed he took the whole thing very well—or perhaps card-sharpers are accustomed to such incidents? Or, as Mrs Anstruther suggests, perhaps he wasn't a card-sharper at all, but simply a better poker-player? We shall never know. The fact remains, to our relief, that the original bridge four have returned to their game and the two young men now play draughts.

My companion in the interlude on deck now rather avoids me, which I can well understand. No man likes to have shown weakness before a woman!—and I have refrained from asking the return of my handkerchief.

Oct. 28th.

There has been an odd sequel. The other, 'something in the City' young man approached me this morning to thank me, very properly, for my exertions; but when I naturally expressed my pity for his friend— motherless and fatherless, forced into Marine Insurance by an un-sympathetic guardian—looked surprised, and assured me that not only were both the latter's parents still living, but that going into Marine Insurance had been entirely his own wish. I was for a moment surprised too; then it occurred to me as only natural that the poor boy had concealed his misfortunes from a companion of his own age. It was only to an older woman like myself he felt able to open his heart!

Oct. 29th.

Today (we approaching our destination) the Captain and I had quite a long talk. He seemed curious to know why I was visiting the Antilles. Naturally I told him nothing of Benny—though sorely tempted to: he is

137

just the type of strong, kind, resolute man to help me find and bring Benny home. But why involve him in purely family affairs? I said merely that I'd always longed to visit San Domingo, also that I had a little business there. For some reason he gave me a long look, and said the islanders were very much attached to the Roman Catholic faith, and strongly resented any interference in it; to which I sincerely replied that though naturally C. of E. myself, I had every sympathy with them—any religion in which one has been brought up and believes in being better left undisturbed, at which he looked relieved. I longed to ask him what was his own creed, and whether it had been a help to him in his own tragedy, but feared to intrude. It occurred to me that he might be a Plymouth Brother, which would explain his reluctance to conduct a Church of England Service.

Now San Domingo almost in sight!

We stay only for a day, while fresh fruit and vegetables are taken on board and the rest of the party pay a visit to the Santana caves; but of course I shall remain longer and in fact shall ask to have my baggage put ashore.

The request was in the circumstances so unusual, again the Captain looked at her curiously. It had been a great relief to him to find he wasn't conveying a missionary in disguise; but that Mrs Price, the very pattern of an English gentlewoman, could have other business in that raffish township struck him as not only improbable but almost unthinkable.

'The trip to the Santana caves won't take more than a day,' pointed out the Captain.

'Oh, *I* shan't be going to the caves,' said Margaret, 'I must start making enquiries straight away!'

Then the half-correct explanation occurred to him: she was after some scallywag remittance-man of a brother ...

'You speak Spanish?' he asked politely.

'No,' admitted Margaret, 'but surely someone will understand English?'

'Ship-chandlers, undoubtedly,' said the Captain.

'They'll be the very ones!' cried Margaret, much encouraged—for surely it was ship-chandlers, of all people, who would know what had become of Benny! 'Where shall I find them?'

'Anywhere on the waterfront. I shall still hold your luggage on board unless you send for it,' declared the Captain. 'You know we go straight on to Trinidad?'

'But put in again a fortnight later on the way back,' pointed out Margaret (who knew the *Alberta*'s itinerary as well as he did himself). 'Perhaps then I'll be able to rejoin you—and another passenger as well!'

So a remittance-man it was, thought the Captain compassionately ...

But if Margaret was stubborn, so was he, and she disembarked with no more baggage than anyone else. It was the Captain's conviction that a day spent wandering alone, unable to speak the language, would bring her to her senses, and that when the rest of the party returned to the *Alberta* so would Mrs Price.

All were glad to be released from the confinement of shipboard, and that the expedition to the caves was to be made on donkey-back gave it the character of a picnic. (All the ladies carried parasols; Mrs Anstruther's had a green lining.) Though to heave up the couple from Sheffield, and the X—s, taxed the guides' strength to the limit, Mrs Anstruther mounted with perfect dignity, while the young man representing a Marine Insurance firm, and the young man who was something in the City, each threw a leg over the flat saddle with such superior looks, one would have supposed them regular followers of the Quorn.

'What on earth made you tell Mrs Price all those whoppers?' asked the latter, as they began to jog uphill.

'They just sprang to mind,' said his companion, 'I suppose because I'd just made a damned fool of myself and wanted sympathy ...'

'And life in Marine Insurance isn't such a bed of thorns after all?'

'Oh, the old man's decent enough,' admitted his companion. 'It's just Braithwaite who's such a damned martinet.'

'But aren't you coming too?' asked Mrs Anstruther, as Margaret alone made no move to mount.

'I'd rather see the Cathedral,' said Margaret. (Not a lie; she would in any case rather have seen the Cathedral than the Santana caves.) 'Cowardy custard!' exclaimed one of the Miss Cooks vivaciously. 'But, my dear, will you be *safe*?' asked Mrs Anstruther anxiously. 'Of course I shall,' said Margaret. 'I didn't mention it, but I have connections here ...' Which effectually answered Mrs Anstruther (though arousing her extreme curiosity), and quenched the Misses Cook.

Nonetheless more than a little apprehensive felt Margaret as the donkeys ambled off and she was left alone on the quay; and it was fortunate that even as she began to search along it for a ship-chandlers the first person she set eyes on was Benny himself—obviously in the pink of health.

A bit fat round the belly, but sun-tanned and bright-eyed, dressed in duck trousers and a dirty singlet, on his head a native straw hat, engaged in loading bunches of bananas onto a trampish looking cargo-boat. Their recognition was mutual, and to each equally astounding.

'Benny!' cried Margaret.

'Sister Meg!' cried Benny. 'What on earth are *you* doing here?'

'I came to look for you,' sobbed Margaret. 'When Sir Roger came back without you, we thought—Aunt Flora and I—you must be sick. So I came to find you ...'

Benny put his arms round her—Margaret smelled the sweat under his arm-pits—and gave her a rough bear's hug. But his eyes and voice were tender as he thrust her away again and looked her up and down.

'You were always my kind sister, eh, Meg? But this beats everything!' marvelled Benny.

'Then you haven't been ill after all?' asked Margaret super-fluously.

'Not a day,' Benny reassured her. 'But I've got married.'

It was the last straw that had broken Sir Roger's back: Benny had married the daughter of a Portuguese ship-chandler.

Chapter Twenty-Two

WHAT AN IDYLL it had been!—though Sir Roger didn't see it as such. They'd been cruising about the Antilles for some eight or nine years: when Benny first set eyes on Carmela she was a little girl playing about her father's shop. He used to give her sweets and stroke her silky black hair. Her father, for the purposes of his trade, had picked up a good deal of English, and so too had she; under Benny's tuition she learned even more, and in return taught him a little Portuguese, so that they could converse quite freely. Sir Roger himself, frequenting an island where Spanish and French also were spoken almost indifferently, never learned a word of any, and would have despised himself had he done so: English was then the world's *lingua franca*, as well established as the Pax Britannica or the superiority of the British Navy.

Then a period of maiden modesty supervened; Carmela still accepted the sweets, but no longer allowed her hair to be stroked. 'Soon I shall put it up, like a young lady!' she told Benny. Her mother also, the ship-chandler's stout wife, by a beetling of the brows warned him off such familiarities. Carmela was now attending the convent school run by the good sisters of Cluny each morning, and in the afternoons wasn't allowed to play about the shop any more; Benny's only chance of catching sight of her was when demure in her mother's shadow both made the ritual promenade round the town square—they walking clockwise, Benny widdershins. Each time they passed each other the wife of the ship-chandler bowed (Sir Roger being an excellent customer of her husband's shop), and Carmela modestly averted her eyes—except for once or twice casting a sparkling, kindling glance, extraordinarily expert in one so young, that told Benny she at least remembered old days. Then as her breasts began to bud her mother guarded her even more strictly—no more promenades!—and Benny was reduced to hanging about under her window.

'If you're dangling after that girl of Delgado's, you're wasting your time,' warned Sir Roger. 'Her virginity's going to be part of her dowry when she marries probably a chief of police.'

Like the Irish priest who warned an ostler against greasing his horse's teeth, Sir Roger was better-intentioned than sophisticated. The idea was put into Benny's head, and during a longer stay in the islands than usual (due to a damaged rudder) burgeoned. The idle reference to a chief of police also carried weight; all the police, in Benny's view (hadn't he been arrested by them?), were brutal louts; the thought of Carmela being placed in one's power was like thinking of a dove being mauled by a cur. In short, he made a proposal in due form, and was accepted before the *Enchantress* sailed.

How should he have been refused? Carmela was not only the Delgados' sole daughter, but sole child; a son-in-law was of the greatest importance to the old man, and that Carmela had caught an *Inglés* filled him with pride. As for Carmela herself she confessed that she'd loved *el Inglés* ever since he'd bought her sweets when she was a little girl, and thus the marriage rites, performed by a liberal-minded Catholic priest, were an occasion for rejoicing all round—except to Sir Roger, who refused even to attend the ceremony and took his yacht home in time for the shooting season.

It was an idyll nonetheless, and idyllic too the little house Benny carried his bride to—so swathed in vines one couldn't see where the vines ended and the walls began. Benny quite longed to show it, and his wife, to Margaret, and immediately proposed, while she was still speechless with surprise, to carry her thither in a one-horse trap with whose driver he appeared to be on familiar terms.

However dumbfounded and dismayed—Benny *married*? Why was Benny married? Had it been a shot-gun wedding, the girl already pregnant by him?—Margaret let him have his way. Up a winding road the trap rattled, then down into a small valley, then up again to the spur of a small hill. What struck Margaret chiefly, at the moment of arrival, was that Carmela was waiting at the little house's gate, as though she always stood there waiting for Benny. Margaret at once appreciated Carmela's prettiness and fondness, but above all the fact that she quite obviously *wasn't* pregnant. She was slender as a willow-wand her mother's bulk would come later—so the worst of Margaret's apprehension was allayed.

'*Cara,*' cried Benny joyfully, 'meet my sister Meg who's come all the way from England!'

Carmela put out a soft little hand that in Margaret's felt like a kitten's paw.

'All the way from England?' she marvelled.

'Because for some reason or other she thought I was sick,' explained Benny, smiling from one to the other with almost equal fondness, 'so she came to look for me!'

'Then I see she loves you just as much as I do!' cried Carmela. 'She shall be the friend of my heart!'

With which, after kissing Margaret on both cheeks, she ran indoors to lay her best table-cloth, and to add a special sauce to the chile con carne, and to spread her best embroidered linen on the spare bed.

For neither she nor Benny appeared to have the least doubt that Margaret was going to stay with them. ('What, come all the way from England,' they protested, 'and then not *stay?*') That Benny wasn't after all sick would simply make her visit more agreeable. ('And if he *were* sick,' said Carmela proudly, 'I would never have left his bed night or day!') Benny in fact proposed taking advantage of the horse and trap to fetch Margaret's luggage from the *Alberta* straight away, and Margaret was far from unwilling—for wouldn't the claiming of her baggage show the Captain she really *had* business at San Domingo? Nonetheless to the note authorizing its surrender she added a brief rider: *Not my cabin-trunk, just the two suit-cases ...*

'Whatever the deuce she's up to,' thought the Captain, 'at least she's enough sense not to cut the hawser altogether;' and to the rest of the party's natural exclamations of surprise when Mrs Price didn't reappear, answered that she would rejoin ship on the way back.

To Margaret, staying with Benny and his wife was another idyll. Carmela insisted on waiting on her hand and foot: each morning Benny summoned the trap again to drive her about the beautiful island, afternoon siestas, in that insidious climate, were so much a matter of course she stopped feeling guilty about them; but most delightful of all were the evenings when they sat together after supper under the bougainvillaea trellis and Carmela sang the little song of *Noche sin Luna*—

> *'Noche sin luna,*
> *Flor sin olor,*
> *Rio sin agua*
> *Cor sin amor—'*

and Margaret and Benny recalled old times.

'Remember when I threw rice at your wedding?' asked Benny.

'Do I not! It took months to get it out of the Crusader's moustache!' recalled Margaret amusedly.

'I never properly told you,' said Benny, suddenly putting his big hand over hers, 'how sorry I was about your sad loss.'

For a moment Margaret was quite startled. It had been so long ago, her sad loss, and so much had happened since—i.e., the establishment of her Community—that she now rarely thought of her late husband at all. Curiously enough, her most vivid memory of him was at the moment when he'd risen in such protective dignity before the horrible old man in the Tuileries Gardens—perhaps because it was on their honeymoon? Nonetheless—

'He was the best and kindest man in all the world,' said Margaret sincerely.

'I'll never forget,' agreed Benny, 'the pains he took with me over Latin. *Caesar*,' pronounced Benny, with a powerful effort of memory, *'Gallam in tres partes dividat*. And what a spread Mam put on for the wedding! I'd never eaten so much in the way of party food before.'

('Party food? What is party food?' asked Carmela jealously.

'The food you give us every day,' said Benny.)

'You were no greedier than any other boy,' said Margaret. 'The worst thing you ever did—oh, Benny, do you remember?—was when you ran off to be a drummer-boy!'

Even after more than twenty years Benny looked sheepish.

'It was all along of Sergeant Butley ...'

'I wasn't supposed to know anything about it,' said Margaret, 'but of course I did. I wanted to dress up as a vivandière and go and look for you!'

'As you've come to look for me now?' said Benny shrewdly. 'You're the best sister in all the world!'

Even twisted roots may still bear fruit—in this case of a strong and genuine affection.

The mutual affection between the young couple was also a source of pleasure to Margaret—Carmela living for Benny as obviously as Benny lived for her. 'How wrong Sir Roger was,' thought Margaret (for Benny had early explained his patron's disapproval of the match), 'not to see they were made for each other!'

All the same it was lotus-land they were living in. Not that Benny was idle; from dawn each morning he worked about the docks like a stevedore, and but for Margaret's presence, Carmela told her, would have been busy in the shop all day. It still seemed to Margaret like lotus-land, and when Benny and Carmela pressed her to stay with them always, her every puritan instinct resisted.

'Why not stay with us always,' pressed Benny, 'and be Tia Margharita to all our children?'

'I would very much like them to have a Tia Margharita!' smiled Carmela.

They were sitting after supper under the trellis, beneath a crescent moon already more refulgent than a full moon over the East Anglian marshes. But it wasn't by the beauty of the scene Margaret was for a moment tempted. Benny was the living being she loved best in all the world, and she felt she could love Carmela too, and all the nephews and nieces so confidently expected ... But the moment passed.

'Because I have duties towards the Community at Cotton Hall.'

'Cotton Hall? What is that?' asked Carmela.

'Tia Margharita's house in England,' said Benny.

'A house of her own! A woman to have a house of her own!' marvelled Carmela. 'Tell me all about it!'

'Later,' said Benny. 'The Community be damned,' he added easily, turning to Margaret again. 'Can't Aunt Flora look after it?'

'She's sixty,' pointed out Margaret.

'And will probably live to be a hundred,' said Benny. 'I always remember her old enough to be my grandmother, and the last time I saw her she didn't look any different.'

Then Margaret took the bull by the horns.

'Come home and see for yourself, Benny,' she urged. 'Though you've let me do what I liked with it, Cotton Hall's still your property, and if you'll come and live in it the Community will find somewhere else. Come home, Benny, and bring Carmela, and let me be Tia Margharita to your children in England!'

The master of Cotton Hall scratched himself under an arm-pit. Probably attracted by the smell of sweat, mosquitoes always bit him worse under the arm-pits than anywhere else.

'I doubt whether the climate would suit her,' said he. (Margaret saw Carmela's soft little hand steal into his and cling there gratefully.) 'I doubt whether the way of life would suit either of us. Besides ... don't you want to see to your house, *cara?*'

Carmela vanished like a ghost.

'Besides,' went on Benny, when he and Margaret were alone, 'I sometimes wonder whether I've any right to Cotton Hall at all.'

'I can't imagine what you mean,' said Margaret.

There was a long pause.

'To tell you the truth,' said Benny slowly, 'I don't think Da was my father.'

Which of course was the truth; but he was still a long way off mark.

For a moment Margaret couldn't believe her ears. Then—

'Benny!' she cried. 'How can you say such a thing? Not your father—? I suppose the next think you'll be saying is that I'm not your sister!'

'No, I'll never say that,' Benny reassured her earnestly. 'You've always been the best and kindest sister a man ever had. Being a half-sister makes no difference. He never felt to me like a father,' went on Benny. 'I don't know how it was, but he didn't. He spoiled me, and left me all the property—*he* thought I was his son all right—but there was never any—what's the word?— filial feeling on my side. He seemed more like an old grand-father.'

'That was because of the difference in age,' said Margaret. 'He *was* old enough to be your grandfather. For that matter he was old enough to be mine too.'

'You still felt like a daughter to him?'

146

'Of course! Why, I remember him riding me cock-horse on his foot, and giving me dolls—'

'He never paid much attention to you as you got bigger,' pointed out Benny.

'That's because he was so fond of his Benjamin,' said Margaret gently. 'Benny, think what you're saying. If we haven't the same father, think what you're saying about our mother ...'

'I wouldn't blame her,' said Benny simply.

He had the air of having thought it all out and come to a satisfactory conclusion.

'Then who do you believe,' asked Margaret, 'really was your father?'

If he'd said Sergeant Butley, a good deal would have been made plain. But no.

'Sir Roger,' said Benny.

Margaret almost laughed with relief; for on a moment's reflection it seemed the most natural thing in the world that Benny, discontented with his own parentage, should pitch on the most glamorous figure he knew as a substitute.

'They could have met while Mam was still quite young,' offered Benny.

'Dear, you know it isn't possible,' said Margaret. 'When Sir Roger came to Cotton Hall to ask if you might go crewing with him, it was the first time she'd ever set eyes on him.'

'Of course she'd pretend so,' argued Benny, 'and so would he, but they might have met for all that, on the salt marshes. I'd like it to have been on the salt marshes, with the sea lapping behind, perhaps after Sir Roger'd been wild-fowling ...'

He obviously visualized a brief encounter indeed; but as obviously, as he'd said, didn't blame Hilda—nor Sir Roger.

'I dare say he didn't even know I was born,' went on Benny, 'but he always had a father-like feeling for me all the same, as I've had a son-like feeling for him. Even when he was so angry with me for marrying Carmela it was because he felt father-like. Don't look so badly, Meg: I'm just telling you why I feel I've no right to the property, and wish I'd only given it you properly as my dear sister and the old man's true child. If I ever come home, that's what I'll do.'

Nothing Margaret could say would move him. He appeared to put Cotton Hall completely out of his mind—though

Carmela for her part, whenever alone with Margaret, chattered about it incessantly, asking where was it in England, was it a big house, was there a bath?—but all with the air of listening to a fairy tale.

So after two weeks in lotus-land, just as the Captain had expected, she returned to the *Alberta* alone—where what happy exclamations on the part of Mrs Anstruther and the Misses Cook greeted her! 'Dear Mrs Price, we quite feared you must have *gone native*!' cried Mrs Anstruther. 'We're so glad to have you back!'

Chapter Twenty-Three

So were the ladies of Cotton Hall glad to have Margaret back, even alone.

'You couldn't find him?' they asked anxiously.

'Yes, I found him,' answered Margaret, 'but I'm afraid he'll never come home.'

'He's not ... *buried* there?' cried the ladies.

'No,' said Margaret. 'He's quite well. But I'm afraid Benny will never come home again;' and gave it as her opinion also to Flora. 'He's married,' she explained to Flora in private conference. '*That* was what so upset Sir Roger: Benny is married to the daughter,' said Margaret plainly, 'of a Portuguese ship-chandler. I know it sounds dreadful, but they're perfectly respectable people in their way, and Carmela is really charming.'

'You met her, then?' asked Flora.

'Of course I met her. I can't tell you how—how heart-warming it was, Benny's pleasure at seeing me again! (And he's fit as a fiddle; we needn't have worried about that!) Of course I met his wife; in fact I stayed with them for a whole week and it was one of the happiest times of my life,' said Margaret enthusiastically, 'in their dear little house, and seeing them so devoted to one another! But I'm afraid, Aunt Flora, it means Benny may never come home again ...'

Margaret told her nothing of his extraordinary delusion as to his parentage; she felt it would only cause distress and to no purpose. But she couldn't help regarding Sir Roger, on the single occasion when they re-encountered, with slight but uncontrollable curiosity.

'All well at Cotton Hall?' said Sir Roger, drawing up his trap beside her in a lane. 'I haven't forgotten young Benny! We'll pick him up next time round ...'

Margaret quite marvelled how she could tell such lies. But he didn't know she'd been to San Domingo, and she wasn't going to enlighten him; it gave her a secret satisfaction to think that while he believed her to know nothing of Benny's fate, she in fact knew all. However she was less concerned with Sir Roger's morals than with his physical appearance. There was no trace of Benny in him except that they both had brown eyes: Sir Roger was fine-drawn as a Regency buck, Benny stocky and broad-beamed as any stevedore. How elegantly Sir Roger's hands flexed the reins, in contrast to Benny's big bear's paws!—that had nevertheless rested on her own hand so tenderly!

'Of course it's just Benny's imagining ...' thought Margaret. Aloud—

'You must give him all our love,' said she, with a calmness Sir Roger appreciated; after their encounter behind a hedge he'd feared that Mrs Price might make rather a nuisance of herself.

It may be said at once that the Community's attempt to breed Angora rabbits was a failure. Margaret had been careful to keep the Misses Cook's address, and they in due course dispatched to Cotton Hall a presumed buck and doe of impeccable pedigree. Only something had gone amiss; it was either two bucks or two does the Misses Cook dispatched, and no fine-furred progeny resulted. Let out of their hutches—for it seemed too cruel to keep them perpetually confined—they rapidly made their way through the wire netting of their run to wreak havoc among Flora's lettuces, until one day when Margaret was absent they disappeared for good. It was to be hoped (at least Margaret hoped) they'd heard the call of the wild and escaped to join their freer kind. But Mr Marjoram, butcher and poulterer, had a couple of skinned rabbits hanging up with their noses in tin pails and his little daughter had a very pretty muff.

Flora was always tough.

But even with Flora anno domini was catching up. She was by no means done for: as Arthur Stacey said, she had her father's stamina. But she began to be an old woman indeed, as often leaning on a hoe as employing it to mulch between the bean-rows, and needed to sleep a little in the afternoons; owing to which new-formed habit she missed, or perhaps one should say avoided, a year later, an unexpected visitor.

*　　*　　*

One afternoon in early spring that still rarity a motor car drove up to the gate and from it descended a middle-aged or elderly lady of distinguished and faintly foreign appearance Though Margaret had never consciously set eyes on her before there was something oddly familiar about her: she was extremely tall, with a long narrow face that even the elaborately curled fringe of dark hair, à la Princess Alexandra, hardly shortened. She was like—

'Good gracious,' thought Margaret, 'she's like Aunt Flora!'

Why shouldn't she be? For it was indeed Flora's niece Sybil Braithwaite, now Mrs Vanek. She for her part naturally didn't know Margaret from Eve, and tentatively produced a visiting-card.

'If Miss Flora Braithwaite still lives here,' said she—and her voice was faintly foreign too –'perhaps you'll ask her to be good enough to let me walk round the grounds a little?'

'Why, you must be one of her nieces who used to visit here in the summer!' cried Margaret impulsively. 'You won't remember me—I was too little—but I'm one of her nieces too. I'm Margaret Price.'

'Price?' repeated Mrs Vanek uncomprehendingly.

'I married the Vicar,' explained Margaret. 'And of course you married too—Aunt Addie told my mother. How glad I am to see you! Just now Aunt Flora's lying down, but I'll wake her at once!'

'No, don't do that,' said Mrs Vanek, whom this surge of family reminiscence, and indeed of family affection, appeared rather to disconcert. 'Please don't disturb her on my account. As I see you accept my credentials, just let me walk round the garden by myself. Is there still the bee-hive lodge?'

'But of course I must fetch her!' protested Margaret, 'and of course you must stay and at least have tea with us! Have you come from London?'

'Say, from Italy!' smiled Mrs Vanek. 'My husband and I are in London on business of his, only for a few days, and I'm afraid I can't spare the time. Besides ...'

'Oh, I know all about *that*,' said Margaret. 'There was some sort of family disagreement, which was why you all stopped coming here. But how absurd to let it matter, after so long!'

'I see you have a very charming disposition, my dear cousin,' said Mrs Vanek, 'but let sleeping dogs—by which I mean no disrespect to my Zia Flora!—lie, and let me just walk round the garden by myself. There *is* still the bee-hive lodge?'

'Yes, but I'm afraid rather dilapidated,' said Margaret. 'Shall I show you the way?'

'Thank you, I know it,' said Mrs Vanek. 'We used to play there as children ...'

With a rather gangling stride, her long skirts trailing over the rank grass, her long feather-boa brushing the rank bushes on either side, unhesitatingly Mrs Vanek made her way down the path to the small ridiculous building and pushed at its door. To Margaret's surprise (she following at some distance, since her company seemed unwanted), it creaked open; a rusty lock had evidently rusted from its socket. Mrs Vanek entered, and closed the door behind her.

She stayed within only a few minutes; and on re-emerging again shut the door and without another word returned to her car and was driven away.

After she had gone Margaret out of curiosity in turn went in. There was a smell of damp and decay; it would have been totally dark, but that four or five tiles had fallen from the roof; through the aperture fell sufficient light to reveal no more than an old croquet-box. Margaret lifted the lid, and inside found a foxed pack of playing-cards, an equally foxed *Old Moore's Almanac*, and what looked like an old Guy Fawkes' mask—she couldn't be sure: the papier mâché had disintegrated more than the almanac or playing-cards, but moustache and beard hadn't totally succumbed; hollow-eyed and lantern-jawed it had almost the appearance of a skull. Then probing further Margaret discovered a skull indeed: a rabbit's ...

'Well!' thought Margaret. 'If these were the sort of things my cousins played with, they must have been very *unwholesome* games!'

Sybil Vanek could have told her that some in a sense had been unwholesome enough, though not to Alan or Alice or Timothy the Scapegoat.

'Tomorrow I'll have it cleaned out,' decided Margaret, 'and it can be used as an extra tool-shed ...'

'I don't know whether I did right or wrong, Aunt Flora,' said Margaret later, 'but this afternoon while you were resting a lady called, and it turned out she was your niece who'd married a man called Vanek and now they live in Italy. I didn't disturb you—'

'Quite right,' said Flora. 'What did *she* want?'

'Just to look at the bee-hive lodge. Aunt Flora, what *sort* of children used to come here on summer visits?'

'Perfectly ordinary uninteresting children,' said Flora. 'I'm glad you sent her packing.'

'But of course I didn't,' said Margaret. 'How could I? It was she who didn't want me to wake you.'

'But she's gone?'

'In a car with a chauffeur.'

'Addie would never have let her daughter marry a man without means,' meditated Flora, 'even if having to live in Italy on 'em. If any other of my relatives turn up, kindly send *them* packing too.'

The next day Margaret indeed had the bee-hive lodge cleared out—playing-cards and mask and *Old Moore's Almanac* put onto the bonfire, and the croquet-box chopped up for kindling. But for some reason or other the place was never much used.

Actually some ten years were to pass before any other of Flora's relations put in an appearance, and this time she herself was caught, as one afternoon halfway down the drive she encountered a middle-aged lady with two children in tow. Flora, by this time getting rather deaf, had heard no car stop at the gate, otherwise she'd have gone back to the house and dispatched Margaret, or one of the ladies, to explain that Cotton Hall wasn't open to visitors; as it was she grimly prepared to do so herself; but before the rebarbative words could form on her tongue—

'Aunt Flora!' cried the middle-aged lady. 'And not a scrap changed! Don't you remember me?'

'No,' said Flora positively.

'I'm Alice—Clara's daughter—now Mrs Burton. Don't you remember how cross Aunt Addie was because I got married before Sybil did?'

'No,' repeated Flora. 'But I've no doubt you are if you say so ...'

'And these are my children Humphrey and Alison,' went on Mrs Burton, with all the lack of social sensitivity she'd inherited from her mother. 'Say how d'you do to your Great-Aunt, Humphrey—Alison, give her a kiss!'

Both children however hung back. Humphrey looked about twelve, his sister perhaps two years older. The appearance of neither particularly recommended them: the boy was too plump, the girl too skinny, and their expressions were sulky.

'Passing by as we were—' Mrs Burton chattered on.

'I thought we came specially,' observed Alison.

'Be quiet, dear!—I did so want Boy and Girlie to see the dear old place where we all had such happy times as children! *I* was always the ring-leader,' said Mrs Burton gaily. 'Once, just to stir things up, I put my best doll on the bonfire and said it was a funeral pyre!—while all the others fled from the grown-ups' wrath!'

If in Flora a memory stirred it was not of happy times when Alice was ring-leader but a more recent one of an equally unwelcome visit of which the brunt had been borne by Margaret.

'You mean you want to see the bee-hive lodge too?'

'Indeed I don't!' exclaimed Mrs Burton. 'It was the one place Alan and Sybil used sometimes to keep us out of! But the big hall, and the minstrels' gallery—'

'I expect they'll be rather piffling,' observed Alison, or Girlie.

Humphrey, or Boy, by a backward glance towards the gate seemed rather to share her opinion. But Mrs Burton shepherded them on towards the house.

'You haven't seen them yet!' she cried vivaciously. 'Aunt Flora, mayn't I take them in for a few minutes?'

Since it seemed the best way to get rid of them, and since she herself didn't expect to return to the house for at least an hour, Flora instructed the party to go up to the front door and ring the bell and when someone answered explain that they had permission to look over Cotton Hall; and then went on down the drive.

Fortunately it was Margaret who opened, and in her Alice found a more sympathetic audience, for Margaret, as had been said, in the goodness of her nature truly regretted the family breach.

'How nice of you to come!' she exclaimed, as soon as Mrs Burton had again identified herself. 'Of course you must look round—and stay to tea! We'll give you home-made bread and honey! Miss Pocock, we've visitors!'

Miss Pocock, foreseeing she'd have to cut bread and butter for three extra, showed less enthusiasm, but politely enquired the children's names.

'Humphrey and Alison—my Boy and Girlie!' Mrs Burton told her.

'I do wish you wouldn't,' said Alison.

'Girlie has just won a junior tennis championship,' explained her mother fondly, 'so is quite above having a pet name! For goodness sake try to be a little more agreeable!' she added. 'And Boy, stop kicking your heels!'

She wanted both to make a good impression. It was why she'd driven them over from Broadstairs. For it had occurred to her in the watches of the night, while her hard-working doctor husband snored beside her (unless roused by some panic-stricken midwife), that there was property going in Cotton Hall in which none of the rest of the Braithwaites appeared to take any interest, it having passed to Hilda's daughter Mrs Price; but wouldn't Mrs Price have to leave it to *someone?*—and why not to a great-niece or nephew? It was from this motive alone that she'd commandeered her husband's car and driven over; and thus Flora's disagreeableness meant nothing to her, so long as the children made a good impression on Mrs Price.

Fortunately Margaret, again in the goodness of her heart, decided that they were simply both very shy and that their mother mishandled them; so she made no attempt to draw them out, but let them stare at the great hall, and up at the minstrels' gallery, without requiring the cries of admiration and surprise prompted by Alice.

'This is where we have our morning prayers, and then evensong,' she explained gently, 'but now we'll have tea here!'

At least the home-made bread and honey in a honey-comb were a success. Humphrey munched with a will—'Darling, *please* don't swallow without chewing!' adjured Mrs Burton—and Alison voluntarily passed a plate to Miss Pocock; and as the rest of the ladies, low-voiced and plainly clad, gathered round, showed a first sign of interest.

'Are you nuns or something?' she asked curiously.

'Certainly not,' said Miss Pocock. 'We are simply Anglican gentlewomen who have retreated from the world to spend our lives in prayer.'

'Don't you do anything else?'

155

'We cut bread and butter for unexpected visitors,' said Miss Pocock.

'Nonsense!' cried Margaret. (But she felt for Miss Pocock nonetheless. How was it possible to explain the ethos of *laborare et orare* to these patent outsiders?) 'It's indeed a place so to speak of refuge, but there are no drones in the hive!'

'Or you wouldn't get such good honey,' said Humphrey—for once winning his mother's smile of approval.

So the visit passed off well enough, though when Mrs Burton promised to bring Boy and Girlie again quite soon, something in Margaret's aspect warned her that it shouldn't be *too* soon. In fact Margaret's manner at this point became quite cool, and Clara drove back to Broadstairs but ill-satisfied with her venture, and in the event it wasn't she but her daughter who paid a return visit.

Chapter Twenty-Four

BENNY ACTUALLY RETURNED to his native shore no more than three or four years later. When the *Enchantress* stopped putting in at San Domingo, and seemed to have ceased cruising round the islands altogether, Benny worried; and when he finally heard, by way of the ship-chandler grape-vine, that the *Enchantress* had been sold (which rumour his father-in-law confirmed), could only imagine Sir Roger at death's door, as so he was.

'Ahoy there, Benny!' articulated Sir Roger feebly, as Benny shouldered his way in past doctor and nurse. 'What a devil of a time you gave me! I hope all's well now?'

'Aye, aye, sir,' said Benny; and under his breath added 'Da ...'

But Sir Roger didn't seem to hear.

'New owner's a fool, mind you don't ship with *him*!' articulated Sir Roger.

'I won't sir,' promised Benny.

There ensued a long pause, during which the doctor took his leave, and the nurse looked ready to pull Sir Roger's eye-lids down. But a little life flickered under them still, and Benny stood stubborn.

'Remember when I took you ashore at Cowes?' articulated Sir Roger.

'Indeed I do,' said Benny.

'And then that damned house party, with the Blue Hungarian band?'

'I wasn't there,' reminded Benny. 'I was fishing with the Strowgers.'

'Sensible lad,' approved Sir Roger retrospectively. 'I'm sorry,' he added, 'about what you told me afterwards about your cook losing her stays on the back-stairs. Their stays mean a lot to a woman.'

Such, however surprisingly in one who had devoted his life to seafaring, were his last words; and if Benny hadn't been home for his mother's funeral, he was for Sir Roger's.

He put up, of course, as usual, at Cotton Hall, and was persuaded to stay longer than he'd intended in order to help decorate the church for Harvest Festival and bawl out the old hymns. Much as he missed the embraces of Carmela the attentions of the Cotton Hall ladies—he the sole male in that innocent harem—were not disagreeable to him; only he felt his Aunt Flora sometimes regarding him with a thoughtful eye.

Flora was by this time nearing seventy, but still upright and stringy, still spending almost as many hours a day in the garden; whether or not she'd live to be a hundred, she looked at least good for another decade. But no more than Hilda had she been able to resist the pious ambiance of Cotton Hall, and her conscience had caught up with her at last.

'Come and talk to me a moment,' ordered Flora, 'before you make off again!'

Thus summoned to her private room behind the stair to the minstrels' gallery, Benny instinctively took the chair nearest the door, prepared, as much as he was prepared for anything, for a renewed appeal to his homing instincts.

'Come closer,' ordered Flora. 'You can't expect me to bawl at you!'

So Benny moved to a chair directly opposite her own across the desk behind which she was seated. Upon it lay a large manilla envelope printed with the words '*Broccoli: sow in late spring*', and Benny, reading them upside down, took heart. Perhaps she only wanted melon seeds from him?

'Margaret tells me,' opened Flora however, 'you've married a very charming wife?'

'She's an angel,' said Benny heartily. (No doubt the envelope was there by accident.)

'And have you children?'

'Three—two sons and a daughter,' said Benny. 'Benito and Juan, and the little girl's Margharita. If you like, we'll call the next Flora.'

'So you expect further progeny?' enquired Flora.

'Well, of course,' said Benny.

'And to spend the rest of your life abroad?'

'Well, of course,' repeated Benny. 'As I told Meg, the life here wouldn't suit either of us ...'

Flora's eyes rested on the envelope in turn. She had taken it out to re-read Hilda's Last Will and Testament and assure herself that what she was about to propose was more or less in line with the latter's intentions. As has been said, its suppression was never hitherto much of a weight on her conscience, but seeing an opportunity to make things straight at last, she was ready to take it.

'Then I wonder whether you'd consider selling Cotton Hall to Alan Braithwaite?'

Benny stared.

'Alan Braithwaite? Who's *he*?'

'Your father's grandson,' explained Flora. 'He used to come here as a boy every summer, and perhaps remembers it, and perhaps would like to come back with his own children.'

'So I dare say he would,' agreed Benny. 'But what about Meg's Community?'

'Of course they would have to find somewhere else ...'

'You mean turn out Meg's Community to make room for a cousin I haven't till this moment even heard of?' protested Benny indignantly.

'It would give you a substantial increase of capital,' pointed out Flora.

'I don't want any substantial increase of capital. As Delgado's only son-in-law I'm due to inherit the whole ship-chandlery business,' said Benny. 'Besides—'

He paused. How to tell the formidable old woman facing him that he had no true right, as he stubbornly believed, to any of John Henry's property? It was beyond his powers.

'I shall leave Cotton Hall to Meg—or give it her now. That's what I'll do,' said Benny happily, 'and while I'm home I'll go over and make the Ipswich solicitors see about it.'

'Since I intend in future to be domiciled abroad,' said Benny, employing what he hoped was lawyers' language, 'and Mrs Price is my elder sister, why not?'

He had decided to say nothing of Margaret's being (which he

159

also stubbornly believed) only his half-sister. He felt it might lead to awkward questions.

The Ipswich solicitors by now saw little profit in looking after the Braithwaite property, and to save themselves trouble let him have his way, only trusting that Mrs Price, in her own testamentary instructions, would have enough family feeling to remember her cousins.

'There must be quite a clutch of them,' said junior partner to senior partner—actually son to father.

'I have no doubt Mrs Price will do what is proper,' said the father. 'What a warm man old John Henry was once!' he meditated. 'And now all that's left is Cotton Hall and a miserable revenue that barely pays the rates. I remember my father—your grandfather—warning him about those railway shares at the time. Well, let the tree lie where it falls ...'

Thus Benny returned to San Domingo with a light heart, where in due course Carmela bore him indeed another daughter (not christened Flora, however, but after herself), and he in due course inherited the ship-chandlery business, while Margaret and the Community, at last secure of tenure, equally flourished.

Thus another chance to have the twisted root made straight (if only by purchase) passed by, and Flora put the envelope marked '*Broccoli: sow in late spring*' back in her desk. Or thought she did: her memory was becoming unreliable.

Chapter Twenty-Five

Now secure of its tenure, the Community at Cotton Hall more than ever flourished. Of its original members only one or two now remained; most had been middle-aged on arrival and the course of nature took its toll. (Lest the little graveyard above the salt marshes should become over-burdened, Margaret always encouraged their relatives to take them home for burial, but as a hearse bore one away a car or bus brought another; there were always more applicants to join the Community than Margaret could easily cope with. She still preferred those of the educated middle-class (of course of the Anglican faith), with a bias in favour of widows. But as though in memory of the 'cellist from Bath, many of the newcomers turned out to be musical: one played the harpsichord, another the spinet, and both brought their instruments with them. Little concerts in the great hall were not infrequent: a focus not only of piety but of music became Cotton Hall, which in turn promoted village prosperity, many music-lovers from quite far afield putting up at the Crown overnight, where after listening respectfully to Bach or Vivaldi they prolonged their pleasure by singing glees. It made a change from the days when Sergeant Butley and his cronies had bawled out their songs there, but some changes are for the better.

However Margaret was aware that except economically the village remained uninvolved, and when one day out of the blue a George Brewer telephoned offering to give an evening of readings from Dickens for no more than a silver collection, she scarcely hesitated before accepting. Dickens, unlike Bach, was of course strictly secular, but wasn't he also a classic? Moreover she felt a duty towards the village, which so regularly shunned Bach, and felt that to hear the death of Little Nell declaimed by a professional entertainer would be an uncommon attraction.

So it proved. The great hall was for once quite thronged with native inhabitants, as George Brewer took his place behind an improvised lectern on a desk complete with glass of water. It was hard to tell his age: he was either about sixty or had got himself up to look so; he'd even got himself up to look like Dickens, Victorian frock-coat and beard and all; and after the pathos of Little Nell, and the humour of Sam Weller, launched so vigorously into the death of Nancy at the hands of Bill Sykes, Mrs Strowger fainted and all left feeling they'd had their money's worth, and some even put a shilling instead of sixpence into the silver collection.

Margaret for her part felt the death of Nancy rather over-doing things, though it was by far the most popular part of the programme; Flora too sat with pursed lips as Mr Brewer thrashed the floor behind the desk in simulated frenzy. They still, the performance over, offered him a light meal of coffee and sandwiches, during which—

'I don't suppose you'd have known me anyway, Aunt Flora,' said Timothy, 'even without this beard.'

For Timothy it was, Timothy the Scapegoat, under yet another *nom de théâtre*, and on his beam ends.

It was extraordinary for a Stacey that he had never made a solid success; all the other Staceys were successful. But Timothy's early burst into fame as Matty Topper, more than thirty years ago, had been in fact the apogee of his career. Thenceforward, with but few ups to vary the downs, all was decline. Australia had been less kind than Manchester to him; he never really caught on in Australia, and presently joined a touring company playing not Shakespeare but melodrama, in which from comic lead (one of the ups) he faded to general utility man. For some years, in a circus, he clowned indeed, and not even as the Chief Clown resplendent in spangles and white stockings (which by tradition may never be splashed or soiled), but as an Auguste, the clumsy oaf over whom buckets of water are poured. Another thing Timothy disliked about circus life was the absence of landladies. The troupe, living under canvas or in caravans, had no need to take lodgings: no lodgings, no landladies, and Timothy missed being spoiled by them. (At least he'd always retained his touch with landladies. One, a widow, while he was still a leading comic, had made honourable advances to him, which Timothy sometimes regretted having refused.)

The circus went to New Zealand and Timothy with it, where he had the ill, or perhaps good, fortune to collapse with pneumonia and was left behind to be nursed back to health in a kindly Cottage Hospital. That he came from Home, from England, interested both nurses and fellow-patients alike, also the visitors of the fellow-patients, and in convalescence he enjoyed considerable popularity: he was always a good talker, and held his unsophisticated listeners spellbound with vivid descriptions of the English scene—though drawing on London rather than Manchester. In the end, in fact, he talked himself homesick, and as soon as he was on his feet again borrowed his fare back to Liverpool.

Thanks to the ministrations of the Cottage Hospital he was in better physical shape than he'd been for some years, and had also borrowed enough money to buy himself a new suit, but he landed with just enough in his pocket to get him to Manchester; where the god Momus, who among other duties looks after Augustes, threw in his way the theatrical agent who'd known him as Matty Topper.

'Hi, Matty,' said the Agent. ' 'Been away?'

'Australia,' said Timothy. 'Marvellous country!'

'But you didn't stay there?'

'Too bloody provincial,' said Timothy. 'If you've an opening for me here—'

'As it happens, I have,' said the Agent. 'Our Baron Hardup's packed it in . . .'

So Timothy was back where he started. (That is, after his brief period of glory.) But he was always popular in Northern Panto, and in summer in Pierrot shows up and down the coast, and for a time didn't do too badly. He ate, as the saying goes, and wasn't eaten. However he had begun to feel his age; a Pierrot's ruff sat uneasily about his neck, and the prat-falls required of Baron Hardup jolted his spine; and then it was that he was inspired to offer recitations from the most popular author of the day, and hanging by Dickens' coat-tails embarked on a new avatar under the name of George Brewer. Again for a time he didn't do too badly. Music-halls gave him a spot in the first half, Temperance and Nonconformist soirées welcomed him. (It was with an eye to the Nonconformists that Timothy had chosen such a reassuringly plain name.) Then at last these audiences too—ah, fickle, fickle public!—tired of him, and his engagement at Cotton Hall was in fact his first for six months.

'I don't suppose you'd have known me anyway, Aunt Flora,' said Timothy, 'even without this beard. I'm your nephew Timothy.'

Over eighty as she was Flora was still capable of handling with aplomb and precision any situation that promised to disturb her peace.

'I've no doubt, if you say so, you were one of the children we were always infested with,' observed she coldly. 'Do you regularly go about the country giving penny readings?'

'Aunt Flora!' protested Margaret.

'Forgive me,' said Flora. 'I forgot it was to be a silver collection. Now as I always go to bed early, I'll leave Mrs Price to show you out.'

She gone, Margaret regarded the Scapegoat with more compassion. He'd unhooked the beard from his ears to reveal a face not lined—no actor's face is ever lined, owing to the constant application of grease-paint and cold cream—but somehow slack.

'I'm afraid Aunt Flora has grown rather crotchety,' Margaret apologized. 'She doesn't like having jokes played on her. It *was* a joke, wasn't it, your coming here in disguise? *I* think it was wonderfully funny.'

She was offering a salve to his pride, and he seized on it.

'Well, of course it was a joke—though a rather expensive one; my usual fee for a Dickens is twenty guineas. But I'd looked forward, you know, to a rather amusing dénouement, and perhaps even having a fatted calf killed for me. But Aunt Flora, like Queen Victoria, was evidently *not* amused. Who are you?'

'Your Cousin Margaret. Of course you won't remember me at all, I was always too little to join in your plays ...'

'Then why does Aunt Flora call you Mrs Price?'

'I married the Vicar,' explained Margaret.

'Whereas my Cousin Sybil,' recalled Timothy, 'married a filthy rich amateur of the arts with a villa in Florence and my Cousin Alan into the *haute bourgeoisie*. For a bunch of cousins we're certainly an odd lot!'

'Are *you* married?' asked Margaret.

164

'I? No. I just live in sin as the mood takes me,' Timothy told her.

'Even illegal unions may be truly loving,' said Margaret kindly.

'You evidently didn't hear: I said, "as the mood takes me," which rather puts loving out of account. I won't bore you with the list of my amours, it would be as long as Don Juan's—besides totally unsuitable for the ears of a Vicar's wife!'

('Widow,' said Margaret automatically—but Timothy, now in the full flight of fantasy, didn't hear.)

'Though I think I may safely tell you,' he went on, 'that one of the most beautiful women on the English stage did me the honour of accepting diamonds from me, as indeed did a lady of title; lesser loves—no, I see you flinch from the word!—lesser *amourettes*, say, were correspondingly less expensive, and indeed asked no more than to have their hands kissed—preliminary, of course, to warmer embraces. Actually the diamond star I gave Ellen Terry—'

Margaret was truly sorry for the poor Scapegoat, but by now she'd had enough. She was no longer the innocent of the voyage to San Domingo.

'Cousin Timothy, what a liar you are!' said she.

Of course he was a liar. To lie was his last defence against the slings and arrows of misfortune. Of course he lied ...

'Tell me why you really came here?' asked Margaret.

The slack face suddenly crumpled.

'Actually, to tell you the truth,' confessed Timothy, 'I thought I might be put up for a bit. One gets so tired of landlady's lodgings. I thought if I came as a gladsome surprise to Aunt Flora, I might be put up for a bit at Cotton Hall.'

Not only his face was slack now, but his whole body inside the antique frock coat.

'I'm sorry, but you must see it's quite out of the question,' said Margaret. 'You must go back to wherever you've come from.'

'London,' said Timothy. (It was actually Salford, where lodgings were cheaper.) 'Even a silver collection will hardly pay my fare ...'

Margaret made a rapid calculation. There must have been at least a hundred people in the hall, half of whom she guessed to have contributed not sixpences but shillings.

'You must have made at least three pounds ten,' said she. 'Of course you can go back to London!'

'To tell you the truth, I'm too whacked,' countered Timothy. 'You've no idea how Dickens takes it out of one ...'

'Then stay at the Crown.'

'The local pub? They'll make me drink. I know my weakness,' said Timothy frankly. 'After the success I've made I'll be stood drinks all round, and then *I* shall stand drinks all round, and end up with a filthy headache and nothing in my pocket.'

Margaret felt it only too probable. Timothy's admission of his weakness (as it had been intended to do), touched her. But what on earth was she to do with him?

'Couldn't I doss down in the bee-hive lodge?' he suddenly suggested.

'Why, do you remember that too?' cried Margaret.

'"Too"? Who else remembers it?' asked Timothy.

'Your Cousin Sybil. She came back here—oh, years ago—and wanted to look at it.'

'Of course, it was the place she and Alan sometimes used to keep us out of,' recalled Timothy, 'but why should I be kept out of it now?'

'Because there's nothing there except a few old tools no one ever uses.'

'Then I'll sleep among the tools,' declared Timothy.

So he did. Where else was he to sleep? Margaret, though with many misgivings, carried down blankets and pillows and an oil lamp from the house and left him to make himself as comfortable as he could. But when she carried down a breakfast tray next morning, he was gone.

Gone absolutely: dead and gone. Sometime during the night his heart had failed him; he lay sprawled like a puppet with broken strings; dead and gone.

Margaret, running back to the house to telephone the doctor—or should it be the Police?—encountered Flora at the back door. As she went to bed early, so Flora always rose early, and had already made herself a cup of tea, eaten a digestive biscuit, and was ready to set forth weeding. Margaret had meant to break the news later, carefully, but meeting Flora at the back door, simply told her.

166

'But why was he in the bee-hive lodge at all?' demanded Flora.

'I let him sleep there,' confessed Margaret, 'because he had nowhere else to go ...'

'Very foolish of you,' commented Flora. 'Now I suppose it's a matter for the Police. Remember we know nothing about him. I'm too old to be bothered.'

'At least we must tell the police his real name,' protested Margaret.

'He gave his name to us as George Brewer, and let that suffice,' said Flora. 'Both his parents are dead long since, and I can't imagine his siblings much interested in his fate. Give me your word, Margaret, you'll say nothing.'

Did she totter deliberately? Perhaps not. She was so old, she quite often tottered. But her hands were less steady than her voice. What if *she* should have a heart-attack?

'I give you my word,' said Margaret wretchedly.

She kept it. All she gave the police was a perfectly straight-forward account of George Brewer's recitation and its success, then his subsequent revelation that he was almost penniless and her own impulsive decision to let him spend the night in the tool-shed. ('Which I'm sure did you every credit,' said the Sergeant politely, privately thinking what a fool she'd been.) So Flora wasn't bothered. It was the police who were bothered, trying to identify George Brewer.

Fortunately there was no suspicion of foul play, the doctor immediately diagnosing simple heart failure. But the contents of his pockets were curiously anonymous: an uninitialed handker-chief, a box of cough lozenges, three pounds seventeen and six in cash, and a pair of socks. In his wallet were, item, a faded photograph of Ellen Terry, item, a leaf torn from an *Old Moore's Almanac*, and, third item, another from *Joe Miller's Jest Book*; but not a letter, not an envelope, not a bill.

'I gather his coming was all fixed up by telephone?' the Sergeant asked Margaret.

'Yes,' said Margaret; and paused. There was one piece of information she could give, she felt, without breaking her word to Flora. 'But I do remember his mentioning, I suppose as a sort of reference, that he'd acted at the Theatre Royal Haymarket.'

'Thank you, that may be very helpful,' said the Sergeant.

But when the intelligence was transmitted to London it bore no fruit, the Theatre Royal professing complete ignorance of any George Brewer.

'Though of course if he no more than carried a spear,' said the casting-director, 'there'd be no record of him. Try the theatrical agencies.'

Painstakingly the police went the rounds, with equal ill success. They unearthed indeed two George Brewers, but both still alive and their whereabouts known ...

In short, the police were baffled; and after the remains of Tim Stacey had lain a fortnight in Ipswich mortuary the Coroner brought in a verdict of death from natural causes, person unknown.

But a body has to be buried somewhere.

Margaret, having kept her word to Flora, still felt a duty to her unfortunate cousin, and offered him burial in the little churchyard above the salt marshes.

She had Mr Ruddock in her pocket, and to the small expenses the ladies of the Community readily contributed. (The tragic death of one who'd been reading passages from Dickens to them only the previous evening was the next most exciting thing that had happened in their small world since Mrs Price went to San Domingo.) Actually Timothy was interred a little apart in the plot by custom reserved for unidentifiable mariners, and when it came to putting a name on the small wooden cross above, Margaret hesitated. To have inscribed thereon 'George Brewer' would be to lie in the face of death.

'Suppose that wasn't really his name?' she asked Mr Ruddock.

'I take your meaning,' said Mr Ruddock sympathetically. Actors in the course of their profession I believe take many false names ... Why not put simply, "A Wayfarer"?'

And as no more than a Wayfarer Tim Stacey was commemorated. The graves of old John Henry and Hilda were of course on the landward, less susceptible to erosion, part of the churchyard, but at least the poor Scapegoat lay more or less among his kin.

Flora for her part thoroughly disapproved of the whole proceedings. But Margaret having kept her word, Flora let her have her way. However as Mr Ruddock intoned the magni-

ficent rhetoric of the Church of England burial service, Flora
was in the garden sowing a catch-crop of radishes.

They had just begun to sprout when a shot fired in the Balkans
turned all the world upside down, and England was at war.

Chapter Twenty-Six

NONE WERE MORE eager, in the common parlance, to do their bit than the ladies of Cotton Hall. It was a genuine source of grief to them that living frugally as they did there was practically nothing they could give up except sugar, but they knitted unceasingly, and Margaret, having achieved her Red Cross first aid certificate in record time, organized a class for instruction of others twice a week. Of course they prayed more than ever—for the brave Belgians, for the men at the front, for the destruction of the Kaiser—but sometimes felt almost helpless against the evil he'd unloosed in the world; and when early in 1915 it was suggested that Cotton Hall might become a convalescent home for walking-wounded officers, all rejoiced.

The proposal came in fact from Alan Braithwaite. By this time just retired from the Treasury, he had like Margaret become involved with the Red Cross, though of course at far higher level. The resources of Military hospitals, before the ever-increasing casualties of trench-warfare, were becoming strained; the walking-wounded were required to find other asylums; and Alan Braithwaite remembered Cotton Hall.

Only with whom should he get in touch? Hilda he knew to be dead, and Benny, he remembered his mother saying, was more often at sea than on shore. Could his Aunt Flora still be alive? In the end it was to Miss Flora Braithwaite he wrote, and in reply received a summons to present himself without delay.

It was Margaret who composed the letter, though Flora signed it; and during the short interval before he appeared a superstitious instinct led her to look in her desk for the envelope marked 'Broccoli' containing Hilda's farewell missive.

She by no means intended to make Alan privy to it at last. Far from it: she simply, superstitiously felt it had better be got rid of for good before he came back to Cotton Hall.

Only it wasn't there. She couldn't find it. Suddenly, as rare things will (to quote the poet Robert Browning), it had vanished.

She remembered clearly its being on her desk during the interview with Benny: then hadn't she replaced it in the secret drawer containing besides only Alexander's farewell note? She thought she had; she must have done ... Only it wasn't there. Flora ransacked the whole desk, turning out how many similar envelopes marked Alyssum (sow in spring) or radishes (early summer) or spring onions (ditto), besides old nursery-men's catalogues and recipes for making rose-hip and bramble jelly; and at last, in her frustration and irritation it was to Alexander's parting note she put a match.

'What a fool I was!' thought old Flora grimly. 'What an innocent, ignorant fool!'

Yet wasn't the fruit of that folly Margaret, now her prop and stay and comfort? As has been said, Flora never thought of Meg as her daughter, but now in her declining years had come to lean on her more and more, which was why she'd signed the letter to Alan Braithwaite.

A day or two later Alan Braithwaite arrived. He hadn't set foot in Cotton Hall since that last family visit a full half-century before: then he'd been not even a school-boy, now he was a man of more than sixty, portly, dignified, striped-trousered, and bearing so strong a resemblance to his late father that for a moment Flora had the illusion that it was Harry himself who had returned. Alan however addressed her as Aunt Flora with complete aplomb. Of course he found her changed, but less than he'd expected; she indeed looked capable of out-living all of them! Margaret he didn't recognize at all, and hearing her address Miss Braithwaite as Aunt Flora, not unnaturally imagined her to be one of his cousins of whom in fifty years he'd lost track, and found her very agreeable. But what should have been a natural flow of do-you-remember over lunch was inhibited indeed, by the family breach. So Flora merely enquired after Addie, hoping she was well.

'My mother died in 1889,' said Alan.

'Of course, how stupid of me,' apologized Flora. 'What pretty bonnets she used to wear!—I remember one with humming-birds on it. But your wife I trust is well?'

'I lost Mabel even earlier,' said Alan sombrely.

'Any children by her?'

Alan shook his head.

'Then I suppose you married again,' said Flora shrewdly. 'Is your second wife well?'

'Unfortunately she didn't survive the birth of our youngest son ...'

'You *do* seem to be unlucky with wives,' said Flora.

After which she left family topics alone and concentrated on practicalities, explaining that all arrangements for turning Cotton Hall into a convalescent home must be made with Mrs Price, since it was now her property, her brother Benjamin having made it over to her when he decided to settle abroad. 'It's with Meg you must make all arrangements,' said Flora. 'Now I think I'll go and lie down.'

Alan Braithwaite had long schooled himself to the knowledge that Cotton Hall would never be his, and was only glad to find in Margaret so sensible and willing a coadjutrix. After lunch all arrangements were indeed swiftly made: Cotton Hall to be subsidized by the Red Cross, but staffed, apart from visiting doctors and therapists, by its own denizens, with assistance of V.A.D.s, or Voluntary Aid Detachments. (All over England such amateur establishments were springing up, and many proved just as efficacious as the more professional.) Alan finished his coffee well satisfied, and was about to take his leave when Margaret held him back.

'Wouldn't you like to walk round the garden a little as your sister Mrs Vanek did?' smiled Margaret. 'How is *she?*'

'Sybil? I rarely see her,' said Alan, without apparent regret. 'She and her husband live in Italy; when war broke out I suggested their coming home, but they prefer to stay where they are. The last time I saw her must have been eight or nine years ago ...'

'When she paid us a visit?'

'She came here? I didn't know,' said Alan. 'Why was that?'

'She wanted to look at the garden again—and the bee-hive lodge. If *you'd* like to see it, it's still standing.'

It cost Margaret more than a little to make the suggestion; since the poor Wayfarer's death there it was a spot she avoided. But it was also the spot where Alan Braithwaite had played as a child, and for him as well as his sister might hold memories he'd like to renew. However—

'Thank you, I won't bother,' said Alan, looking at his watch. Then he looked at Margaret. 'But if you've time for a stroll with me, that I should enjoy very much.'

'I should enjoy a stroll too!' said Margaret.

At fifty-one she was still a very nice-looking woman. About the squirrel-brown eyes that had charmed Mr Price were only a few lines, otherwise her skin had all the smoothness and freshness that can be the reward of living in country air on a plain diet and with a good conscience. Her dark reddish hair still had no grey in it, and though she dressed it very plainly showed its abundance in the thick plaited coils at her nape. Her chief attraction however lay in her expression, which was one of extreme benevolence lightened by humour.

Alan Braithwaite felt more and more liking for her, while she for her part was pleased by his indifference to the bee-hive lodge. (He must have played there, she thought—feeling still a revulsion from the rabbit's skull—just because the other children wanted to.) Strolling between the flower-beds, chatting of what expenses the Red Cross would allow—would they perhaps include train fares for visiting relatives?—fully half an hour passed before Alan looked at his watch again.

'Of course I'll drop in from time to time to see how you're getting on,' he promised.

'I hope so,' said Margaret.

'Or if you ever have any difficulty, don't hesitate to get in touch with me.'

'I won't,' said Margaret. 'I'm very glad we've met at last! But how little I know about you!' she added. 'You spoke of your youngest son: how many others are there? What are their names?'

Over Alan's face dropped a stoic mask.

'James and Henry ...'

'Much older?' hazarded Margaret.

'Old enough to enlist. Of course they volunteered.'

'How splendid!' cried Margaret.

'And were killed,' said Alan bleakly. 'The life of a second lieutenant in the trenches averages, I am told, six weeks, and they conformed to the norm. It seems they grew to manhood just in time to be butchered.'

'I'm sorry,' said Margaret inadequately. Her heart was torn by pity, the tears sprang to her eyes, but what else was there to say? *'There is some corner of a foreign field that is for ever England,'* or, *'Greater love hath no man than this, that he lay down his life for his friend'*? They were beautiful words, and true, but by now alas become hackneyed ...

'I suppose I may still count myself lucky,' said Alan Braithwaite. 'My youngest boy, Matthew, my Benjamin, is barely in his 'teens, and the war can't go on for ever.'

With which stoic in striped trousers he left.

The good impression he left on Margaret wasn't however shared by Flora. To Margaret bringing her a cup of tea—

'He has all his father's pomposity,' she observed, 'which is saying a great deal.' (The truth was she wanted to have a low opinion of him. It is always more satisfactory to have wronged a person of whom one has a low opinion, than one of whom one has a high.) 'I've rarely met a man I so immediately disliked.'

'Aunt Flora,' said Margaret, 'he's lost two sons in the war.'

There was a moment's pause. Then—

'As unlucky with his children as with his wives,' said Flora heartlessly.

The tea slopped into the saucer as Margaret's hand shook. Then she forgave. Flora was so old; and the old dislike having their emotions touched as much as they dislike any other disturbance.

Shortly after there came a less expected visitor, as Meg encountered approaching the house a powerful, heavy-set middle-aged man in the uniform of the Merchant Navy; and immediately fell into his arms, for it was Benny.

It had taken a European convulsion to bring him home, but England at war, how could he stay away. To Benny, it was as simple as that.

'But Carmela,' cried Margaret, the first exclamations and embraces over, 'how could she let you?'

'Well, she created no end at first,' admitted Benny, 'but I just took no notice. She'll be all right, she's all the children—we've seven now—and actually Carmela knows as much about the ship-chandlery business as I do ...'

With seven children, and a ship-chandlery business on her

hands, Margaret could well see that Carmela would have little time to spend in lamentation, but it struck her that Benny himself showed unexpected insouciance at being parted from the charming little creature Meg still remembered with fondness.

'Actually she's got as stout as her mother,' remarked Benny. 'And my word, what a tongue!'

'No more *noche sin luna*?' asked Margaret regretfully.

'What, you remember that?' said Benny. 'I haven't heard it now in years ...'

He couldn't stay even overnight; he was only on two days' shore leave—one of which, it must be confessed, though Benny didn't, he'd spent painting the town red in Glasgow—but how rejoiced were all the ladies, even those who didn't remember him, as well as Margaret to see him! If no fatted calf could be killed, they brought out all their best of eggs and cheese and honey and jam for a high tea of such splendid dimensions, Benny declared he hadn't had such a spread since Margaret's wedding breakfast. Only Flora, ever a realist, told him he was a fool not to have stayed out of harm's way where he was.

'But *you* don't think I'm a fool?' asked Benny of Margaret before he left.

'Indeed I don't!' cried Margaret. 'I think you're absolutely splendid! Why I'm crying is just because I'm so proud of you!'

Again he gave her his bear's hug and went off to rejoin his old tub of a tanker. Of course he'd have preferred to wear Navy uniform, but at his age had had to settle for the Merchant Marine, and therein did his loyal patriotic duty like a true son of Sir Roger.

Chapter Twenty-Seven

As a convalescent home for walking wounded officers
Cotton Hall proved a great success. Only some dozen could be
accommodated, even though the ladies now slept even two or
three to a cubicle like old lags in a condemned prison. ('Or in
the Dorm!' giggled one boarding-school bred lady to another.)
In time they adopted a uniform of a grey overall, or smock, and
a grey headscarf, which indeed gave them a rather nun-like
appearance, but was convenient and to Margaret at least
becoming.

The great hall was filled with chess- and backgammon-
boards, and tables for jigsaws and ping-pong, for by such simple
means, in that pre-psychiatric era, was it hoped to mitigate the
loss of an arm or leg. The ladies would have been glad to
surrender it altogether to their poor patients, except that the
latter seemed quite to like hearing them sing hymns there
morning and evening; the very regularity of the life soothed.
Also helpful was the presence of the V.A.D.s—by a fortunate
chance all rather pretty young things whose usefulness, though
they scrubbed floors and washed dishes with a will, lay rather in
a tendency to flirtatiousness. As the ministrations of the ladies
soothed the troubled breast, those of the V.A.D.s stimulated the
sexual instinct; and altogether no Red Cross visitor had any
criticism to make of Cotton Hall—except the absence of a fire-
escape.

'A fire-escape?' repeated Margaret. 'Why should we need a
fire-escape? Of course I know some of our patients smoke—'

'Ah!' said the Red Cross visitor.

'—but they're all perfectly conscientious about putting their
:igarettes out. We have ash-trays in every room and corridor.'
And regularly empty the butts out of piss-pots, she might have
dded; but forbore.)

A fire-escape was nonetheless erected, at the expense of the Red Cross: a spidery iron affair which by no means improved the look of Cotton Hall's west front. However, as the tendrils of a baldschuanicum began to envelop it, it became quite a rendezvous for the patients and V.A.D.s. Sometimes Margaret, passing beneath it, heard therein rustlings as of nesting pairs, but sensibly took no notice.

They were an ordinary enough, run-of-the-mill walking-wounded who at Cotton Hall tried out their artificial limbs and flirted with the V.A.D.s: the single exception was a Captain Gilbey of the Gurkhas, who instead of experimenting with an artificial left arm preferred to keep an empty sleeve pinned across his breast and sling his jacket over his shoulder hussar-fashion. Tall, thin, pallid instead of being bronzed, he had an air of almost Byronic melancholy about him, and was rumoured to woo a V.A.D. with poetry instead of stolen kisses. Many of the other patients had brought with them such trophies as German trench-daggers and de-fused hand-grenades, which Margaret let them keep under their beds—almost an arsenal was Cotton Hall, besides a convalescent home!—but Captain Gilbey had a kukri, the wicked curved knife that could slice a man's head off while he slept; and this Margaret, in case he should nocturnally run amok, secretly abstracted and kept by night under her own bed. He was a little too fond, perhaps, of referring to the days he'd spent shooting with hill-rajahs in the Himalayas, perhaps a little too emotional about his Gurkhas cut up at Festubert, but all the same, though not particularly popular with his fellows, a source of interest and even pride to the ladies of Cotton Hall. He always addressed Margaret as Mem-Sahib, and referred to her as the Mem.

The rest called her simply Ma Price. After having no children at all, Margaret now had a dozen.

Every now and then, when he had shore leave, Benny dropped hook at Cotton Hall just as he used to do when sailing not under the red ensign but with Sir Roger Wynstan, and these were always occasions for rejoicing. Even the walking-wounded responded to his vigorous presence, as to a gust of sea air blowing through the sometimes too quiet rooms and corridors, and he initiated them into the game of Crown and Anchor, sometimes called Housey-Housey, with marked therapeutic effect.

'To be frank,' he once told Meg, 'I think what you're doing now is a damn' sight more useful than coddling a parcel of old women.'

'But you approved of the Community!' cried Margaret. 'Why else did you give me Cotton Hall?'

'Just to be rid of it,' said Benny.

He was always careless about property.

Not much longer alas would Benny come back to bellow out the old hymns. Early in 1916 Margaret received a brief message, a telegram from the Merchant Navy Authorities: lost at sea.

It was the severest grief she had ever known—more severe even than the death of her husband. Mr Price had at least died in his own home, surrounded by every loving care, but Benny tossed in the cruel Atlantic waters. Then she took comfort from the thought that he'd died in defence of his country, and leading the Community in hymns at a memorial service—which of course included *For Those in Peril on the Sea*—not her voice cracked, only her heart.

Even unsummoned, Alan Braithwaite soon reappeared. It would be wrong to say that he'd immediately seen in Margaret a replacement for his second wife; but he was a man who was happier with a wife, a domestic man, who disliked coming home to an empty house as much as he disliked not being seen off in the morning; the years that had elapsed since the birth of Matthew had been a period of discomfort to him. There was always an occasion for his coming—the fire-escape, for instance—but one day in 1917 it was no more than a shortage of paper towels he came to investigate, and after briefly and competently promising to have the matter taken up at Headquarters, he and Margaret again found themselves strolling in the garden.

'You I believe lost your husband many years ago?' opened Alan Braithwaite.

'More years than I like to remember,' said Margaret. 'I've never told you how sorry I am for *your* loss.' (Or losses, she might have added, but sensibly let it be understood that the reference was only to his second wife, she who'd borne him three sons.) 'If you'd like to talk about her, please do.'

But this was the last thing Alan wanted. He wanted to talk not about the past but the future. So he took the plunge.

'I imagine we're both past the age for romance,' said Alan Braithwaite, 'but there can still be a great comfort in companionableness ... Margaret, my dear, is it possible you would think of marrying me?'

In the circumstances it wasn't badly done. It was even rather well done.

'I shan't ask for an early answer,' added Alan before he took his leave. 'Just think it over. I know you have many commitments here, but as to the hospital we could find a matron, and is the community to absorb your whole life?'

*   *   *

How kind he was, how understanding! How agreeable it would be to have some strong masculine guide which for all her outward competence Margaret sometimes felt in need of!

The only trouble was that Alan Braithwaite wasn't really her cousin: he was, or so she believed, her nephew.

It was a point Margaret had quite forgotten, during their pleasant cousinly intercourse; now she remembered it.

It was obviously necessary to write to him before he returned, and never was a letter more difficult to compose; for wouldn't to put the truth plainly—'Dear Alan, I am so sorry, but I am not in fact your cousin, as I think you imagine, I am your aunt'— make him feel something of a fool? So in the end, after making several drafts, Margaret summoned to her aid another masculine guide —her late husband.

'Dear Alan,' wrote Margaret.

'You hardly gave me time to say how grateful and touched I was by your offer; and indeed I have, as you asked me to, thought it over. But however regretfully —and indeed it is with regret—I must refuse. The memory of my dear late husband is still so alive and precious to me, not even the kindest and best of men could make me ever forget. Perhaps you would say you wouldn't wish me to forget, any more than you yourself would forget. But both of us with so much on our hearts, I believe it would be best we should remain just truly affectionate friends ...'

It will be seen that she omitted any reference whatever to Cotton Hall. A man like Alan Braithwaite—indeed most men, Margaret rightly felt—would far rather prefer, as a rival in her

179

affections, the memory of a husband rather than devotion to duty.

Thus another chance to make the twisted root straight was lost, for had they been able to wed Cotton Hall would have passed into Alan's hands just as Hilda had intended. But it wasn't to be.

The evening after her letter was posted Margaret ascended the stair to the minstrels' gallery and stood looking down.

Among the ping-pong tables and chess- and backgammon-boards the ladies were gathering for their evening hymn. Once again it was *Now The Day is Over*; and several heads lifted from chess- or backgammon-board, as the ping-pong balls ceased to flip; a gunner lieutenant even joined in. It was still a faint sound enough, until a V.A.D., glancing up and perceiving Margaret, urged her to come down and lead them in the alto.

'Come down and sing with us, Mrs Price!' called she.

'It's better as it is,' thought Margaret.

Not long afterwards Alan Braithwaite married the secretary seconded to him by the Red Cross, a very well-bred young, or rather middle-aged, woman, who naturally adored him, and to whom he never mentioned Cotton Hall.

Margaret was unsurprised that her letter had received no answer, and Flora for her part definitely welcomed the cessation of Alan Braithwaite's visits.

'He always set my teeth on edge,' she remarked. 'I never knew how you could put up with him.'

'He was as good and kind as could be,' said Margaret loyally. 'You're unfair ...'

'At my age, so soon for the ferry, I hope one can be as fair or unfair as one likes,' said Flora.

'So soon for the ferry? Nonsense!' cried Margaret. 'Aunt Flora, you'll live to be a hundred!'

But Flora was a mere eighty-six when she died. She was still leaning, however impotently, on a hoe when her heart suddenly and finally failed and she was carried into the house on a wheel-barrow.

Again, it was a simple funeral in the little church above the salt-marshes. It was war-time; too many graves were being dug overseas to make one in England of much consequence. But all the ladies of the community attended, and several of the walking wounded officers as well, it affording a welcome break in routine. Among the simple flowers on the coffin one of the ladies had imaginatively introduced a head of lettuce, and Margaret herself went down to the estuary and picked a bunch of sea-lavender. Flora had never shown any particular liking for sea-lavender, but Margaret felt it a proper tribute from the countryside where she'd always lived. As she followed the coffin with downcast eyes Margaret suddenly perceived a last grain of rice lodged in the Crusader's moustache; and stooped to pick it into her palm.

When anyone, and particularly a woman, dies at the age of over eighty there can be an immense amount of detritus left behind: Margaret faced the necessary clearing up of Flora's effects with her usual conscientiousness but with a sinking heart. It seemed Flora had never thrown away a single garment she'd once worn; in an attic cupboard Meg discovered even a whalebone crinoline and the wide flounced petticoats that went with it. There were bustles, and the skirts, narrow in front but lavishly draped behind, that went with bustles. To any historian of fashion the contents of Flora's cupboards would have been treasure-trove—but Margaret's only concern was how to get rid of them. In the end (as practical as conscientious) she bundled them all into potato sacks and let Mr Marjoram have them, he being in serious need of some dunnage to re-inforce the bank that sheltered his pig-sties from the wind across the marshes. Hitherto he'd always used trusses of straw, but now farmers were so careful of their straw, a truss couldn't be got for love or money! So he was very thankful to Margaret, and only regretted that the community's well-known vegetarian habits prevented his offering them even a few sausages.

There was also the accumulation of papers Flora had kept in her desk, but here Margaret's task was easier, since they seemed all to be either gardening bulletins or packets of seed by now probably long infertile, and these Margaret simply consigned to the bonfire; among them Hilda's farewell letter, which Flora had absent-mindedly let slip between the pages of a seed-merchant's catalogue.

Her death made more difference to Margaret than the latter expected. Mistress of Cotton Hall as she was, there had always been Flora in the background: the archetypal ancestral figure. Now that figure was withdrawn, and Margaret felt the lack. She didn't let it appear, however. Competent and serene, Margaret was still the Cotton Hall's moving spirit; and when after the cessation of hostilities it was finally closed down, the last day was rather like an end-of-term breaking up. As to a popular head-mistress, the ex-patients pressed on her not only a round-robin of thanks, but also small gifts they'd made themselves: pin-cushions shaped like a Mills bomb, paper-knives honed from Jerry trench-daggers. Margaret kissed them one and all, so did the ladies kiss them; it was like end of term at a girls' school.

Chapter Twenty-Eight

HAPPY WERE THOSE, and most were, who had fond families to welcome back a wounded hero; happy too the odd solitary whose only ambition was to get away from an institutionalized life; and happiest of all should have been Captain Gilbey ...

'And where are you bound for?' asked Margaret.

'Oh, back to the Hills,' said he. 'Perhaps first to Kashmir, then up to the high hills again. A rajah there's always been rather a pal of mine ...'

But the brave words didn't altogether carry conviction. They sounded—rehearsed.

There was then a brief pause, before, to Margaret's extreme surprise and embarrassment, he brushed his single hand across his eyes and brought it away wet.

'Is it because you won't be able to handle a gun again?' asked Margaret gently, remembering his tales of shikar.

'No, not that,' mumbled Captain Gilbey. 'I could be as happy with a pair of binoculars ...'

'And think how glad your rajah will be to see you,' persuaded Margaret, 'after all you've been through!'

'Not he,' said Captain Gilbey. 'I may as well make a clean breast of things,' he suddenly added. 'My Gurkhas were cut to pieces at Festubert and I—I survived. Some damned stretcher-bearers carried me back to base. I can never show my face in the Hills again.'

What a masculine tragedy, thought Margaret! She felt for him as much as she could; but Cotton Hall, as a convalescent home, was being closed down.

'Haven't you anywhere to go here at home?' she asked.

'No,' said Captain Gilbey, regaining a little control of himself. 'I was the black sheep of the family who 'listed for a soldier—and by God the Army made a man of me! If I gave India the best years of my life I don't regret it. But sooner than go back to that suffocating provincialism I'd wear my medals and turn a barrel-organ in the street ...'

Again, Margaret felt for him; but a last Red Cross visitor just then arriving called her from his side; whom she impulsively invited to share her, and Captain Gilbey's, distress.

'Captain Gilbey? But he was never in the Gurkhas,' said the Red Cross visitor, surprised. 'He was in the Army Service Corps.'

Margaret was surprised in turn.

'You're sure?'

'Of course I'm sure. We had all the names and regiments from the War Office. I'm afraid, dear Mrs Price, he's been pulling the long bow!'

Margaret suddenly remembered Timothy the poor Wayfarer, who'd also told lies; but final compliments exchanged, returned to the impostor with a stern face. It was always difficult for Margaret to look stern, but for once she achieved the unwonted expression.

'Captain Gilbey,' she said plainly, 'I think you've been lying to me. You were never in the Gurkhas at all.'

He made an attempt to look as affronted as astounded; but had less control over his features than Margaret, and the effort failed.

'I suppose it was bound to come out some time,' he sighed.

'Then I hope the Gurkhas weren't really cut up at Festubert either?' said Margaret.

'They may have been. I wouldn't know. Actually I was in the A.S.C.'

'So I've just learned,' said Margaret, 'and I think you should be thoroughly ashamed of yourself.'

'They did a very useful job,' pleaded Captain Gilbey.

'I'm sure they did,' said Margaret. 'That wasn't what I meant; I meant for all the lies you told us. When I think how I slept with your kukri under my bed—! Where did you get *that*?' demanded Margaret.

'In a junk shop, when I was a boy,' confessed Captain Gilbey. 'I'd had it for years. I suppose that's how it all started— dreaming dreams as a boy does—'

'And where,' interrupted Margaret, 'did you dream these boyish dreams?'

'Actually in Wolverhampton ...'

'Then that's where you must go back to,' said Margaret, 'and stop trading on the Gurkhas.'

(As Sergeant Butley had traded on Balaclava. Was it possible that Balaclava too had been a myth?)

'Only all my people there upped sticks and made for a new country,' said Captain Gilbey resourcefully. 'The suffocating provincialism got too much for them too—and I honour them for it! In Australia, but for an unprecedented series of droughts—'

'They'd now be cattle barons,' supplied Margaret. Captain Gilbey was obviously about to embark on another series of lies, and she grew impatient. 'In any case you can't stay here, because we're closing down.'

'Why not?' said Captain Gilbey. 'Won't you want a handyman gardener about the place?'

What a declension, from being the intimate of hill-Rajahs. ('Only of course he never *was*,' Margaret had to remind herself.)

'You've only one arm,' she pointed out with rare unkindness.

'I could at least keep the compost-heap going,' suggested Captain Gilbey humbly. 'There's some sort of chemical stuff you put on it ... And I wouldn't ask more than my keep; my disability pension would look after my smokes and the occasional pint. I could hoe and plant all right; give me a free hand and I'll guarantee you peas in May ...'

So Margaret let him stay. What else could she do? As it turned out she acted not only humanely but practically, handymen-gardeners being then so hard to come by, they were heard of asking no less than five pounds a week, whereas Captain Gilbey asked nothing except a home.

He was found quarters in the lodge built like a Swiss cottage and spent most of his evenings at the Crown, where one day idly observing Sergeant Butley's cartridge-pouch on the mantelpiece of the snug he had the curiosity to ask how it had got there.

'Where did that come from?' he asked. 'It's not any modern issue ...'

''Tis an antique,' said the barmaid. 'It's been there since the year dot. We keep it as an antique.'

*   *   *

185

The First World War ended before Alan's youngest son Matthew could be swept into the holocaust; but otherwise the once flourishing clan of Staceys and Braithwaites was terribly diminished. Like their cousins, both Stacey boys volunteered and were in due course slaughtered; in Florence the Vaneks, unable to get enough fuel to heat their villa, almost literally froze to death in the winter of '17, though the cause was officially given as influenza. There was a good deal of influenza about, though not until after the war ended did it become a plague almost on the scale of the Black Death; by a bitter irony of fate the survivors of Passchendaele and the Somme returned home to succumb not to bullets but to a bacillus; among them George Braithwaite's single son Humphrey.

No special train now would have been needed, to carry old John Henry's descendants to Cotton Hall. The elder generation had in the course of time naturally passed on—George, the family always believed, nagged to death by his wife, though Clara at least had the grace to follow him to the grave within a couple of years: there survived, of the children who had summer-visited in 1860, only Alan and Alice, and of the younger generation, who had borne the brunt of the War, only Alan's youngest son Matthew and Alice's daughter Alison. Had Adelaide rejoiced in having only grandsons? She was lucky to have died before the holocaust . . .

Moreover the tenacity of life which had so distinguished John Henry seemed to have been transmitted only to Flora: both Alan's younger brothers had predeceased him. He, as has been said, after his disappointment over Margaret married again, but his bride was beyond the age of begetting any further progeny, and only Matthew remained to carry on the once pullulating family line. It was a satisfaction to his father when he married early (and impeccably: to the daughter of a Lord of the Treasury) and rapidly sired two baby sons and a baby daughter. Alan would have liked to think of them as the heirs to Cotton Hall; but was aware that he only indulged a fond fantasy.

Chapter Twenty-Nine

THUS COTTON HALL reverted to its original function as a place of retreat for Anglican gentlewomen. How empty it seemed at first, without the V.A.D.s and walking wounded! Clearing chess and draughts and backgammon boards and ping-pong tables from the great hall the ladies were quite surprised by its size, and sleeping again only one to a cubicle quite missed the boarding-school bedtime camaraderie. It took a little readjustment to return to a quiet life of prayer, even though it was so to speak on a raft of prayer they'd survived the war. Serving meals, making beds, emptying slops, they'd still gone on praying, and now that their prayers for victory had been granted, those that remained switched to praying for the League of Nations.

Those that remained: of Margaret's original flock time had inevitably taken its toll; the death of Flora, as though a foreshadowing, had been followed by two or three more, so that towards the end of the war the surviving ladies had been almost driven off their feet; and now Margaret surveyed their diminished number with dismay, for Cotton Hall, even in peace-time, was a big house to run.

She needn't have worried. Almost to her surprise, there were more applicants then ever to join the community, after the long toil, and losses, of the war. Again Margaret could pick and choose, and again chose widows; among them a Mrs Lennox who'd lost two grandsons on the Somme, a Mrs Hume bereaved when the *Hood* went down, and a young Mrs Packett whose newly-wed husband had been killed only days before the Armistice. For her Margaret felt a special sympathy, also was glad to see a younger face among so many middle-aged and aging ones. Mrs Lennox turned out to be a bit of an authoritarian, and Mrs Hume a bit of a whimperer, but the ethos of

Cotton Hall soon transformed all three into dedicated bedes-women of the League of Nations.

They paid a good deal more for their keep than the original ladies. Though the trickle from John Henry's estate would still have just kept Cotton Hall on its feet, extra revenue was becoming important in the harsher post-war days, and Margaret was always realistic.

Thus happily and calmly Cotton Hall resumed its pious routine; until one day, when Margaret was supervising Captain Gilbey's attack on greenfly on the runner beans, a car stopped at the gate and set down a portly middle-aged woman dressed all in black who at the sight of Margaret broke into a tottering run and threw herself on the latter's neck.

'Tia Margharita!' cried she. 'Oh, Tia Margharita, I come to you at last!'

It was Carmela.

It was Carmela, she who'd sung *Noche sin Luna* under a grape arbour in San Domingo with her hand nestled in Benny's like a kitten's paw—but now how changed! Despite Benny's warning Margaret was totally unprepared for her sheer size; she was almost as stout as Hilda had been—but unlike Hilda kept her bulk in bonds by obviously very powerful corsets. Between broad bosom and broader hips was a waist of no more than thirty inches or so. (Cut the lace, and what a bursting forth of grateful flesh!) But it was Carmela nonetheless—indubitably it was Carmela—and Margaret unhesitatingly took her in.

It was a painful story indeed she had to tell. Benny away, her own son, her own eldest son, had stolen the ship-chandlery business away from her, and at the news that his father would never return had simply draped a scrap of black over the sign for two days and then invited all his friends to a drinking party. 'You married an Inglés,' Benito told his mother, 'now let the Inglese look after you!' (A married man with three children, glossed Carmela, of course he wanted the business—but still, what barbarity!) In her distress she went to the British Consul, but the British Consul demanded papers, and Benny had left none; so Carmela made for England aboard a cargo-boat her father had been used to kit out and turned up at Cotton Hall.

The achievement was no mean one. Landed at Harwich she and her cabin-trunk spent the night at a Salvation Army hostel, attempted to interest an immigration officer in her plight, he and when next day, in charge of a Salvation Army captain, she proved as uncooperative as his more dignified confrere at San Domingo. Naturally enough he'd never heard of Cotton Hall, also Carmela's admission that she was penniless did nothing to promote his sympathy. Carmela would have been in sad case indeed had not a hand been taken by a lady of title waiting in an outer office for news of a quarantined Siamese cat.

'Cotton Hall, did I hear you say?' she exclaimed. 'Cotton Hall, where I've heard such beautiful Bach played? Is *that* where you want to go?'

'Because that is where my Aunt lives,' explained Carmela. 'My Tia Margharita, Mrs Price.'

'Mrs Price is your aunt? What an extraordinary thing!' cried the titled Bach-lover. 'I'd simply love to see her again! I've a nephew who plays the viola quite beautifully, and now the war's over why shouldn't the concerts be started up again? I'll drive you over tomorrow!'

But alas for her hopes; when next day they arrived at Cotton Hall Carmela threw herself so impetuously out of the car and then vanished that the titled Bach-lover, after waiting minutes, pushed Carmela's cabin-trunk out alongside the gate and then drove away again, having fruitlessly squandered more petrol than she could spare.

So there Carmela was; and what on earth was Margaret to do with her? Carmela for her part seemed happy as a bee.

'To stay here in peace and quiet is all I ask!' said she. 'Why did you never tell me, Tia Margharita, yours was a house of religion?'

'If you mean a nunnery, it's nothing of the kind,' said Margaret. 'It's simply a place of retreat for Anglican gentle-women.'

'But you wear habits, like religious?' pressed Carmela.

The mistake was pardonable, as the ladies passed to and fro in their grey smocks with their scarves over their hair.

'We dress as we do for convenience, and to obliterate all distinctions,' said Margaret.

'I think you are religious all the same,' decided Carmela positively, 'even if not true Catholics. Oh, how happy I shall be to stay here!'

At which point Captain Gilbey hauled in the cabin-trunk left by the gate.

Naturally Margaret consulted Alan Braithwaite. Hadn't he told her he was always there to be consulted?

She didn't this time summon him to Cotton Hall, however; he was married to a new wife. It was over the telephone that she recounted Carmela's piteous tale—and into, she feared, unsympathetic ears.

'It seems to me the woman is simply imposing herself on you,' said Alan. 'Whatever you do, don't allow it. Get rid of her.'

'But she's Benny's wife!' pleaded Margaret! 'Or rather widow ...'

There was a slight pause.

'I suppose she was legally married to him?'

'Oh, I'm sure so,' said Margaret. 'It was just before I went out.'

'You went out to San Domingo?' asked Alan, startled.

'Yes, when we thought he was ill ...'

'He was always a nuisance,' recalled Alan. 'I remember the trouble my father had when he ran away to sea ...'

Of course it hadn't been to sea Benny'd run off, but to join the army in the wake of Sergeant Butley; however Margaret let the error pass.

'At least he was definitely in the Merchant Service in the war,' said Margaret. 'He used to come here on leave, and I had the official notice when he was lost at sea.'

'Then it was you he gave as his next of kin?' pounced Alan—still suspicious of any legal union.

'I suppose because I was in England,' said Margaret reasonably, 'but Carmela heard too, so he must have given hers as well. (In this she was wrong; how Carmela had heard of Benny's old tub being lost with all hands was by way of the ship-chandlery grape-vine.) 'What I want you to do is find out whether she's entitled to any pension—as I'm sure she must be. Benny didn't leave any papers with her, she doesn't know how to make a claim, but I'm sure if you went to the right quarters—'

'I'm afraid the Merchant Service isn't my pigeon at all,' said Alan.

'But it's for Benny's wife!' pleaded Margaret.

Alan Braithwaite was a less conscientious man than his father, also wasn't Benny's god-parent. However he put a few enquiries to a man he knew in the Admiralty, who transferred them to a high-up official in the Merchant Marine, who turned the matter over to a clerk.

'If the cadavers of all the good men lost at sea were laid end to end,' said the clerk, 'they'd reach to the Horn and back. This chap seems at least to have rated a telegram, but otherwise I'm sorry I can't be more helpful.'

So Alan was forced to report that the chances of Carmela's getting a pension seemed to be slim, and as the best he could do offered to pay her fare back to San Domingo, to get her off Margaret's hands.

Carmela however refused the proposal point-blank.

'Never, never will I go back,' she declared, 'to beg bread of a son who has behaved so! For besides all else he heaped every insult on me for having married an Inglés—he said he would rather be half negrito and stand up for his own people in the coming revolution!'

'But you have other children?' prompted Margaret. 'How can you bear to leave *them*?'

'All my daughters are married into the Police,' said Carmela, 'and let my other sons follow their brothers-in-law into politics! *I* wish no guns hidden under my bed to shoot poor people with when the revolution comes!'

In short, by sheer passivity Carmela made herself a refuge from all contrary winds at Cotton Hall.

That it was a strictly Protestant community in which she found herself troubled her not at all. 'Of course you will all go to Purgatory at least,' she regretted, 'but even out of that I may be able to pray for you a little, so kind you are to me!' and when Margaret offered to investigate the possibility of attending a Roman Catholic church at Ipswich, she sensibly refused. 'Without a motor-car, however would I get there?' said Carmela practically. 'Also when I married your dear brother —for of course he became a Catholic first—the Padre told me that for bringing even one soul to the true Faith I might be absolved for almost anything!'

This was the first Margaret had heard of Benny's change of religion. He'd said nothing of it to her. But then he wouldn't, thought Margaret, possibly to save her pain but also quite possibly because it seemed of no importance to him. Perhaps oddly, in one so dedicated to the Church of England, Margaret now felt it of no importance either: dear good Benny was certainly in Heaven—a proper Anglican Heaven, with no nonsense about Purgatory! What sometimes a little troubled her was the thought that but for his impetuous generosity towards herself he might have left Cotton Hall to Carmela. But what would Carmela have done with it, except perhaps sell it to the first comer and take the proceeds back to San Domingo there to live as a fat idle dowager? Much better, thought Margaret, to respect Benny's wishes and leave well alone, even though it meant giving Carmela a permanent home at Cotton Hall.

And Carmela settled in very comfortably. The pious ambiance suited her; it reminded her of the time when she'd gone to school with the good sisters of Cluny. 'If I had not married your brother,' she told Margaret, 'I might well have become a religious myself!' Margaret rather doubted it; if Carmela hadn't married Benny, thought Margaret, she would probably have married a police officer. But now widowed of Benny, and the ship-chandlery business stolen from her by her son, how could she be better off than at Cotton Hall?

She was by no means unuseful there. Were the ladies vegetarian? Carmela cooked them enormous, delicious meals of spaghetti and macaroni. While each swept her own room to the glory of God, Carmela went down on her knees to tackle the floor-boards of the great hall scarred by the legs of ping-pong tables. 'Such a floor as this, old oak, should be shining!' she told Margaret. 'Cotton Hall has for the last four years been a convalescent home for walking-wounded,' said Margaret. 'If they could walk, they should have put felt slippers on!' said Carmela, not quite comprehending. 'I shall need at least three more tins of floor-polish!'

She was useful everywhere. When new sheets were needed, it was Carmela who marked them—not in Indian ink, but in convent-taught cross-stitch. She also, in the superfluity of her beneficent energy, darned Captain Gilbey's socks for him.

Chapter Thirty

FOR CAPTAIN GILBEY rapidly became Carmela's chief ally at Cotton Hall. She always referred to him as el Capitán and addressed him as Señor. She thought it quite wonderful that after his long and distinguished services in the war (with her it was possible for him to draw the long bow again), he had found peace and fulfilment in humble service to a community—as though El Cid, or Don John of Austria, had so condescended. He for his part, as he always addressed Margaret as Mem-Sahib, addressed Carmela as Señora.

They began to run the garden in cahoots. Captain Gilbey planting and pruning, Carmela mulching and weeding (her energy really was super-abundant!), they were able to take in more ground; grew so much, in fact, in the way of peas and broad beans and lettuces, surplus to Cotton Hall's needs, that they were able to sell it—not in the village, of course, which grew its own vegetables, nor at a stall outside the gate, against which Margaret absolutely set her face, but to green-grocers raiding the countryside from as far afield as Ipswich. To one used to running a ship-chandlery business it was money for old rope!

The profits from this trade were punctually turned over to Margaret —'So I may pay a little for my keep!' explained Carmela pathetically. (Actually when she arrived at Cotton Hall Carmela had some fifty golden sovereigns distributed about her person, which she now kept concealed under her mattress—for why squander unnecessarily, when all were so kind?) Naturally a small percentage was kept back for herself and el Capitán, of which, equally naturally, she took the lion's share; and if Captain Gilbey suspected he was being short-changed, he made no objection. He was developing a great admiration for la

Señora; he admired, besides her business acumen, the broad bosom that overhung her stays, and the broader hips that swelled so voluptuously below.

'Do you know,' murmured Mrs Hume to Mrs Lennox, 'I once saw him *pinch her behind*?'

So had H.R.H. once pinched Hilda's behind; for men will be men and women women at whatever age. Captain Gilbey was no more than thirty or so, Carmela almost forty, but her black eyes hadn't forgotten how to shoot a sparkling glance as they'd once shot sparkling glances at Benny during the *pasear*. She was undoubtedly stout, but Captain Gilbey had always liked fine women. They formed the habit of sitting together, in their leisure moments, on the embowered fire-escape—Carmela stepping out upon it from a second floor window, Captain Gilbey, Romeo-like, swarming up from below, and sometimes, when he felt particularly dashing, sliding his one arm round her tightly corseted waist. Quite soon it was always to the Señora he brought a first picking of new peas, or a first bunch of radishes, or a mushroom sprung up in the turf of what used to be the croquet lawn.

'Penguins, I believe,' once observed Mrs Lennox, 'court their mates with pebbles. Not that I mean anything against Captain Gilbey's peas—they're quite delicious; it just crossed my mind.'

It crossed Mrs Hume's mind as well that Captain Gilbey was perhaps paying Carmela inappropriate attention, but when she drew the fact to Margaret's notice, in Mrs Lennox's presence, she was gently snubbed.

'They are both of them in rather difficult situations,' said Margaret, 'and naturally feel a sympathy for each other, which I hope no thoughtless remarks about penguins may disturb.'

'I didn't make it *to* either of them,' apologized Mrs Lennox.

Nonetheless not only she and Mrs Hume but most of the other ladies observed the alliance between la Señora and el Capitán with a disapproval which Margaret had she been less pure-minded might have put down to subconscious jealousy. In any case it made her like Caroline Packett—whom she'd begun to call Caro—all the more, in that she at least never made inappropriate jokes. Margaret herself was only glad to have two such faithful servitors, and not for worlds would have put them out of countenance.

*   *   *

194

She was kinder to uninvited callers than Flora had been, and made a point of never refusing to see one, if only to explain that Cotton Hall wasn't open to visitors; so when one day in early summer Carmela reported having let in a young lady, Margaret immediately made her way to the lobby where the young woman waited.

At first glance Margaret took her for about nineteen. She was fairly tall, light-eyed and fair-haired, with the unmistakable look of a daughter-at-home. Her navy-blue coat and skirt looked quite new, but was so extraordinarily badly cut that the long double-breasted jacket would have gone twice round her narrow bust, and the skirt was longer in front than behind. On her head she wore a straw hat trimmed with field flowers, which looked somehow inappropriate.

'I'm sorry,' began Margaret briskly, 'but I'm afraid we're not open to visitors—'

'You're Mrs Price,' stated the girl. 'I remember you. Don't you remember *me*? I suppose it's not surprising, after all these years and when we only had tea here. I'm Alison.'

Then Margaret indeed remembered the lanky, sulky child brought to see her by Mrs Burton.

'And you've come to pay us a visit again?' said she kindly. 'How nice of you! How—' a second memory resurged—'is your brother?'

'Dead,' said Alison briefly.

'The dreadful war?' cried Margaret.

'Not in the war,' corrected Alison. 'It was the influenza that finished him off. If anyone in our family died a hero's death it was my father, who worked himself into the grave after his junior partner joined up. But I haven't come to bore you with all that.'

'Just to have tea with us again?' said Margaret, touched.

'No,' said Alison. 'To stay.'

It was then that Margaret noticed the suitcase, and flinched.

'My dear child'—she began.

'I'm thirty,' said Alison.

Margaret was astonished. At first sight she'd taken her for about nineteen—though now belatedly realizing how many years had elapsed since that original visit she saw it to be impossible. As though meeting her thought—

'One can't really grow up, in Broadstairs,' said Alison. 'A

daughter at home in Broadstairs leads a very restricted life. Even in the war I wasn't even let be a V.A.D. because of mother's nerves.'

(Though Margaret couldn't, Flora would certainly have recognized in Alice daughter of Clara certain inherited characteristics.)

'Then I'm not surprised you want a change,' said Margaret. 'But why come here—to an even quieter place than Broadstairs, where there are at least—' another memory revived—'tennis tournaments? And I'm afraid you got a wrong impression of Cotton Hall altogether: it's not in any sense a guest-house—'

'You said it was a refuge,' stated Alison.

'Did I? I suppose one could call it so,' admitted Margaret. 'But why should you need a refuge?'

'I've just missed my third period,' said Alison.

Again it was a pathetic tale Margaret had to listen to, after she'd taken Alison up to the room behind the minstrels' gallery and comforted her with a strong cup of tea and told Carmela they weren't to be disturbed. Quiet as it was—or because it was so quiet—Broadstairs had at least taken in wounded soldiers, many of whom, in their blue suits and red ties, still lingered disconsolately on its promenade; and it was to one of these Alison had lost her virginity. He used to make little water-colour sketches of the sea and sands; naturally Alison, one of whose own few hobbies was sketching in water-colours, took an interest in him. ('It was so unexpected, in a common soldier,' she explained.) They became, though of course her mother knew nothing about it—quite friends, and he showed her a derelict beach-hut he'd made into a sort of studio, where no one else came ...

To cut matters short, in the derelict beach-hut, while her mother rested after lunch, common soldier as he was he took Alison's maidenhead before being pronounced fit to return to civil life, and of his present whereabouts she knew no more than the babe unborn.

'But he must have told you something about himself!' protested Margaret. 'What was his name?'

'Basil,' said Alison. 'At least that was what he said it was; but it might have been Tom, Dick or Harry ... He used to call *me* Clara—not for my grandmother,' added Alison, with a faint smile, 'but after Lady Clara Vere de Vere ...'

196

'He can still obviously be traced,' said Margaret practically, 'if he has any sort of disability pension. Would you marry him?'

'One day his wife came down,' said Alison. 'I saw them together on the promenade. Of course that was *after* ... But I wouldn't have wanted to anyway—I mean, a common soldier!'

Margaret regarded her now with less sympathy than she'd hitherto shown; and remembered to ask a question she should have asked before.

'Have you told your mother?'

'It would kill her,' said Alison. 'She's nearly seventy and I'm all she's got left. You don't know how conventional people still are, at Broadstairs. I know lots of other girls have war-babies, but not at Broadstairs. And soon I'll begin to show ...'

'Is that why your new coat and skirt's so badly cut?' asked Margaret.

Alison nodded.

'How clever of you to guess! Soon I'll begin to show,' she repeated. 'Mother hasn't noticed anything yet, but of course she soon will, and I shan't be able to play in the tennis tournaments. So I told her I wanted to come and look you up at Cotton Hall, and because I think she's always wanted to get in touch with the family again she let me.'

Then she suddenly put her head down in her hands and burst into far bitterer tears even than those shed by Captain Gilbey.

'I've tried everything!' sobbed Alison. 'I've tried Epsom salts and cold baths and quinine—'

'Then that was very wicked of you,' cried Margaret, 'and let me never hear you speak of such a thing again! To destroy a God-given life—'

'I don't suppose God had much to do with it,' sniffed Alison, with a dreadful cynicism that shook Margaret's heart. 'I don't feel in the least like the Virgin Mary ...'

'I am making every allowance for you,' said Margaret, 'but please don't blaspheme. Of course you must have your child!'

'Then will you let me stay and have it here,' demanded Alison, 'where nobody knows me? If not, I'll just have to swim out to sea and drown myself!'

Thus to prevent Alison committing the mortal sin of destroying a God-given life Margaret was forced to enter upon a course of deception as alien to her nature as would have been the turning of Cotton Hall into a road-house.

For of course she let Alison stay as she'd let Captain Gilbey stay and Carmela stay; but how easy those prior acts of benevolence compared with this! Immediately, in the little room behind the minstrels' gallery, Margaret had to begin weaving a web of deceit.

It would of course be simple enough to explain to the other ladies that she had a great-niece staying with her at Cotton Hall, so long as Alison's pregnancy didn't become apparent—but what when it did? Would it not be better to present her at once as a war-widow?

But Alison's left hand was bare. Margaret hesitated only a few painful moments before slipping her own wedding-ring off her finger from below her husband's signet. (In all her life those were the only two rings Margaret had ever worn. They hadn't thought about engagement-rings when she married Mr Price.) Alison accepted the sacrifice with self-centred casualness, but at least intelligently.

'And what's to be my married name?' she enquired.

'Wayfarer,' said Margaret. 'No, of course that won't do: Palmer.'

So as Mrs Palmer, a pregnant war-widow, Mrs Price's great-niece was received as a supernumerary lady into Cotton Hall.

She settled in very acceptably. All the rest were extremely sympathetic to her; it was considered particularly *nice* of her, for example, that she insisted on wearing a grey smock just like everyone else—though in fact as Alison had brought only one suitcase with her, this was more a matter of practicality on her part than niceness. Mrs Lennox even imported a case of Beaujolais to help put colour into her pale cheeks, and though Cotton Hall, except for a little brandy kept in the medicine chest in case of emergency, was strictly tee-total, Margaret raised no objection; and it was another proof of Mrs Lennox's uncommon strength of mind that she never took a glass herself.

Margaret in fact often regretted that she and Mrs Lennox were almost of the same age; she felt that Cotton Hall, after her own demise, would have been safe in those authoritarian hands. Margaret didn't often think of death, she was too busy, but as she had told Hilda, we must all go when our Maker calls us, and looking ahead she sometimes worried. Could Mrs Hume perhaps be her successor? Margaret doubted it; Mrs Hume, though strong on prayer, was altogether too vague to make any sort of an organizer. So Margaret gradually began to give Caroline Packett more and more responsibility. But all this lay in the future, as Alison sipped her Beaujolais and knitted tiny garments.

Besides playing in tennis tournaments at Broadstairs she'd also played in amateur theatricals. Now her smiles were only appropriately melancholy, and her occasional tears swiftly and bravely dried. When Margaret wanted to summon a doctor to examine her she stoically refused. 'After all, it's a perfectly natural process!' she pointed out—and here had the backing of Carmela, who had at once taken the greatest interest in her condition.

'Am not I as good as any midwife myself?' cried Carmela. 'I will watch over her like a mother!'

Margaret looked at Carmela's stout matronly figure and was reassured. There was something ... not exactly coarse, but so to speak *earthy* about Carmela, that promised she would take a childbirth in her stride as easily as she'd taken over the running of a kitchen garden.

'She is carrying it low!' chuckled Carmela. 'It will be a boy!'

So no doctor was summoned, and Margaret felt Alison had come to accept the prospect of maternity at least without the panic she'd shown on arrival. Watching those inexpert fingers muddle with the wool, Margaret sometimes smiled tenderly: Alison might not yet actively desire her baby, thought Margaret, but as soon as she held it in her arms of course, of course she would love it!

Such had not been the case with Flora a long life-time ago. When Margaret as a new-born babe had been placed in Flora's arms Flora had felt nothing but repugnance. But of course Margaret was unaware of this depressing example, and Alison played her part wonderfully well, when anyone was looking.

Chapter Thirty-One

ONLY CARMELA WASN'T taken in. Without a word on the subject openly spoken between them, between the daughter-at-home from Broadstairs and the woman from the Voodoo island of San Domingo there was immediate rapport.

Carmela had seen too much of life not to know whether a girl wanted her baby or didn't, and weren't there enough children in the world already? So she gave Alison good advice.

'Tia Margharita urges you to take walks about the grounds,' said she, 'but *I* could show you exercises far more useful that you could do in your own bed ...'

They consisted, the exercises recommended by Carmela, of a series of jerking movements—knees drawn sharply up to waist level, then a twist of the abdomen before they straightened and the programme was repeated. 'Twenty times each night,' assured Carmela, 'and you will have nothing to worry about!'

Margaret never witnessed these exercises, as Alison jerked and writhed in her bed, for it would have been unkind to let her know that her milder recommendations were considered insufficient.

As once a crinoline, so now the grey smock Alison insisted on wearing effectually concealed a swelling shape. Not that concealment was necessary, at Cotton Hall, but Alison was indeed glad of the garment the afternoon her mother paid an unannounced visit. She had the wit to slip the wedding-ring from her left hand to her right even as Mrs Burton stumped up the drive; Alison, just returning from a regulation walk, had fortunately seen her coming. In fighting trim was Mrs Burton, for she had grown tired of not having a daughter at home, and nearing seventy as she was her step was firm and pugnacious on the gravel and her tongue sharp.

'What a fright you look in that outfit!' she said at once. 'Aren't you going to kiss me?'

'It's just what all Great-Aunt Margaret's ladies wear,' explained Alison, having obediently pecked a cheek smelling of violet-powder. 'I didn't want to look any different ...'

'Well, I hope she'll at least give me a cup of tea,' said Mrs Burton, 'after I've driven all the way from Broadstairs in a hired car!'

'Actually she's taking choir-practice,' lied Alison. 'Tea won't be till half-past five.' (It was then three.)

'Can't you tell her I'm here?' enquired Mrs Burton angrily.

'No,' said Alison. 'You don't realize, mother, what an orderly life we live here. I certainly couldn't break in on a choir-practice.'

Mrs Burton drew a deep offended breath.

'What you see in your Great-Aunt Margaret—!' she began; then decided on more direct tactics. 'I always knew perfectly well why you wanted to get away from Broadstairs, but just because you didn't win a tennis-tournament is no reason for dressing yourself up as a nun. Go and get your things together and come home with me at once.'

It was at this moment that a first pang wrenched Alison's womb. She had to bite her lips before she could reply.

'Only I'm not ready to, mother. You probably won't believe me, when I tell you I've found at Cotton Hall such peace and serenity—'

'Fiddlesticks!' said Mrs Burton. 'You're simply afraid you won't find a partner for the doubles. Go and get your things at once!'

'I shan't!' cried Alison, resourcefully reverting to childishness. 'I shan't, I shan't, I shan't!—and I wish you'd go away!'

In earlier, juvenile tantrums she'd been used to hurl herself to the ground and cry herself into hysterics, and looked ready to do so now. Apprehensive as well as discouraged, Mrs Burton did go away, mentally promising herself to return in another month or so, when Alison should have got over her inexplicable infatuation with Cotton Hall.

In the event she had no need to. At supper that night, after evensong, Alison caught Carmela's eye.

They always went to bed early, at Cotton Hall, but for once

201

Carmela pottered about the kitchen later than usual, keeping a kettle simmering. She also carried up to Alison's room clean sheets and towels from the linen-cupboard, and the little bottle of brandy from the medicine chest, so that all was prepared when about two o'clock in the morning Alison gave premature birth.

She was less stoical than Flora had been. Carmela had to stuff the sheet almost halfway down her throat, to stifle her cries. But it was over at last, and out at last the little embryo emerged as Alison shudderingly closed her eyes ...

As for Carmela, she had seen unwanted little embryos before. They were not to be smacked on the bottom like a full-term child, but ... disposed of. Good Catholic as she was, however, as soon as she had made Alison clean and comfortable (and given her enough of brandy to induce obliviousness) she made the sign of the cross in water on the potential brow before gathering the carnal detritus into a slop-pail, and then, while Alison still lay panting, carried it out into the garden, and got a spade and under a witch's moon buried it as casually as she'd have buried a puppy or kitten; and only after dawn had broken went and roused Margaret.

'All is over,' announced Carmela sadly. 'A miscarriage in the night ...'

'But why didn't you fetch me?' cried Margaret.

'There was no time—and what could you have done that I could not? She suffered very little, scarcely at all,' said Carmela, 'for one four months gone. We should now I think let her sleep.'

'But the ... baby?' cried Margaret.

'I myself christened it, and now it lies in peace.'

'But where?'

'Not in any part of the garden where it is likely to be dug up,' Carmela reassured her, 'in a part where nobody now goes any more ...'

It was actually among the roots of the briar-bushes surrounding the bee-hive lodge that Carmela had dug the small grave, and indeed no one went there any more.

The sad news, when relayed to the other ladies of Cotton Hall, aroused universal sympathy, but commiserations were mute as Alison herself begged them never to speak of it.

'Please, please don't let anyone talk to me about it!' implored Alison. 'Please don't let anyone talk to me about it ever again!'

'But what will you do now, my poor child?' asked Margaret compassionately.

'I suppose go back to Broadstairs,' said Alison.

And as soon as she was recovered, back to Broadstairs she went.

'Thank you very much for having me,' said Alison, returning her borrowed wedding-ring; and left to try and pick up a partner for the doubles.

Alas, she played in the doubles all too soon; fell while reaching to return a high lob and never recovered from an injury to a back already weakened by her miscarriage. So in a way Alison killed her mother indeed: Mrs Burton without a daughter having nothing left to live for, within a couple of years was dead too; and that was the end of the George Braithwaites.

Chapter Thirty-Two

THIS WAS THE SINGLE episode in Cotton Hall's history that left Margaret unhappy. However irrationally, at the thought of the little embryo buried somewhere in the garden, she felt guilt. Of course Carmela had acted for the best according to her own lights, and had indeed saved an infinity of trouble: Margaret still felt guilt; and it was perhaps partly because of this that her feelings towards Benny's widow began to alter. She didn't yet positively dislike Carmela, but she began to—particularly as the latter, as though now feeling herself on firmer ground, started asking questions she'd never hitherto have dared to put.

'To whom will Cotton Hall eventually pass?' asked Carmela inquisitively. 'Mrs Palmer is of course your great-niece, but not, I think, to her?'

'Indeed no,' said Margaret. 'She's not at all the sort of person to undertake such a responsibility.'

'And Mrs Lennox is almost as old as you are yourself!' lamented Carmela.

'Of course it should be someone much younger,' agreed Margaret.

She was actually thinking of Caroline, or Caro, Packett, in whose good sense and good will she had come to have ever increasing confidence. Like Margaret herself, Caro was both compassionate and resolute—gentle as a lamb with those older ladies who sometimes scamped their God-glorifying duties, but bold as a lion when confronted by an Income Tax official enquiring whether or not Cotton Hall was a registered charity. (Since there seemed some tax advantage in its being so, Caro said, certainly, and left him to make his own investigations; and the wheels of Inland Revenue, if they ground surely also grinding slowly, gained at least a respite.) Margaret had in fact almost already made up her mind that Caro Packett was to be her successor, and had begun to give her more and more responsibility, but this how could Carmela guess? All she heard was, *someone much younger*, and Margaret completed the illusion that it was to be herself by the kindly if ill-considered remark—for she felt guilt also at beginning to dislike Carmela—that nothing had ever made her so happy as being able to give Benny's widow a home.

Thus the colloquies on the fire-escape became more enthraling than ever as she and Captain Gilbey envisaged the possibilities.

'For when Tia Margharita dies—and she is seventy—and leaves Cotton Hall to me, do you know what I shall do with it?' said Carmela. 'I shall turn it into an hotel!'

'With bar?' said Captain Gilbey eagerly.

'Naturally with a bar. It is from a bar most profit is made. But also of course with a restaurant, specializing in Spanish dishes, but with the steaks, home-grown vegetables.'

'What a woman you are!' said Captain Gilbey, quite lost in admiration.

'Of course I should need a man to help me run it ...'

'At your service!' said Captain Gilbey, sliding his one arm round her thirty inch waist and applying a definite pressure. 'You'll need not only a maître d'hotel, Señora, but a husband!'

'Me at my age to think of marrying again!' giggled Carmela.

'Don't you know how I've always admired you?' said el Capitán.

'Without my corsets I am really very big!' sighed Carmela.

'I like big women,' said Captain Gilbey. 'One of the Rajah's wives in Kashmir weighed sixteen stone, and I damn' nearly lost my head over her!'

It will be seen that their conversation sometimes strayed from the minutiae of hotel-keeping, but never for long.

'A car park,' said Captain Gilbey, a few evenings later. 'If people come in cars they'll want a car-park.'

'We will asphalt the croquet lawn,' said Carmela, who had evidently given the matter thought already. 'It is nothing but waste space.'

'Remember when I brought you a mushroom from it?'

'And all the ladies were jealous?' giggled Carmela. ('Take your arm away, bad boy!) They will be more than jealous when I tell them they must find somewhere else to go and pray!'

Captain Gilbey however retained a certain loyalty towards the Mem-Sahib, and even though all these happy plans could be activated only after her death, was slightly troubled.

'The Mem wouldn't like all her old pussies turned out ...'

'Old pussies? Old cats!' retorted Carmela vigorously. 'Listen, *amigo*, if you are to be squeamish, tell me so now and I will find someone else to help me. When I turn Cotton Hall into an hotel there will be no room in it for the ladies! As I said, they will have to find somewhere else to go and pray!'

It was by pure chance that Margaret overheard. She commonly took a stroll round the garden in the evening, returning to the house sometimes by the front door, passing the long east windows, sometimes, as on this occasion, by the back, passing under the fire-escape; the thick swags of baldachin veiled her, a slight breeze stirring among them muffled her still light footfall from the ears of the self-absorbed pair of plotters above; and so Margaret heard, and heard enough.

If necessary, she could be as tough as old John Henry himself. Next morning—

'I have decided it is time for you to go back to San Domingo,' Margaret told Carmela. 'Of course your passage will be paid—'

'But whatever should I do in San Domingo?' cried Carmela.

'Open an hotel,' said Margaret.

The three words were enough. There needed no more to be said to make Carmela understand her plans would never come to fruition. How did Margaret know of them? 'She has eavesdropped,' thought Carmela angrily, 'upon me and el Capitán!'—never doubting but that Margaret had done so deliberately. Indignation swelled her large bust and sparkled in her eye—but only for a moment; even as she perceived (the exchange about old cats returning with particular vividness) that her goose was cooked, she was thinking how to salvage some of the stuffing.

'You have guessed my ambition,' she confided blandly. 'Tia Margharita, who reads everyone's heart! Indeed I should like to open an hotel, at home in San Domingo.'

Margaret was surprised but relieved, for if that was the line

206

Carmela intended to take—to pass a sponge, so to speak—over the entire conversation on the fire-escape—much unpleasantness might be avoided. She still requested that Carmela should take the next available boat.

'When friends must part, it is best to get it over quickly,' agreed Carmela. 'How much?'

'How much?' repeated Margaret.

'An hotel cannot be set up without a little capital.'

'With all your connections there, I'm sure you'll have no difficulty in raising it,' said Margaret. Then she remembered Carmela was Benny's widow.

'A hundred pounds,' said Margaret.

Carmela was naturally emboldened to try her luck further.

'A hundred is very little.'

'Take it or leave it,' said Margaret, with a touch of old John Henry in her voice. 'In any case, you will leave by the next boat.'

Of course Carmela took it, and the next boat as well. She'd cooked her goose and knew it, and in the circumstances the stuffing might have been worse.

She also took back with her to San Domingo the fifty golden sovereigns she'd brought with her. During all her sojourn in England she hadn't had to break into one of them, thanks to the hospitality of Cotton Hall. She'd also have liked to take back a few pairs of the sheets she'd marked in cross-stitch, but Margaret supervised her packing.

So back to San Domingo went Carmela, and Captain Gilbey, the poor fool, went with her, to be unpaid barman in whatever raffish hostelry Carmela succeeded in establishing. To him it was like his dream of going up to the high hills—that is, until he awoke to the unpleasant reality of a bed under the bar because all the rooms were occupied by the police and their doxies. Carmela never married him after all, but now and then, for old times' sake, let him pass his arm about her waist just as she'd been used to do when they sat together on the fire-escape.

The extrusion of Carmela from Cotton Hall was heartily welcomed by the other ladies. 'She was taking too much on herself altogether!' pronounced Mrs Lennox. 'Stopping Mrs Price from calling in a doctor!' remembered Mrs Hume. 'Poor, poor Mrs Palmer!'

'She was extremely useful in her way, particularly about the garden,' reminded Margaret fairly. 'We shan't be sending vegetables to Ipswich any more!'

'And a good thing too,' observed Mrs Lennox. 'Though of course I never said so, dear Mrs Price, I always thought it a mistake for Cotton Hall to have any sort of commercial dealings ...'

She had every right to speak. When she died a year later she left the community, via Margaret, the sum of forty thousand pounds.

As though they had antennae for any transference of property, the Ipswich solicitors about this time wrote pointing out that Mrs Price hadn't yet made a Will; they hoped to take her instructions without delay. But Margaret refused the offer— though not from the superstition felt by many otherwise quite well-balanced people, that to make a Will is practically to invite one's decease. (Young people enjoy making Wills, leaving their books and bicycles and tennis racquets to cousins.) Margaret simply hadn't made up her mind. 'I quite understand your concern,' she wrote back, 'but coming as I do from a long-lived family—' which was true; John Henry and Flora had died at over ninety and eighty respectively—'I fail to see any immediate necessity; but in due course hope to leave all in order.'

The Ipswich solicitors sent even the senior partner to reason with her, whom Margaret received with her usual benignity— and stubbornness.

'Might it not after all be left in God's hands?' said she finally. 'Would you care to stay for evensong?'

'Thank you, no,' said the senior partner.

Chapter Thirty-Three

NOW FINANCIALLY BUTTRESSED by Mrs Lennox's bounty, Cotton Hall again entered on a halcyon period. Caro Packett turned out all Margaret had hoped, as kind and competent, compassionate and firm, as Margaret herself had always been. In time, oddly enough, there grew also to be a physical likeness between them: on arrival at Cotton Hall Mrs Packett had been rather pretty: now as the years elongated and hollowed her cheeks and pushed back her hair-line, she too began to resemble a Holbein; by many who didn't know the Hall's history they were taken for mother and daughter. Again thanks to Mrs Lennox's bounty, a new handy-man gardener could be paid a properly economic wage, and as Captain Gilbey's replacement, if less glamorous, was even more efficient. (He also was an ex-serviceman, but with a full complement of limbs.) Bach was once again played in the great hall, and the nephew of Carmela's titled saviour, though off his own bat, found his way into a string quartet.

The years sped smoothly, and swiftly. Caro Packett was middle-aged while Margaret still thought of her as a young thing, and Margaret herself was of course growing older. She was seventy, she was eighty, but just as Flora had done continued straight-backed and alert, though she occasionally went to bed early, when Caro brought her supper on a tray. (Not Hilda's supper of a pork chop; usually an omelette.) Now and then one lady had to be replaced by another, but all, selected by Caro, shared the ethos of Cotton Hall; and almost two decades passed in such serenity, it seemed as though He for whose sake the community swept and garnished indeed bent a benevolent eye on their endeavours.

Then He averted it.

Who could have foreseen that at the end of that happy period Cotton Hall would have become an embattled field whereupon a war was waged as bitter as that between the storks and pygmies?

It began with an urgent call from Mr Ruddock in the guise of a billeting officer. Cotton Hall had of course already been shaken by the outbreak of another war, and was fully prepared to take in walking-wounded again, that heroic period having become quite legendary in its annals. So Mr Ruddock's proposal at first aroused only extra enthusiasm.

When war broke out in 1914 only a few months' hostilities was envisaged: in '39, more realistically, a grimly determined nation foresaw that perhaps years stretched ahead before the defeat of a Europe dominated by Hitler. So the embattled islanders took their measures, one of which was to evacuate their children before the bombs fell on London, and it was on this errand that Mr Ruddock, alerted by a brother priest in Islington, now came, asking if Cotton Hall could receive perhaps a dozen evacuees. He was getting old himself, Mr Ruddock; his dear wife had predeceased him, all his children had left home, the little church above the salt marshes, however sparsely attended, was his only link with the world. When the call came from London he was almost too ready to respond to it, considering how very quietly the ladies of Cotton Hall were currently living. However there could be only one answer, and for the next few days Cotton Hall buzzed like a bee-hive.

The sexes of the children expected were as yet unknown—or rather, the proportion of the sexes; since they came from a Junior school, ages eight to twelve, there would be both girls and boys. Margaret and Caro Packett organized two dormitories on the topmost floor, and set aside a portion of the great hall for meals and recreation. Camp beds and bedding flowed in from the newly-formed Women's Voluntary Service; beside each bed was set up a little table (they were mostly card-tables, dating from the period of the walking wounded) upon which to display photographs of loved ones—of Mum and Dad, perhaps a big brother in the Services or an auntie in the A.T.S. Margaret and Caro thought of everything; and Mr Marjoram sent up three pounds of sausages from his secret store.

'I'm afraid they won't be arriving until later than we expected,' reported Mr Ruddock, 'the coach was late starting. They won't be here till seven.'

'Then the poor little mites shall have supper straight away!' cried Margaret, surveying the trestle tables (contributed by the Scouts) ready laid with egg-cups to receive boiled eggs and mugs to receive fresh milk. 'The very moment they get here, so they'll see they're welcome!'

The coach was even later than had been apprehended, but at last, in charge of two school-mistresses, one old and one young, the children arrived; dumb, defenceless, labelled like so many parcels. Some clutched an untidy bundle of clothing, some a badly wrapped packet of food; very few a toy. They were not the sort of children who had toys. They were not the sort of children anyone at Cotton Hall, or in the village, had ever seen before.

They were urban slum children. It was as though the pages of Dickens had been re-opened and out swarmed all the juvenile delinquents from Fagin's cellar and even Tom All Alone's.

'They've pee'd,' said the young schoolmistress encouragingly. 'We stopped the coach on a common. They won't want to pee again just yet.'

'I can't tell you how sorry I am, Mr Price,' apologized the elder schoolmistress, handing over their ration-books, 'to dump them on you like this, but we've got to go back with the coach at once because there's another batch waiting to be evacuated— isn't there, Miss Pye?' 'Another load of trouble for *someone*,' agreed Miss Pye bleakly. 'I hope you've brandy on the premises?' 'A little,' said Margaret. 'Do you need some now?' 'No; but *you're* going to,' said Miss Pye ...

At this point all the children were looking too cowed to be dangerous. Their only links with the past about to vanish altogether, half were in tears—or rather snivelling. Naturally they had no handkerchieves; the mucus from their dirty noses flowed unchecked into their open, adenoidal mouths. Margaret seized a napkin from the table and wiped left and right— swiped, almost, left and right, scrubbing down their unresisting faces with a violence by which she was herself alarmed. There was no gentleness in her touch; there was only disgust; she saw Caro Packett looking at her in surprise, and attempted to cover her all too natural reaction with a false, bright smile, while the children looked more cowed than ever.

'That's better, isn't it?' demanded Margaret brightly. 'Now

supper, supper, children, before you even wash! A lovely brown egg for each of you, and a glass of milk before you go to bed!'

Many of the children didn't even know how to use an egg-spoon. Caro went up and down the tables crushing shells for them, but was met with almost Sir John Falstaff's distaste for pullet-sperm with his brewage—in this case, fresh milk. 'Aren't there any fish and chips?' they whined. 'No,' said Margaret sharply—and was about to add that many poor little children would be glad of their nice eggs when she remembered that these *were* the poor little children of nursery legend. Bread and jam however went down better, then, after a long procession to the lavatories—though it was but an hour since they'd pee'd on the common, they were bundled into their beds, still unwashed, in their ragged underclothes.

'Go and scour the village,' Caro bade Mrs Hume, 'for absolutely anything a child can wear!' Again, the W.V.S., and the Mothers' Union, rose to the occasion; Mrs Hume returned with her arms full and a couple of Scouts panting behind; their booty included, besides all the children's gear stowed against the next jumble sale, a pair of black crêpe-de-chine camiknickers heroically contributed by the barmaid at the Crown. Even by this time it was only half-past nine, but it felt like two in the morning as Margaret at last shut herself in her own room and knelt in agonized prayer.

'O Lord,' prayed Margaret, 'let me not hate these children. Let me remember what dreadful circumstances they come from, what dreadful danger they are escaping. Let me not be disgusted beyond endurance. Let me discover good in the least promising. Let me be able to keep a guard on my hands, and not hit them.'

When Flora, long ago, had prayed in church, it had always been with the addendum, If it be Thy will. This time Margaret left her Maker no such discretion.

Despite the procession to the lavatories, most of the children that night wetted their beds.

They were urban slum children. Some were undernourished, some verminous. They were quarrelsome beyond belief. Their school, which should have been a unifying element, might not have existed: the fact was that many rarely, if ever went to school—their names simply appeared on its register, and thus they were swept up into evacuation. (Mrs Black, the elder teacher, had been quite surprised to see so many unfamiliar faces, but not Miss Pye, who knew more about the incidence of truancy.) Thus they were sadly lacking in any *esprit de corps.* Siblings clung together, as did those from the same street or tenement. Otherwise they were united only by a common refractoriness to their new surroundings.

The single desire of the children was to get back —back to the fish-and-chip shops, back to their quarrelling parents, back to their uninhibited guttersnipe lives. So they began by wetting their beds.

It might of course have been simple incontinence. A wetted bed, in such homes as they came from, meant no more than a clout on the ear; but Margaret always suspected them of deliberate offensiveness, so that they should be sent back. But she was equal to them. Even while their bed-linen next day steamed in the laundry, she sent to the Scouts for rubber ground-sheets.

Immediately however (possibly owing to Divine intervention?) she kept her hands at least under control, and helping Caro Packett bath the children next day, didn't once rub soap into their eyes.

They showed an unexpected prudery. To be naked, even in a bath, appeared to offend some deep-seated instinct. They clung to their urine-contaminated rags as though clinging to some last shred of decency. But Margaret was firm; naked into water dosed with disinfectant went each child, and on emerging submitted peaceably enough to be clad in unfamiliar garments—except that two rivals for the crêpe-de-chine camiknickers came to fisticuffs. That there were sausages for breakfast also helped to pacify them. They liked sausages, and ate up Mr Marjoram's bounty at one sitting.

'What shall we do now?' asked the children.

'Make a bonfire of all your old underclothes,' said Margaret.

It was a far crueller thing than slapping them or boxing their ears or twisting their arms. As their pathetic familiar garments went up in flames many a child whimpered—and Margaret was pleased to hear it whimper.

To begin with they played card games all day. Outside, Cotton Hall's garden and the countryside beyond lay burnished under a sun as glorious as in the equally ominous year of 1914. The children stayed indoors playing beggar-my-neighbour or rummy on the tables dedicated (Margaret had hoped) to photographs of their nearest and dearest. But none seemed to possess any such photographs. Some of the boys had pin-ups of nudes, but these went onto another bonfire. (All except a selection stuck into a stamp-album.) Again, it was far crueller than slapping them or boxing their ears; but Margaret at this one and only period in her life was cruel.

'Oughtn't they to be doing lessons?' suggested Mrs Hume— · but apprehensively, in case she herself should be detailed as instructress. (When in early days she asked the children to repeat the Lord's Prayer—'Our Father which art Ernie Bevin!' they had chorused.)

'Of course they should,' said Margaret, 'but it would take a lion-tamer ... If the billeting authorities wanted them to be taught,' she added more reasonably, 'they should have supplied a teacher. We must just let them run wild.'

It was early days, the children huddled over their card games. As yet they weren't running wild at all; but all too soon they were.

It was the Albert Buildings mob who on their first penetration outdoors discovered the dilapidated bee-hive lodge and made it their headquarters, defending it in pitched battles against the Cock Street lot. They all enjoyed pitched battles, however, and in due course the Cock Street lot were admitted too, there to smoke and plan nefariousness.

All save the very smallest smoked. Where did they get their cigarettes? Sad to relate, from Mr Marjoram's errand-boy, in exchange for their sweet-coupons. Sweet-coupons were much in demand among the toothless village grannies who had no use for a tobacco ration; cleverly, the errand-boy demanded not money but actual cigarettes in exchange, thus avoiding all suspicion of illegal trading; all *he* asked for, handing over the packets of Woodbine or Gold Leaf, was a page with a nude on it from the hidden album. But Mr Marjoram once catching him drooling over a particularly luscious full-frontal blonde, an investigation ensued; the whole system was discovered and put a stop to, leaving only Mr Marjoram the better off for half-a-dozen nudes in Technicolor.

But the smoking didn't stop. Like so many Robinson Crusoes marooned on an island called Morality, the pygmies fell back on their native ingenuity. They dried grass, they dried leaves, and

214

tamped them into cylinders of toilet-paper, and however disagreeable the first experiments, went on smoking. They particularly liked smoking in bed, and Margaret, expecting every
night to see Cotton Hall go up in flames, thought thankfully of the fire-escape.

Because the pygmies, unlike the walking wounded, didn't
even use their piss-pots. They stubbed their cigarette butts out
anywhere—on a window-ledge, on the floor beside their beds—
and it was only a mercy they didn't leave them to smoulder
under the blankets.

They began to run wild at last.

However urban-bred, they rapidly discovered the joys of
poaching, and with snares ingeniously constructed of elastic
bands and bobby-pins wrought havoc in the surrounding
spinneys. Mostly, not knowing what to do with a rabbit when
they'd caught it, they left it to strangle, for they were naturally
cruel. Nearer home they pulled fledglings out of their nests and
then stoned them to death for sport, meanwhile setting traps for
the parent birds. They hung about whenever a pig was
slaughtered—so indeed had many of the village urchins always
done, but with less esurient pleasure ...

Margaret began seriously to reflect on the doctrine of original
sin. There seemed no other explanation for the children's
badness. Even the little girls were bad. Sister defended sister, but
there was no amity among them, only hair-pulling and small
thefts of a hair-slide or hair-ribbon. They watched their brothers
stone the fledglings without protest, and like them saw a pig's
throat cut with pleasurable excitement.

'But we were never like that?' thought Margaret, remembering her own and Benny's childhood.

Then she recalled how carefully Benny had been tutored by
Mr Price (all his feral instincts assuaged by going fishing), and
how she herself had been under the rule of Hilda and Flora.
Three adults upon two children, as Margaret now saw it, had
laboured to root out original sin, which was probably the right
proportion ... The children now in her charge, she told herself,
had had no such advantage; but didn't hate them any the less.

From poaching they proceeded to attempts at robbing the
village hen-coops and duck-ponds, but here the village deployed
its own defences against them, by setting its urchins on guard by

day with licence to use catapults—so had the children home-
made catapults, but the villagers were better shots—and by
night turning out the newly-formed Home Guard, who also
frustrated an almost frivolous attempt to fire a hay-rick. ('Tis
not the Germans us have to fear,' Corporal Strowger told his
superior officer Captain Marjoram, ''tis they varmints at Cotton
Hall.' 'Setting fire to a rick!' exclaimed Captain Marjoram.
''Twould well might have made us a target for enemy aircraft!
What did you do to 'em?' ''Took the hides off them,' said
Corporal Strowger. 'I doubt if they'll try firing ricks again ...')

Attempts at arson at any rate ceased, for the simple reason
that the Home Guard were bigger than the children. A superiority in physical strength was the only superiority they recognized, and they couldn't compete with for example a
Strowger.

So the pygmies learned to leave the village alone, and
concentrated all their powers of destruction upon Cotton Hall.

It was quite surprising what damage a few children could do to
a substantial stone-built house.

They began by breaking windows. To break the ground-floor
windows was easy enough—any lump fallen from John Henry's
increasingly dilapidated crenellations did the trick—but the
upper ones presented problems which the children had to solve,
and did, by applying a swinging-ball technique. Armed with
more lumps of stone netted in string, from the fire-escape they
swung left and right—they were really very ingenious
children—and had all the upper west windows smashed within
weeks.

As to the ground-floor windows, Caro Packett simply had
them boarded up, there being no plate glass at that time
available, and this produced within doors a perpetual twilight
that the children rather appreciated, as making it easier to jump
out on the ladies from behind doors; but through the upper
floors of Cotton Hall blew in wind and rain soaking all the
children's beds. Little cared the children; whether a bed was
soaked in rain or urine to them was all one.

They also levered drainpipes from the walls, so that the rain-
water accumulating behind the battlements seeped through the
roof and spread wide stains across all the attic ceilings before the
paper actually peeled off, and this again was a source of pleasure

216

to the pygmies, as they traced fanciful ressemblances to Hitler or Donald Duck.

They also got to work on the fire-escape, and succeeded in prying off several rungs whose absence they hid with trails of baldschuanicum, to make booby-traps. (They themselves would never be booby-trapped because they knew where the gaps were; they just hoped one of the ladies might be.)

Within doors, their evil-doing was comparatively passive, producing only an increasing squalor as the lavatories weren't flushed and the dishes they were supposed to wash piled high, then toppled, then crashed. Bang-bang, it's a bomb!' cried the children gleefully hopping amidst the shards they made no attempt to clear up. Not a finger would they lift in any helpful way.

When Cotton Hall was a nursing home it had been regularly visited by persons in authority. No such persons visited it now. Money orders arrived punctually in payment for the children's keep, but otherwise, having once been got out of London, they seemed totally forgotten. Now and then, but very rarely, a parent turned up to give a kiss and some more sweet-coupons, but either the parents had forgotten the children too, or, which Margaret thought more probable, were glad to be rid of them.

Mr Ruddock did his best, but as the children swiftly realized, was by no means a person of authority. He couldn't, like a copper, have them up before a magistrate and put on probation. When he tried to impress upon them how fortunate they were to be taken away from the bombing and into the kind care of Mrs Price, they at best regarded him bleakly and at worst yelled Yah-boo.

It was no wonder that the ladies fled.

'Dear, dear Mrs Price,' they apologized in turn, 'my old mother' (sometimes it was an old aunt, or even old cousin) 'really needs me beside her, in these terrible times!'

It was the hardest thing Margaret had to bear, seeing her community disintegrate. But she didn't blame them. Sweeping and praying to the glory of God was a very different thing from cleaning up after a pack of hooligans who regularly blocked the lavatories with Comics.

'Will they ever come back?' wondered Margaret. 'Will there ever be a community here again?'

She began to feel it unlikely. Everything passes, everything changes; what had once been a place of repose and retreat was now a bear-garden. The single oases of peace and cleanliness were Margaret's room behind the minstrels' gallery, and that because she always swept and dusted it herself and locked the door even when she was absent for even ten minutes, and Caro's, who took the same precautions. Meanwhile between them, with no more aid than Mrs Strowger and Mrs Cable impressed from the village, they soldiered gallantly on; and sometimes, watching Caro Packett's invincible diligence and courage, Margaret let herself hope again; for if anyone was ever able to revive Cotton Hall, it was surely Caro Packett.

'Unless it's burnt down first!' thought Margaret grimly.

But no such disaster was to occur. Mr Ruddock (he who'd been so anxious to receive the children) had written letters of increasing urgency asking for someone in authority to come and see for themselves how impossible the situation had become; but authority had its hands full, and there was no response. Now, after observing Cotton Hall's increasing dishevelment until he could bear it no longer, he took the desperate step of calling in the Sanitary Department, an Inspector from which thoroughly agreed that Cotton Hall could no longer be considered an acceptable refuge even for evacuees; adding that he hadn't seen such squalor since he was assigned to the Isle of Dogs.

'No blame can attach to Mrs Price,' said Mr Ruddock. 'I rather blame the billeting authorities ...'

'In any case the children must be got away at once,' said the Sanitary Inspector severely. (As though it were Margaret who had blocked the lavatories and Caro who had broken the windows.) 'London's comparatively quiet; they must go back to their homes at once.'

Evidently even billeting authorities had to bow before the Sanitary. Within days another coach arrived, this time on a return journey, and gladly the children piled into it without a backward glance. The walking wounded had left behind them pin-cushions and paper-knives and a round robin of thanks, but not so the pygmies, who returned to their deplorable homes without a backward glance, and even cheered.

'I don't believe it,' said Caro, 'that they've really gone. It's too good to be true.'

'Have I ever told you,' asked Margaret, 'how fond I am of you?'

Caro smiled. It was like Margaret, she thought, that the moment the pygmies had departed she could dismiss them from her mind.

'Not in so many words ...'

'I may almost say I love you,' stated Margaret judiciously, 'almost as much as I loved my brother Benny. You both understood what I was trying to do at Cotton Hall.' (So far as Benny was concerned this was a fond illusion. If Margaret had wanted to turn Cotton Hall into a cats' home little would Benny have cared.) 'If I leave it to you, if the ladies ever come back, you'd always look after it?'

'Always,' promised Caro. 'I am honoured,' she added formally, 'by your trust in me.'

'I'll see about it tomorrow,' said Margaret, 'or the day after. I don't know why I feel so tired ...'

'Perhaps it's an occasion for the last of the brandy?' suggested Caro.

So in the last of the brandy that had eased Alison's parturition they drank to a happier future, and at parting for the night, for the first time in their lives, they embraced.

Only for some reason—perhaps the brandy?—Margaret couldn't sleep; and at about two in the morning, imagining she smelt fire, got up and half-sleepwalking stumbled her way out onto the fire-escape; where as no alarm was raised she stood for some time unapprehensive, while her thoughts began to wander.

'Poor Carmela!' thought Margaret. 'Was I unkind to her?' But no, she reassured herself. 'She'd have turned Cotton Hall into an hotel ...'

As the breeze stirred in the baldschuanicum her thoughts strayed back further: to Benny sitting beside her wrestling with his Latin verbs, to Benny belting out the old hymns in the little church above the salt marshes; to the Crusader's brass from which for years she gathered grains of rice ...

And then suddenly, looking up at her from the fire-escape's foot, she saw Mr Price; and all the years since they were married were obliterated like a dream.

'Francis!' called Margaret gladly; and ran down to him so

219

impetuously, she wasn't aware of her foot not touching a missing step.

'And left no Will after all!' sighed senior to junior partner in the firm of Ipswich solicitors. 'I suppose we'll have to make a search; there must be at least one blood-relation ...'

There was; Alan Braithwaite's Benjamin, his son Matthew, he who alone of the clan—too young to fight in the first World War, too old to engage in the Second —had survived to prosper, and who with his wife motored from London to survey his dilapidated inheritance.

Caro Packett received them with stoic amenity as they stared blankly at the boarded-up windows and then entered the defiled rooms.

'The evacuee children did all this?' asked Matthew almost incredulously.

'They were very energetic,' said Caro. 'That is, in a destructive sort of way ...'

'What a terrible time you must have had!' cried Matthew's wife.

'Yes, we did,' said Caro moderately. 'The place simply ... disintegrated. I know there's a terrible lot to be done, but if you'd ever want to come back yourselves—'

'Usen't there to be some kind of religious community here?' asked Matthew. 'I remember my father speaking of it.'

'I'm afraid that's disintegrated too,' said Caro. 'But there's some money left that you could use on reparations, if you'd ever think of coming back.'

'Of course we will!' suddenly decided Matthew's wife. 'Darling,' she addressed her husband, 'haven't we always wanted somewhere in the country? It'll be the very place to bring the children for the holidays!' Then she turned to Caro. 'Mrs Packett, would you possibly consider staying on here until I can come myself? And even afterwards, perhaps, to help with the children?'

'After her recent experience I should think Mrs Packett never wants to see a child again,' observed Matthew.

'Thank you,' said Caro, to his wife. 'I should like to very much, because it's my home.'

Thus the twisted root was made straight at last, as a new

generation of Braithwaites, the great-grandsons and great-grand-daughter of old John Henry, returned to Cotton Hall.